the
FINAL
SEASON

the FINAL SEASON
State of Grace

E. C. Putnam

TATE PUBLISHING & *Enterprises*

The Final Season
Copyright © 2009 by E.C. Putnam. All rights reserved.

No part of this publication may be reproduced, stored in a retrieval system or transmitted in any way by any means, electronic, mechanical, photocopy, recording or otherwise without the prior permission of the author except as provided by USA copyright law.

This novel is a work of fiction. However, several names, descriptions, entities, and incidents included in the story are based on the lives of real people.

The opinions expressed by the author are not necessarily those of Tate Publishing, LLC.

Published by Tate Publishing & Enterprises, LLC
127 E. Trade Center Terrace | Mustang, Oklahoma 73064 USA
1.888.361.9473 | www.tatepublishing.com

Tate Publishing is committed to excellence in the publishing industry. The company reflects the philosophy established by the founders, based on Psalm 68:11,
"The Lord gave the word and great was the company of those who published it."

Book design copyright © 2009 by Tate Publishing, LLC. All rights reserved.
Cover design by Amber Gulilat
Interior design by Nathan Harmony

Published in the United States of America

ISBN: 978-1-60799-934-8
Fiction: Sports
09.09.01

For Vicki

Acknowledgments

Special thanks to Tate Publishing for agreeing to publish my work. To Donna Chumley of Acquisitions for making the decision to offer a contract after my long search, to Audra Marvin, my editor, whose skill and shepherding have allowed my story to be told in the best possible manner and to Amber Gulilat, whose outstanding cover design sets the stage for the story perfectly.

I am forever grateful to friend and author Milam McGraw Propst for all her encouragement and assistance in the process. Without her help, what was a difficult journey could very well have become an impossible one.

Thanks also to bestselling author Deb Smith of BelleBooks, who offered wonderful encouragement and direction, even though her publishing house was not the right fit for my work.

This book is a story about family and could not have been possible without my family: my wife, Monti; daughter, Jennifer; and son, Harris. They are my gift from the good Lord and my treasure. Thanks also go out to my sister, Betty Ann, and my cousin Tommy, who were always ready with an encouraging word; and also to Tommy for his assistance as a proofreader.

This story was inspired by the 2001 season of the Sprayberry High School baseball team, the players, coaches, and family members, and especially the mother of one of the players, Mrs. Vicki Gabriele. Her sudden and tragic passing in 2002 led to my development of the story, and this book is dedicated to her memory.

No acknowledgment is complete without offering thanks for our very existence and any good that comes from our efforts to the good Lord, and for the greatest of all gifts that our Creator sent us: himself in the form of Jesus Christ.

Preface

This book is a novel. Although it is a work of fiction, the story can and should be likened to a cable that is formed by wrapping many strands of wire around a larger, stronger, central wire. Likewise, this story was created by wrapping many individual strands of fact and fiction around a central core of fact. The majority of these strands are fact. The factual spiritual core occurred in the life of the author. It is related in the story by the father to the son. This miraculous event might be described as a spiritual intervention, a God moment, or perhaps as an "infusion of grace." In any case, the story could not have been written without it.

Therefore, this book can best be described as a novel about the truth.

Chapter One

It is August 9, 2001. It is eleven months since I lived, and I am flying. Here I am, streaking above the clouds, released from the earth's surface like some sort of freaking, supersonic Homo sapiens. The wind is with me, strong at my back, and I am airborne. Two amazing events: I lived, and I am flying.

It's five thirty p.m., Eastern Standard Time, and I'm in seat 16C, Delta flight 1029 bound for Atlanta, Georgia. I'm just passing over Philadelphia to my left, with that fifty-mile-per-hour tailwind rushing me on toward home, and I am alive.

Eleven months ago at this exact time, I dwelled in anesthetic limbo. I cannot be sure which part of the procedure the surgeon was involved in at the moment. Possibly, he was completing his bronchoscopy, discovering no CA tumors, but only scarring. Perhaps he was in the process of slitting my lowermost throat to send a probe behind my breastplate on a retrieval mission for lymph cells—the second level of the recon. If the cells had been invaded, no further surgery would be in order, but a hideous trip down radiation lane and/or a debilitating stroll through chemotherapy-ville would ensue. So the cells were harvested in earnest, captured and secured as if a micro-treasure, and routed post haste to lab land for appraisal.

Now, at this present moment in time, I can gaze out the

window—actually more of a porthole—at a beautiful view of the sunset, so spectacular that it is humbling. A porthole—a porthole on a flying ship! Why does this seem so incredible, so awesome to me now? I've flown many times before and many times have enjoyed the amazing beauty of this experience. But this time is different.

I think it's part of what happened to my outlook when I faced my possible end time. When old man Mortality—I call him Mort—slapped me with a lung mass during an annual physical, I had to contemplate the possibility of cancer, the possibility of the end of my life—game over, sayonara, adios. That's when I developed a different appreciation for life. It's kind of hard to explain, nothing especially deep or philosophical, just the moment-to-moment *living* of life. Like watching the wind rustle the leaves of the trees, putting them into a fluttering dance of nature, or checking out the birds, squirrels, and chipmunks feeding in our backyard. And the look in the brown eyes of our husky-shepherd mix as he sidles over to sit beside me and get a reassuring head scratch. These kinds of experiences became very soothing to me.

Time out, the flight attendant has arrived with my libation: Maker's Mark. Maker's Mark—quite a coincidence, or is it irony? That irony thing always mixes me up. In front of me sits a label that reads "Maker's Mark," but as I turn to my right and gaze out my porthole, I can experience the exquisite visual of the true Maker's mark. Who are we that God Almighty should allow this vision of his world, twilight, and beauty from twenty-five thousand feet? A sunset seen from above, filled with radiant hues of purple, red, and shades of gray I can't remember ever seeing before. It's unfortunate but understandable that this beauty and serenity seem lost on most of the otherwise-occupied passengers of Delta flight 1029.

Then I was nowhere. Where else but limbo is your spirit when your body and brain are anesthetized? Is your soul also in the hands of Sir Anesthesiologist? Do angels hover about your body as Sir A tweaks the flow of vital sustainers to your self in neutral? Of course, I can't say with certainty that the Almighty's winged servants held vigil over the ER-ensconced me that day. But I can say for certain that angels were present, maybe not by my side, but for certain in that purgatory dubbed "surgery waiting."

Surgery waiting is the place where the very act of *waiting* turns the minutes to hours. Especially when there are two procedures to complete before the main assault on the lung mass can be executed and it is known if CA has found a home there. I know the waiting turned the minutes to hours for my wife, Jessica, and her twin sister, Monica, as they waited for six hours with my cousin, my sister, and my sister's best friend in hospital purgatory. And it was also that way for my friend and fraternity brother Big Dan, who waited and then picked up my children and brought them to the hospital after the surgery.

Flight 1029 has just passed over Asheville, North Carolina. Imagine that. One hundred plus of us Peter Pans are soaring over the Blue Ridge Mountains in the gloaming. Soon the flight attendant's soothing voice informs us that the pilot has begun the final descent into Atlanta. Holy mackerel, we are flying, not just traveling; we are flying! Flying like the pterodactyls of prehistoric times; flying like the majestic condor or the amazing hummingbird. Our feet are on the floor, but below our feet is more than twenty thousand feet of nothing but air.

Alexander the Great conquered all or most of his known world. What would he have given for this ride in window seat 16C—maybe a quarter of his domain, or perhaps even half? What an absolutely incredible experience it is to *fly*, and yet we take it for granted. For us it's simply the fastest mode of transportation. But what would Julius Caesar or Christopher Columbus or Leonardo da Vinci have given to experience what I and my fellow aviators are experiencing today? To fly is truly miraculous. And that's why I'm documenting this experience. The good Lord and modern medicine have granted life after cancer to me, and I want to remember the amazing things I'm privileged to encounter along the rest of the way.

Since I'm in my fifties, I'll have to write them down 'cause sometimes I can barley even remember what day it is. Time. How awesome it is that I've been given more *time*, the most precious gift there is.

One month and two days after my flight, this miracle of flight was turned into terrifying death for hundreds of airline passengers and thousands more on the ground in the horror of 9/11. I can't imagine what it was like to be sitting on one of those doomed jet airliners; it's unfathomable. So many unknowing victims, so many with no possible idea the end was at hand.

At least for me, I have the advantage of knowing that the end may be looming ahead. The chest X-ray taken during my recent annual physical shows another suspicious lung mass. The surgeon commander felt he had destroyed the enemy some eighteen odd months ago. The tumor and its housing lobe were removed, and all signs were favorable. But there are no guarantees in life, as was made excruciatingly clear on September 11, and Mort seems to be at it again, whispering in my ear that time may now be running out.

On my way home from work today, after I received the bad X-ray news, I detoured by Saint Jude's Church. I sought solace here when I learned about the abnormal X-ray the first time too. And again, it's strange to be back in the church of my youth after all the years and experiences that have passed since I served Mass here as an altar boy. But there is much-needed and gratefully accepted serenity to be found in God's house. I don't know how people cope with the tragedies of life without God's grace, and I'm grateful that I have this haven of spirituality. I can't find all the answers here, but I can find peace and also a few smiles.

I truly believe I have received a lucky break in knowing that I may be facing my final year, or months, or whatever. And now I'm looking forward, with hope, to a different kind of final. My son and his teammates are headed toward their final high school baseball season; a season filled with much promise, and a season which will begin shortly. Who knows, it may be my final season also. But I'm choosing to take this season one game at a time. I've decided that whatever medical procedures are in my future will come after the season. I learned to cherish the day-to-day beauties of life in my first brush with Mort, and I'm not going to spoil this season with recovery downtime, fear of the disease, or the disruptive forces these things would ply on me and my family. I've had too much fun through all these years of baseball—twelve to be exact—with my son and many of his buddies and their parents. It may be selfish. Heck, maybe I've lost my mind, but I don't want to ruin this last one. I hope if the news is eventually bad that my family won't resent my decision. That's probably not a fair expectation, but I have a choice, and I'm choosing to enjoy this final season. And like the wise man of baseball, Mr. Yogi Berra, says, "It ain't over 'til it's over." So for me, it ain't over.

Chapter Two

The last Saturday in January brings parent workday at the field, and I'm extra glad that it's finally here. This year the dads are doing minor, sprucing-up type landscaping around the field and putting yellow plastic piping around the top of the fences in the outfield and down the foul lines. The players are painting the wooden bleachers (and each other) and doing general cleanup. We've caught a break with the weather. It's in the high forties with a bright sun to warm us a bit. And it feels great to be out here with the parents and players again.

Four of us dads are wrestling with the yellow piping. We've tried various ways to spread the slit in the bottom to get the dang thing onto the top of the eight-foot fence, but nothing is working very well. And of course there are a few pinched fingers and muffled angry responses as we attack our chore with determined resolve, pliers, hammers, and a screwdriver. Luckily, two of the dads are tall enough to get good leverage on the top of the piping and smack it down onto the fence once we can pry the slit open a bit. The plastic would be much easier to manipulate if the temp was in the eighties instead of the forties. Now, for the past two hours, we've been four men wrestling with a yellow anaconda, staggering and fighting down the left field fence and across the outfield fence. I have to admit, I've wondered a few times how many of our guys might deposit home run balls over this new fence top as we snake along its length.

As we huff and puff and strain down the last section of the right field fence, we notice two dads putting piping down the right field foul line. When I see there are only two, I think, *Poor devils; there's no way*. And then when we see their method, I now think, *Ugh, we're such morons*. They're simply pushing the tube back against itself once they have one end on the fence. One man holds the attached part down and pushes the open piping down as the other pushes the tubing back against the installed part to open the slit. I have to admit I feel more than a little dopey. But what the heck, we four wrestlers fought the good fight and bonded a little during our taming of the yellow python. At least I take a little solace in pointing out that one of the two efficiency experts is a Tech grad like me. He must have graduated in some engineering discipline, not management as I did.

Throughout the day, the mood and camaraderie are upbeat as we all realize a chance for a special season lies just ahead. The opening game is still over a month away, but this work session is the unofficial start of the campaign. And I'm happy to say that the blue sky and warm sun feel and look like harbingers of good fortune. And even though we've still got some winter to get through, I've found at least one good thing about the gloomy grey season. The sunrises on my way to work and the sunsets on my drive home are spectacular this time of year.

February 26 is the initial Baseball Booster Club meeting for this year. Coach Pat Welsome opens the meeting with a discussion of his past teams and our team. This year's team has eleven seniors, five of whom are pitchers. Pat relates that he had five senior pitchers in 1994, and the team came in second in the state tournament. He says he had two senior pitchers and a team of kids that simply would not be beaten in 1996, and they won state.

I remember those finals vividly, like it was last week. It was a great victory too, coming against Sandy Pines's major rival, Northlake. Two high schools located about four miles apart vied for the top-level state championship; it was terrific! The Panthers and the Hornets split the opening doubleheader, and then the Panthers took the deciding game four to three.

Our family had a special interest in the Sandy Pines baseball program even back then, since Coach Welsome and his family had been our next-door neighbors for six years. His wife, Sarah, and my wife, Jessica, had both been pregnant when the Welsomes moved in next door in 1981. Sarah delivered first, a boy—Justin—born July 25, and Jessica delivered our first, Kimberly, on September 12. Justin was a freshman on the state championship team in 1996, and I clearly remember going onto the field to congratulate Pat after the final victory.

The infield was a madhouse of joy. Players, students, family members, and friends celebrating the ultimate victory, a state championship won in the third and deciding game against their archrival. The atmosphere on the home field was dizzying. I found Coach Pat between home plate and the pitcher's mound. His eyes were brimming with tears of joy, and I was truly happy for him. *How great*, I thought, *to be able to grab the top prize in your profession.*

Champions. How many times do you get the chance to enjoy that title? Four of *this* year's seniors, including my son, Woody, won a youth baseball state title in the summer of 1996 also. Maybe I will be fortunate enough to greet Pat on the field after another championship game this spring. Hey, baseball and life; anything can happen.

    Coach says it's up to these kids and how bad they want it. How much are they willing to give? Listening to Pat, I realize that this is what I've been waiting for; this is what has been buoying me up these past few months. This is what can take the focus off my health situation, shut Mort up for a while, and give me something else to concentrate on besides the guilt of keeping my condition from my family. This season that's finally here is the blessed distraction I've been looking forward to for weeks now. I can feel the adrenaline surge and swirl in my stomach, and it's good. It's good because it means I'm truly alive. I'm actually excited to be nervous. A week from this Wednesday it begins: the final season. This spring is gonna be one to remember.

    And the coming of this spring, as always, will bring excitement and anticipation to every baseball fan. Perhaps baseball's connection to spring is part of its great attraction. It seems so appropriate that America would embrace a sport that flows with the coming of a new season, a coming out of the bleak days of winter into the explosion of nature that spring initiates. The settlers hoped for another year of growth for their crops, their families, and their lives. And baseball fans hope that this new season will be *the one*. The one in which their team can win the region, the state, the World Series, or just the park championship. No matter how dismal the previous season, the fans still hope for newfound success with each new season, each new spring. Indeed, baseball hope truly does *spring eternal* in the spring.

    Our final season will start well before the blustery cold of winter finally gives way to the first warm breaths of spring. But the knowledge that the warmth is coming will arrive with that first pitch.

Chapter Three

Friday, March 1, the phone in my office rings while the Information Technology man and I are sharing some stories concerning the Monty Python comic sound effect he has installed on my e-mail. I see on the caller ID display that it is my home phone number ringing in, so I use my gag answer line (borrowed from my son, Woody).

"911, what's your emergency?" Wow, how things change in an instant and how ironic my phone greeting was.

Woody is on the line. "Dad, I messed my back up really bad. I'm going to Medfirst; do I need money?"

I am almost surprised when an eerie calm comes over me and I don't start screaming in panicked anger, "For crying out loud, son, this may be the last baseball season of my freaking life! How could you rob me of my last chance to see you play? What the heck brainless teenage move did you pull to create this snafu?" But I don't; I keep control and quite simply ask him what happened.

Turns out it was a typical teenage stunt. Seems Woody was trying to dunk a basketball during gym, and they put a folding chair under the basket to make the dunk more available to those in the five-feet-eleven height range, namely Woody. So he springs off the chair, gets too far under the basket, and grabs the rim. But his fingers slip, and down he goes, landing on his left hand, wrist, and hip. He says he thinks his wrist and hand are okay, but it feels like hot pain shooting down his left leg and his lower back.

Again I'm tempted to scream, and again I don't. "I guess I don't need to yell about how this should not have happened, Woody," is my reply.

"No, I know how stupid it was, and I'll never do anything this dumb again," he answers.

Fat chance, I think to myself.

"I'm going to go now and get it checked," he finishes.

"Ok, son. Good luck," is my deeply inspiring reply.

Nerve pain shooting down the leg could mean possible disc damage. What the heck, this could be it. The season ends before it begins. All my planning and rationalization down the drain for some bonehead stunt. I know how selfish that sounds, but I'm fighting a sense of panic here. Then I remember the predominant truth in baseball: sometimes you get the bad bounce. Injury is always a possibility, either before or during the season. But in my own way I'm unrealistically expecting not to have any bad luck or any bad bounces right now.

Anyway, even if this final season is over before it gets started, at least I was blessed with last season. I've been shown how precious life is, and I have been gifted with many more days than I might have had, the treasure of time. So I know I shouldn't harbor any disappointment or bitterness if I don't have any more baseball days ahead. In the grand scheme of things, I guess it doesn't much matter. And at least Woody didn't compound his spill by getting his front teeth caught in the net and ripping them out. That was the fate of one of our football players back when I was in high school.

Football practice was moved into the gym because of bad

weather, so our five-foot-nine running back decides to dunk a football by running up and jumping off—you guessed it—a folding chair, just like Woody. Great minds think alike, huh? I think all of us are a little goofy as teenagers. That memory brings me back to earth. It could have been worse and makes me realize that right now I think I'd just like to hug my son and tell him it will be okay. Maybe that's the most meaningful act one human being can perform for another: to put your arms around someone you love and assure them that things are going to be okay. I hope that Woody is all right and offer up a quick prayer that he is.

If he's not, we'll both have to accept the consequences of his choice. I've tried to teach my children that all choices can have unwanted consequences. And unfortunately, I've taught them through example a few times.

Three summers ago, while body surfing in New Smyrna Beach, Florida, I chose to try to ride an ocean wave that I knew was too vertical, rising over me like a curling, spitting mini-avalanche. I'd been body surfing on Florida's Atlantic coast most of my life. I knew better than to try to catch this wave.

The wave broke straight down on me and drove me toward the ocean's floor. It was as if Poseidon had stepped firmly in the center of my back and stomped me straight to the bottom. With the water racing around and past me, I just managed to get my hands out in front of my body and went rigid to take the impact. Then my body, now a human projectile, reached bottom. My left hand hit the sandy floor first and instantly, with a loud, sickening crack, the force transferred up to and dislocated my left shoulder.

I spent six weeks sleeping in the recliner because I couldn't find a painless position lying in bed. I endured fourteen weeks of gradually lessening pain in my shoulder and daily therapy exercises. And I went five months without golf. How did I ever survive five months without golf? All because of a split-second bad choice.

So if a dad in his late forties can make a really bad choice like I did, how can he raise Cain at his eighteen-year-old son for making the same kind of choice? Again, great minds think alike.

Woody is all right. Turns out it's just a bad bruise. Take it easy for a few days and apply ice; whew, not such a bad bounce this time after all.

It's good he's okay because time is really beginning to fly now, like a roller coaster car that's passed over the high point of the track and is beginning to hurtle down the steepest side. It's Sunday before the first game, senior picture day. The photo shoot is taking place at an antique Southern house of some import, although I'm not sure exactly what that import is. I wanted to bring my camera for some candid shots, but of course, forgot it.

It's hard to believe I've known many of these parents for eight years now, and all but one of the eleven seniors played PONY Baseball together at Jones Park. And the one who didn't, we know from church. This is the baseball culmination of all those years, and we've experienced so many thrills and disappointments together. I wish there was some way to make time slow down and let us linger in this season for a little extra while. But at least we parents have *this* season.

Surrounded by our kids, I can't help thinking about the three thousand plus from 9/11 and the many parents who never got to see their children's final seasons or even their first seasons. To be sure, there are many horrors in life, and as

I watch the eleven seniors all decked out in tuxedos, milling around together for the group shots, I recall another of those horrors. A sudden chill slides down my spine as I recall my senior year in high school and how many American eighteen-year-olds who graduated that year went off to Vietnam.

The name of one of those Americans—one of my classmates—is etched on panel thirty-nine west, line fourteen, of the Vietnam Memorial in Washington, D.C. He lost his life in March of 1968 during the Tet Offensive. The Vietnam War took him a few months short of the first anniversary of our high school graduation. He was probably less than a year older than our boys.

And Vietnam took my brother-in-law's legs and left hand. It took his limbs, but it did not take his spirit. He was an officer, a ranger in the 101st Airborne. He and my sister met in college. They were married in October of 1967, and he left for Vietnam in November. He was an officer who planned to follow in his father's footsteps as a career soldier. He wasn't an eighteen-year-old draftee, but he was attempting to lead his patrol comprised of those young draftees through a mined hedgerow when he stepped on one of the devices. Somehow he survived, and they raised two children together. He went on to become a national commander of the Disabled American Veterans in the early 1980s.

It's strange how we describe our athletes as heroes or their achievements in games as heroics. The true heroes have endured incredible struggles, nightmares, pain, and suffering.

I spent my Vietnam-era military service on the other side of the globe. I served in a navy anti-submarine-warfare helicopter squadron in the North Atlantic and Mediterranean aboard the USS *Intrepid*. We hunted Russian subs about as far away as you could get from the steamy nightmare of Vietnam. I don't regret it.

Back at home I mention my thoughts to Jess. "You remember me telling you about my high school classmate that was killed in Vietnam?"

"Yes, I do. That was a tragic and sad time," she answers before I continue.

"I was thinking about that today, watching the boys posing for pictures and horsing around. When I was that age, Vietnam was less than a year away for some of us."

"I don't even want to think about that. These are boys, our children. I can't begin to picture them as soldiers. It was terrible enough when my brother was over there and then when we learned of the awful injuries Chad suffered. The thought of my son going to war—it doesn't compute; it's unimaginable," Jess answers.

"Who knows what the war on terror will bring, but at least these eleven seniors can still be boys this spring. Boys playing baseball in the warm sunshine of Georgia, not boys at war in some jungle or desert halfway around the world," I say.

"Amen," Jess adds.

I think, *And we can be watching high school baseball games instead of the nightly news for casualty numbers.*

Monday's local paper has the high school baseball preview, and our big rival, Northlake, is displayed in color pictures on the front page. Northlake's head coach and his number-one pitcher are featured. The overview article, of course, mentions Northlake's head coach and Hardison's head coach, but no mention of Sandy Pines's coach, Pat Welsome. I don't know whether to regard that as a mere oversight or a dig at our coach and our program. You'd think a past champion with eleven seniors might generate a little extra ink, but oh well, "he who laughs last."

All the county teams are reviewed, and the write-up of Sandy Pines is a good one anyway. Coach Pat restates for the press what he spoke to us parents. This team can be as good as they want; it's up to them. Boy, how I wish I could instill some perspective into these seniors, but it's basically impossible to bring a sense of urgency to teenage boys, and that's just human nature.

Chapter Four

It's here. It's finally game day, and I go down the roster with great anticipation in the visitor stands. It's about an hour's ride west on Interstate 20 from our neighborhood to St. Stephens, the site of our first game. St. Stephens is a 4A program, and we're 5A, the highest level in the state of Georgia. But from everything I can learn, this is a good team the Panthers are taking on today, and it's early in the season; anything can happen (and usually does).

I check out the players as they take the field for pregame warm-ups, starting in numerical order with the seniors.

At second base is Bob Birdsong. Bobby's only five feet six, but like most not-tall ball players, he's a real scrapper.

At third base is Woody Pelham, my son. Woody stands about five feet eleven and weighs in at a wiry 175 pounds. We'd both like for him to be catching this year, but shortly after the season began last year, about three games in, it became evident that Woody needed to be at third. The move was necessary to put the best infield on the diamond, and that meant Woody and his strong throwing arm would reside at third last season and this.

Behind the plate is Major Thomas. Major is a solid six foot one, 210-pounder. Major is our primary power hitter entering the season. I'm hoping some of these other seniors will come up with a little more pop in their bats now that they have another year of physical maturity on their side. I'm sure Coach Pat is hoping the same thing.

At first base is Terry Davidson. Terry measures in at six feet and 190 pounds. He's an excellent defensive first baseman and seems to hit with power in spurts, having hit two of his three home runs last year, not only in the same game, but also in the same inning.

In center field is Phil Tinsley. Phil stands six feet one inch and tips the scales at 185 pounds. Phil has signed a letter of intent to play college ball next year as a pitcher. He's a lefty with good control who spots his pitches well.

In right field is Hunter O'Brian. Hunter is a rock-solid six foot one, two-hundred-pounder, cut from linebacker/fullback stock. He was a hard hitter during the football season, and let's hope he can direct those hard hits to the baseball this spring. Hunter's the one senior who didn't play at Jones Park, but he was an altar boy at St. Francis church, so I've been watching him grow up on Sundays instead of Saturdays.

In left field is Jason Michaelson. Jason is another six-footer, and he weighs in at 190 pounds. Jason, a fine contact hitter, is a good buddy of Woody's, and I took him with my first draft pick when I coached the twelve-year-old Astros at Jones Park.

The final starting senior is pitcher Danny White. Danny is a lanky six foot three, 185-pounder. He's signed as a pitcher for college next year, and he, like Phil Tinsley, is a southpaw. I can remember Danny as a skinny little six-year-old at Jones Park, jumping around on the bases, causing all kinds of havoc for the other six-year-olds on the diamond.

The other seniors include:

Hank Jackson, a six foot four, 190-pound, right-handed

pitcher. Hank's dad helped me with a broken fan belt at an all-star game near Six Flags. Our kids played on a traveling team together as nine-year-olds—half as old as they are now, that's amazing.

Mike Drew is a five foot eleven, 170-pound, left-handed pitcher. Mike is an excellent off-speed pitcher, a fine lefty junk baller. Mike will probably sign to play college this spring; he's being scouted.

Allan Christopher is a six foot two, 190-pound, right-handed power pitcher. Allan has also signed to play college ball, and he can really bring it. It seems rare to have two left-handed starting pitchers and only one right-hander. I hope that works to the Panthers' advantage.

The other starter is junior shortstop, Pat Messina. Pat is six foot one and weighs 190 pounds. Pat's our other football player, having manned the strong safety position on this year's football squad. We'll need excellent ball-hawking abilities at the shortstop position; as always, the shortstop's play is critical to the success of the team.

That completes the starters and seniors, and I believe I've chewed my first-game quota of antacids; so at last, it's time to *play ball!*

Chapter Five

The first pitch of the final season comes at 5:33 p.m. on Wednesday, March 6, 2002. And it's a called strike to our leadoff hitter, pitcher Danny White. Danny takes the next pitch for ball one and then hits a hard grounder that the shortstop can't handle—E6 and our first base runner of the year. Woody steps in next and tugs at the tops of the shoulders of his jersey to loosen it up, a ritual he has employed since he was eight or nine. I don't know about him, but my adrenaline is really pumping now. He takes the first pitch low for ball one and then rips a line shot straight at the shortstop, who snags this one with no trouble. Shoot! Ain't it weird how there's so much space on a baseball field where there isn't anybody, and yet so many balls are hit directly to where the fielders are standing?

Hunter steps to the plate now with one on and one out. Uh-oh, make that two out and none on; the pitcher just picked Danny off first base before delivering a pitch to Hunter! That makes Coach Pat anything but happy. Hunter grounds the next pitch to third and is thrown out to end the inning. Well, at least we had one base runner for a while.

No drama in the field as St. Stephens goes down one, two, three to complete the first inning.

Major reaches first on an error by the third baseman to lead off the top of the second, and then he is promptly picked off by the pitcher. I'm not looking in Coach Pat's direction this time. Two runners picked off in two innings, ouch. Phil Tinsley coaxes a walk, and glory-be, he doesn't get picked off. However, he does get put out at second when Terry hits a grounder to the third baseman, who throws to second for the force-out. Pat Messina flies out to center field to end the top of the second inning.

St. Stephens can do no damage in the second either. Nor can they mount any kind of effective attack through the next two innings. Sandy Pines goes in order in the third. That's once through the Panthers' batting order with no luck. It is the first game, though.

Woody leads off the top of the fourth with a hard hit ground ball toward third. The third sacker gets to the ball, bobbles it, and throws late to first. Woody's safe with a hit in my scorebook, but the scoreboard shows an error. The Panthers' official scorebook also records the play as an error. *What the heck?* You'd almost think I was biased. Unfortunately for Woody and Coach Pat's blood pressure, he gets picked off first. Oh my gosh. Now that's really embarrassing! Two guys before you have gotten picked off, and you're number three in only the fourth inning. That's bad base running, really bad base running. Hunter strikes out, and then Major flies out to right field for the third out.

Phil leads off the top of the fifth in a scoreless game and reaches first on an error by the shortstop. Since they only play seven innings in high school baseball, crunch time comes early. *Man, it's time to get something going, boys.* Terry puts down a bunt that the pitcher mishandles, and we've got men at first and second with no outs and no hits yet. Not only no hits in the inning yet, but no hits in the game yet.

Pat Messina follows next and delivers a hard hit grounder that looks like it's gonna sneak between the shortstop and second base, but the shortstop makes a great stop and then throws the ball away at first, allowing two runs to score and putting Pat at second. Now there's a runner on second, no outs, two runs in, and still no hits. Things stay wacky, though, as Jason lines out to a diving center fielder, who rolls to his feet and doubles up Pat, who is trying to tag up and make it to third. Bobby grounds out to the shortstop to end the top of the fifth inning with the Panthers on top two to zero.

Danny has pitched a great game going into the bottom of the fifth, but he begins to tire. And it's getting pretty cold now with the sun down and the wind stirring up a good bit. This is high school baseball, and the weather is still more winter than spring. With two out and two on, Danny hits a batter to load the bases. *Gulp.* Coach Pat sees Danny has gone as far as he can tonight and brings in Mike Drew, our lefty off-speed twirler, to shut the door. Danny moves to center field. Phil moves to left field, and Jason comes out.

The next batter for the St. Stephens Crusaders rips the second pitch he sees from Mike between shortstop and third. Woody dives to his left as my jaws clench and my teeth grind, but he can't reach the shot. The third-base coach is hollering and waving the runners on as the crowd roars. Phil charges the grounder in left field, comes up with it cleanly, and guns it toward home. Here comes the runner and here comes the ball; it's gonna be really close! The runner slides, but the throw has reached Major's mitt first, and he applies the tag while blocking the plate. Out! Now that's what I'm talking about. *Way to laser beam it in there, Phil!* Maybe we can pad our lead in the top of the sixth.

The Crusaders bring in a fire-balling junior relief pitcher. He was catching the first five innings, and he faces only four batters. Hunter smacks a double, the Panthers' first hit, but the inning ends with him stranded at third.

In the bottom of the sixth, with two out and no runners on base, Mike hangs a curveball to their burly designated hitter, and he loses it over the left field fence; home run, tie game. Just like that, with one swing, we go to the seventh and final inning all even. I like the way the seven-inning game magnifies the importance of each inning, every play. But boy, I sure do prefer to be ahead when we reach that seventh inning.

The Crusaders' fire baller works his magic in the top of the seventh, getting two strikeouts and a pop-up to the first baseman. *Where are our bats?*

Phil comes on to pitch in the bottom of the seventh. Jason comes back in to play left field. Starters are allowed to reenter the game in high school baseball. Major's dad, John, Allan Christopher's dad, Mack, and I are all standing at the fence down the left side of the ball field so we don't have to look through the backstop from the stands. So what happens next takes place right in front of us.

The Crusaders' leadoff hitter taps a slow roller right at Woody, but in his effort to come up with the ball quickly and make the throw, he brings his glove up too soon, and the ball rolls under his glove and right between his legs. *Holy cow!* I can't believe it, right through the wicket! That might be the winning run. I've got to get a grip before I have a major meltdown.

"Okay, guys," we all holler. "Turn a double play!" *Please God, please let them turn a double play*, is my silent plea. Phil wn and strikes out the next hitter. Okay, a double ds the inning now, and we can play some more baseb... he next batter lofts a dying quail fly ball toward the left field line, and Jason comes running over to flag it down. But we three dads watch in horror at what unfolds before us.

Jason stretches with his glove hand across his body to make the catch on the run, but the ball pops out of his glove! *Oh no, I can't believe it.* It looks like my boys, Woody and his bud Jason, are combining to lose the season opener right in front of my disbelieving eyes. And I'm now squeezing the chain link fence so hard that it feels like my fingers are going to dislocate at the knuckles.

But wait! There is chaos on the base paths because the runner at first has had to hold up, thinking that the fly ball would be caught. Now the runner races for second as Jason fields the ball on one hop. Mack hollers, "Second base!" but Jason is looking at third and starting his motion to throw there. *Oh no, no, no, no, no, no!*

Mack screams again, louder this time, "Second base!" Jason hears him, turns, and fires the ball to second base, forcing the lead runner out. *Hallelujah! Thank you, Lord, and thank you, Mack*, I think. Phil strikes out the next batter for the third out, and the game goes into extra innings. Woody and I can now breathe again, and my fingers are still attached, although the knuckles are throbbing steadily.

The top of the tenth inning finds the score still tied two to two. Phil, who has continued to pitch superbly, leads off the inning with a single, only our second hit of the game. Terry then puts down a sacrifice bunt that travels a little faster than he hoped toward the mound. The fire baller charges the grounder as his catcher yells, "Second base!" The pitcher fields, wheels, and rifles the ball to second. But it's high, pulling the second sacker up and off the bag as Phil slides in safe. The second baseman tries to salvage an out and hurries a throw to first, but it's wild and goes into the St. Stephens dugout. Coach Pat races to the infield to confer with the men in blue, and they properly award two bases to the runners, bringing Phil home with the go-ahead run and putting Terry on second. *Holy mackerel!* A sacrifice bunt meant to move a runner into scoring position at second base gets him all the way home with the go-ahead run in the top of the tenth inning. Ain't that amazing? The inning ends for the Panthers before any more runs score, but hopefully that one will be enough.

Right-handed power pitcher Allan Christopher comes on to pitch for the Panthers in the bottom of the tenth with a three-to-two lead. He mows the Crusaders down in order while my stomach attempts to tie itself into a granny knot, and Sandy Pines opens the season with a thrilling, improbable, one-run win.

This could turn out to be the best possible opening game for our boys because they faced adversity together and pulled together as a team more so, I believe, than ever before. It was not pretty; in fact it was down right ugly, uglier than a mud fence. But they fought and scratched together and in the end tasted victory. And it wasn't a mighty blast of a home run that won it for them. It was the lowly sacrifice bunt that turned into the big blow.

If this had been a hockey game, the three stars would be awarded as follows:

Third Star goes to Mack and Allan Christopher—Mack for verbally guiding Jason's throw to second to cut down the lead runner in the bottom of the seventh; and Allan for overpowering the Crusaders in the bottom of the tenth and never giving them a chance even to hope for a rally.

Second Star goes to Terry Davidson for getting down two intended sacrifice bunts successfully. Bunting seems to be becoming a lost art, but it's an art Coach Pat firmly believes in, and Terry got the job done, resulting in the win. You never know what will happen if you can just put the ball in play.

First star goes to Phil Tinsley, of course. All Phil did was cut down the tying run at home with a rocket peg from left field, pitch three superb innings, overcome some fielding pitfalls in the process, then lead off the tenth with a single, and eventually score the game-winning run.

Wow, it was truly crazy, even agonizing at times, but a *W* is a *W*. And you have to take them any way you can get them, pretty or ugly. Oh, by the way, Woody made a great running catch of a foul pop-up going away from the infield and toward the left field side fence. At least I'm told he did. I missed the play because I decided to use the restroom while our guys were in the field and had to walk up the hill to the football field facilities. I heard a roar from the crowd as I was heading back, but of course I was too late to see the play. Murphy strikes again!

Jessica hasn't traveled to this first game with me since I took the day off to play golf in the area and reach the field early without having to rush. So my ride home in the dark is a solitary one. Mort seizes this opportunity to mess with my head a bit. As I exit I-20 onto I-285, I think I can hear his whisper. "That was a pretty good game, wasn't it? The first game of the season is a win. But is it really worth risking your life for? Do you believe Jess would agree that it's worth dying for?" I counter Mort with the Lord's Prayer, said in thanksgiving that I'm here to experience the games and in hope that I'm doing the right thing.

Chapter Six

Home opener question: *Can you learn more from a hideous, error-driven loss or from a miraculous comeback?*

The sky is an overcast gray, and there's a cold wind blowing, both possible forebodings of impending doom, not to mention less-than-picture-perfect baseball weather. But still, it's the home opener for the senior Panther eleven, and fellow students fill the stands and jack up the excitement meter. Yep, there really is a buzz in the air.

The park looks great with the black windscreen above the newly painted black retaining wall beyond the fence in the outfield. The gold lettering of *Sandy Pines Baseball* on the windscreen rises above and beyond the outfield fence to enclose and insulate the park from busy Evergreen Boulevard.

Allan Christopher is our starting pitcher, and Phil Tinsley has moved to the leadoff spot, dropping Danny to second and Woody to third in the order. Being at home, the nerves are a little calmer, the stomach a little less jumpy.

Both teams go quietly in the first, but the Hardison Indians put together two hits and one run in the second. Hunter starts off the Panther second with a single, and Major follows with a walk. Terry is next, and he sacrifice-bunts the runners up a base. Luke Williams, a six foot, 185-pound sophomore catcher, is the designated hitter this game, and he steps up and rips a double to left field—plating Hunter. Sophomore Joe James is courtesy-running for the catcher, Major Thomas, and he is gunned down at home. Tied score at the end of two.

The Indians add a run in the top of the fourth behind a single and a double. But the Panthers answer and then some in the bottom of the fourth. Terry follows Major's single with a shot over the left-field fence for a two-run dinger—the first home run of the season for the Panthers. We lead three to two.

After one out in the top of the sixth, the Indians' third-sacker launches a solo shot over the center field fence, and we're tied again. The next batter flies out to center, and then the nightmare begins. Woody misplays a medium-slow roller to his left, and the Indians have a runner at first. After the following batter singles, Coach Pat brings on Mike Drew in relief. With runners on the corners, Mike tries a pickoff throw to first. It's wide left, and the go-ahead run scores.

My gut spins, and my heart sinks. This is the part of the game that just flat out hurts. And right now I can't say who feels worse: Woody, Mike, the Pelham parents, or the Drew parents. My bet is on Woody, since I know he's thinking he should have ended the inning three batters ago. But now the nightmare takes on a burgeoning, gluttonous life of its own as a single, two walks, and another E5 bring five more hideous Hardison tallies across the plate.

I'm tempted to curse at the top of my lungs for the frustration and pain I feel for Woody. It's only a game, but this just is not fair. Woody's mistakes are from trying too hard and the mounting stress of the errors. He's playing like the fate of the world hangs in the balance with his every move. Heck, he's playing like he knows about my health issue and as if his performance can determine my fate as well as that of the team.

How can I change that focus? How can I take that crushing weight off the shoulders of my eighteen-year-old?

Our family has seen its share of real-life tragedies: Jess's mother's sudden death of heart failure at age fifty-four, her brother's suicide, the passing of both of my parents—real, heartbreaking, devastating tragedies. Was it too much to hope that we could have smooth sailing in this silly game of baseball? I know it might be selfish to keep my situation to myself now, but I'm sure it's right that Woody doesn't have that extra burden to bear, especially the way the season is starting out. *I am right, aren't I?*

Bottom of the sixth, and the Panthers are down nine to three. Woody leads off with a single to left field. I'm proud he kept his chin up and his head in the game after the disastrous fifth. Hunter O'Brien then strokes a shot to the gap in right center, and Coach Pat waves Woody to third, where he is cut down by an excellent relay. The ball had already reached the third baseman's glove by the time Woody went into his slide. *Good freaking grief, when will the personal nightmare end?* Major Thomas then doubles to score Hunter. Terry singles, and then Luke Williams reaches base on a miscue by the shortstop. Pat Messina, Phil Tinsley, and Bob Birdsong add three more singles in a row to plate three more runs. That closes the scoring in the sixth, and it's now nine to seven. *Holy mackerel, they're fighting, but can they make it all the way back?*

Pat Messina moves from shortstop to the pitcher's mound for the seventh and possibly final inning. He's greeted by a double off the bat of the Indians' leadoff hitter. Even though the next two batters go in order, Woody's torture has continued. On a pitch in the dirt that's blocked by Major, the runner at second takes off for third. Major is forced to make the throw to third from his knees. The throw is slightly high and Woody, again in his haste to make a play, hurriedly brings his glove down to tag the sliding runner, but the ball tips out of the webbing of his glove and into left field. That runner scores, and it's now ten to seven in favor of the Indians when the Panthers come up for their last at bat in the bottom of the seventh. *Jiminy crickets, was I really in a big hurry for this season to start? Can Sandy Pines tie it up and force extra innings? Can they pull off a miracle and win it in their final at bat?*

My gut churns as I pace the planks of the left field foul line bleachers—far from the crowd in the stands behind home plate. It's good here away from the crowd, and I can see over the side fence by standing on the bleachers. A few of us dads congregate here for an unobstructed view of the game.

Woody leads off the bottom of the seventh and reaches first when his shot through the left side of the infield is ruled an error on the college-signed shortstop. Hunter is next up, and he draws a walk. Woody takes third on a wild pitch, and runners are on the corners with slugger Major Thomas at the plate. I have a good feeling Major might lose one and tie this thing up. Major tries to fulfill my premonition with some mighty cuts but goes down swinging. Terry is up next, and I'm hoping for another dinger from him. Heck, he hit two in a game last year; he can do it again. But no. Terry matches Major's fate and also goes down swinging for out number two. *Well, that's not what we wanted or needed now, is it?*

It's the bottom of the seventh, two on, two out, and the Panthers are down by three runs when sophomore Luke Williams steps to the plate. What pressure for the youngster, but he's a good hitter with a natural, solid stroke. Here's hoping. And the sophomore delivers a mighty blast skyward toward center field. The crowd roars. I pick up the ball at its apex and watch as the center fielder races back toward the fence. Time seems frozen as the fielder reaches the fence, but his sprint is in vain as the horsehide flies high over his upturned face and the fence! Tied game and pandemonium. Ain't baseball beautiful? I feel like I'm back from death's door again. *Finish this thing now, guys, while you're on a roll.*

Pat Messina and Bobby Birdsong string back-to-back singles together, and that sets the table for last game's hero, Phil Tinsley. And Phil does not disappoint. He laces one to center, and Pat comes home with the miraculous winning run. Pandemonium II—this is getting to be too much! What fantastic, gutsy finishes this team has come up with. And, oh yeah, the Pelhams are redeemed again. Deep breaths of relief are followed by a few lingering nervous twists in my gut.

What a great clutch home run by sophomore Luke Williams. Will he ever hit a bigger one than his first?

This living moment to moment can be darn tough during baseball games, especially baseball games that matter as much as these do to me. It ain't for sissies. But when the outcome is a *W*, it feels mighty good. It's also a bonus good feeling to pick out the parents of the player who has made a big play and enjoy the huge smiles and shouts of excitement that follow. I think sharing in that joy maybe increases it in some way or another.

Chapter Seven

Stone Ridge comes calling. In the third game of the Dugout Tournament, which opens the high school baseball season in metro Atlanta, the Panthers face the Stallions at home. It's a beautiful, spring-like Saturday, and happily the game takes on the same aura in a breathe-easy fashion.

Phil Tinsley gets the start for Sandy Pines, and the Stallions go in order in both the first and second innings. The Panthers also go one, two, three in their first at bat but scratch across one run in the bottom of the second without benefit of a hit. The Stallions answer back with a run of their own in the top of the third.

But in the bottom of the third, the floodgates burst open as the Panthers score eight runs by collecting hits from DH Luke Williams, Hunter, Terry, Woody, Pat, and Jason, along with Danny and Hunter reaching base as hit batsmen. Pat Messina had the unique experience of scoring twice in one inning, having reached base once via a walk and once with a triple. Phil had a unique experience of his own, making the second and third outs of the same inning. That's a memory that probably won't be cherished. In all, twelve Sandy Pines batters went to the plate in the bottom of the third.

The Stallions go in order again in the top of the fourth,

and then the Panthers add six more runs on hits from Danny, Luke, Hunter, Major, Woody, Pat, and Jason. Senior pitcher Hank Jackson bats for Phil in the fourth and then comes on to pitch in the fifth inning. Hank sets the Stallions down one, two, three, striking out the final batter to end the game fifteen to one with the mercy rule in effect. *This is more like it.* Next game is Wednesday on the road.

Chapter Eight

Game four is on the road but not really for me. Basken High School is a good thirty-five to forty miles from Sandy Pines but only about five miles from my office. And the Internet directions make finding the field a cinch. I like it when it works out that way. No ducking out early and rushing to make it home in time for the game or having to leave even earlier to get to an away game. This is nice for a workday game.

Both sides go one, two, three in the first inning. Major starts off the second inning with a hard liner to center field for out number one. Luke reaches first on an error on the Rebels' third sacker. Woody steps in and promptly spanks one deep to the right center field gap. It's way back, and I think it's got a chance to leave the park, but it bangs off the top of the fence. I don't mind saying it's mighty fine to see Woody really get a hold of one finally. Jason follows with a walk, and then Pat rips one the shortstop can't handle, and two runs score on the E6. That's all the Panthers can get in the second.

The Rebels answer in the home half of the second. The first man up draws a walk off Danny, and that's never a good sign. The next batter slams an opposite field shot over the right field fence to knot the score at two. After the Panthers go one, two, three in the third, the Rebels follow a single with a double to go up three to two after three. Looks like another nail-biter may be brewing. I figure that's okay. There are probably a lot more to come, and it sure beats having to score four or five runs just to catch up.

Pat leads off the fifth with a walk and eventually scores without the aid of a hit, and the game's tied again. The Rebels fail to answer in the fifth. So it's all knotted up, not unlike my gut, with two innings to go.

With one on and one out in the top of the sixth, Woody smashes a single up the middle, and runners are at first and third. A passed ball by the catcher scores Major and gets Woody to second. Jason and Pat draw walks, Bob singles. After a pop-up out to the catcher, Terry smacks a double, and then Hunter reaches first on an E6. Major and Luke put singles back to back. There are two on, two out, and seven runs across when Woody comes to bat for the second time in the sixth. *There's no pressure, so just swing away.* And Woody does just that.

He launches a high drive to deep center field. It might be; it could be. The center fielder comes streaking toward right center giving chase, but is this one the big fly? Not today. The center fielder lays out at full speed, skids along the grass, rolls over twice, and comes up with his glove raised in the air. Unfortunately for Woody (and me), the ball is in the fielder's glove. *Did he catch it on the fly?* He's the only one who knows for sure. That's out number three, but the Panthers now lead ten to three. I'm thinking two things: *The Panthers oughta be able to hold this lead, and Woody shoulda had an extra bowl of Wheaties for breakfast.*

Danny sets the Rebels down in order in the bottom of the sixth, striking out the last two batters. And in the seventh, with one out and two on, he again Ks the final two batters for a complete game victory. Danny pitched a great game, fanning a total of eight and giving up only four hits. The Panthers are looking good so far even though the real test—region play—is still a ways off.

I'm beginning to wonder if Woody's hitting isn't based on a lunar cycle. He didn't hit in the first game when there was a full moon, and he hit better on Saturday when the moon was coming off that cycle. He hit even better tonight. Wow, maybe I'm creating a new baseball superstition, as if there weren't enough of those already. I know it's a crazy idea, but he did hammer the ball tonight. He finished the game two for four, but it could have been four for four with two homers. I know, *coulda, shoulda, woulda,* but at any rate, he's hitting the ball hard, and I can breathe easier.

Hammond is coming up next at home. Woody has a bunch of buddies from grammar school days on this team, and they're all excellent ball players. Woody has always played well against this team, and I hope he can again. They're in our region, and even though this is another Dugout Tourney game, it would be good to put a whipping on a regional foe early in the season.

Chapter Nine

It's another beautiful, sunny day for a home game—the kind of weather for which baseball was invented. It's a Friday, best night for a ball game, and it will have to last me awhile since there's not another game for ten days. I'm not excited about Mort having that much time to grind on me without the distraction of baseball. It's a five o'clock start and windy, blowing out. The infield is in shadows and the outfield washed in bright sunshine. It's definitely a pitcher's advantage to start.

And the pitchers do start strong. Woody's four buddies on the Lancer squad are hitting in the first four spots in the lineup. Phil has gotten the start today, and he strikes out the first two batters he faces. He has the three-hole hitter down one ball and two strikes before surrendering a double. But Hammond's first ends without harm as Woody's fourth buddy to bat in the inning grounds out to the shortstop for out number three.

The Lancers' pitcher has an even better start, pretty near perfect to be exact. The Hammond hurler gets the first three Panther batters to go down swinging. Three Ks to start off the game. That's pretty impressive, not to mention a little nerve rattling.

Things can turn quickly, though, and after the Lancers

fail to score in the top of the second, the Panthers strike for four runs in the bottom of the inning. You know, I'm enjoying making these entries in my scorebook. The inning doesn't start well, however, as Major follows the same path as the previous three Panther hitters with a strikeout. That's four in a row. Woody bats next and draws a walk on four straight pitches. That's odd for a pitcher who has K'd four in a row. Danny's grounder to the second baseman moves Woody to second with one out. Jason works another base on balls out of the Lancer pitcher, and then the hit parade begins. Pat belts a double, Bob a single, and Hunter a double before Terry draws another walk. Terry is caught stealing to end the inning, but the home boys are up four to zero.

The Lancers' leadoff hitter, a Division I college signee, starts off the top of the third with a solo blast off the fence and windscreen that protect Evergreen Boulevard. Another run scores after a walk, a fielder's choice, and a double to make it four to two after two and a half innings. Sandy Pines gets a run in the bottom of the third on a two-bagger by Major and a single by Danny to go up five to two.

The Lancers scratch out a run in the top of the fourth to make the score five to three after three and a half innings. The Panthers answer back in the bottom of the inning. Pat opens the home half with a double. Bob sacrifices Pat to third, and Hunter plates him with a single. Terry doubles to put runners at first and third. After Luke hits a soft liner to the second baseman for out number two, Major comes to bat.

The Lancers fear the slugging catcher, whose double the previous inning was a mile high and windblown to the warning track in left center field. Had Major not gotten under the pitch, it was headed for Evergreen Boulevard. So Hammond's coach likes his chances against Woody better and gives Major an intentional walk; turns out to be a wrong decision. With the count one ball and one strike, Woody sort of one-arms a pitch that's down and away to the base of the right center field fence, clearing the bases ahead of him and stopping at second with the Panthers up nine to three.

Some things turn out so sweetly.

A groundout to the pitcher ends the inning one batter later, and the score remains nine to three heading into the fifth inning. That's good.

The Lancers plate one in the top of the fifth, and the Panthers go one, two, three in the bottom of the inning for a nine to four score after five. That's not as good.

The sixth starts with a single by the Lancers' number-nine hitter. He's batting ninth; he's not supposed to do that! Their leadoff man, who homered earlier, draws a walk, and their catcher, Woody's bud from grade school, follows with a triple to right center that scores two. Now that's not too friendly! He later scores on a single before the inning ends. The score now stands nine to seven, advantage Panthers.

Hunter leads off the Sandy Pines sixth with a single and is moved to second on a sac bunt by Terry. Hunter takes third on a grounder back to the pitcher that results in an out at first. He then scores on a balk, and that's all the damage the Panthers can do in the sixth. But a three-run lead is better than a two-run lead with just three more outs to get.

Coach Pat brings in Danny on two days' rest to close out the Lancers in the top of the seventh with the Panthers holding the lead ten to seven. The seventh, eighth, and ninth batters are due up, and the first man up gets things rolling with a double—not good. Number eight in the lineup draws a walk but is picked off by Danny—better. The next batter also walks to bring up the home-run-hitting leadoff man—getting worse. He is hit by a pitch to load the bases—worse still. Ouch, a single, two walks, and a hit batsman. We're lucky there's one out.

My gut is hoping for a double play, but worse turns to worser, or is that worserer? A single is followed by another hit batsman, another walk, and another single. When the dust settles and the inning is finally over, the Panthers come to bat down eleven to ten in the bottom of the seventh. Consecutive errors with two out puts two runners on and brings hope, but the threat dies with the third out, and the Panthers have a bitter pill to choke down. To make the pill even bitterer, they have to chew it for ten days before the next game. No miracle tonight.

Sandy Pines gives up the four runs in the final inning this time. You win some, you lose some. And it seems like some, you give away. The Panthers were excessively generous hosts this evening. *Can you keep that in mind, Lord, when our boys are in need of a little generosity from the opposition?* Well, I guess it's not really right to pray for your opponent's misfortune and maybe not even for your team to be victorious. But you still pray for the players, that they can do their best and that they not suffer injury.

Chapter Ten

It's lucky for me the ten days off come at a time when my cousin and a couple of his buddies from Rome, Georgia, are making their fifth annual trek south to the Florida Space Coast. I'm happy to hook up with them this year for the trip to my sister's condo on the beach and a game or two at the Braves training complex in Orlando. My son's baseball games have done the job of distracting me from my medical situation by giving me something I truly enjoy to concentrate on, but I'm glad to have this trip in the meantime. The team has ten days to digest a blown lead, but I don't want ten undistracted days to spend debating Mort.

The beach is an incredible elixir for me. I've loved it here since I was a small child, and when I get my first glimpse of the ocean as we travel down A1A the last few miles to the condo, I get the giddy little kid excitement all over.

That night, late—about midnight—my cousin and I head down to the beach for some moon bathing. It's a terrific night, the sight of a thunderhead out at sea illuminated by a three-quarter moon to our southeast, and the sound of the waves makes me feel like I'm cheating to be experiencing something this awesome.

My cousin was born in Orlando, and my family used

to come visit his family in Winterpark for a few days, and then we'd all head for Coco Beach or New Smyrna Beach. We're the same age, and after his family moved to Atlanta, we attended grammar and high school and brothered around through summer vacations also. I know he feels the same about the seashore as I do.

As we sit, listen, and watch, the cloudbank at sea entertains us with changes in shapes, and I'm tempted to ask his opinion on my cover up. Obviously, he doesn't have the same emotional investment in me as my family, and I'm wondering what he might think about keeping the news from them. Mort is quite adept at guilting me, and that guilt is beginning to eat at me more and more. I'm curious to see if another opinion might support my decision because that decision is beginning to seem more and more idiotic.

But I choose not to spoil the moment of solitude with a nasty dose of reality—maybe later. And besides, the soothing sound of the waves and the relaxing feel of the sand between my toes have silenced Mort for the moment.

The visit to the shore was great. The Braves won one game we saw and lost the other. Of course, I became anxious for the next Panthers game while watching the pros work out the kinks for the upcoming season. I was happy for the balm of the ocean but ready to return to the baseball wars of Region 6, 5A. I kept my news to myself.

Chapter Eleven

The night before the season resumes, Woody and I have a talk about what the other region teams have been doing while the Panthers have been off. Since the Dugout Tournament games ended, Sandy Pines has had no further games scheduled before the region schedule begins tomorrow. Some of our close rivals and neighbors have been playing other metro Atlanta teams and fattening up their team and individual statistics. I don't know why Sandy Pines didn't have any games during this stretch, but then again, I don't know a lot of things.

While we're talking baseball, Woody mentions that he has a hard time going to sleep at night because of a lot of stress he's been feeling: baseball, high school, college, college baseball, and last but not least, the senior prom. He's been worrying about us spending the money for a tux, etc., for the prom when he isn't even dating one particular girl. I reassure him that the cost isn't a problem and that he shouldn't miss the prom. It's too big an event and too big a part of high school memories to miss. I also do my best to reassure him that we'll find him a place to walk on if he doesn't land anything in the way of offers by season's end. I just hope and pray that he can relax enough to do his best.

I'm sure he can play at some college level, but he needs to

quit worrying so much and give himself a chance to do his best. That's what I want to see most: Woody and his teammates at their best. *Just do your best, and let the chips fall where they will.* I don't know how much our conversation helped Woody; I hope it did him some good. But it certainly convinced me that I'm doing right by keeping my situation to myself. Woody definitely doesn't need that added burden. Mort let me know that he wasn't happy with this realization.

Game six brings Baxter High to our field to open region play. This will be the first of ten region games, three before spring break. After those ten games, the teams will be seeded based on records for the final four region games to decide which teams will make it into the state tournament. Another of those many things I don't know is how they seed after the ten games, but I do know that this is one of the toughest regions in the state, if not *the* toughest. All the region games will count in the final standings with the final four games somehow arranged to even the competition, since all teams won't play all other teams twice.

I'm having one of those "it's a small world" encounters at today's game. While checking out the Internet Web site of the University of Florida's baseball team, I notice one of their signee's names is Ziniski. And he is from Baxter High in Georgia, and his parents' names are Michael and Rita. Now, Ziniski isn't a common name in the metro-Atlanta area; in fact, I haven't heard it since I graduated from parochial school. In fact, I attended eight years of Catholic school with a Mike Ziniski, and I'm betting he's Brad Ziniski's dad.

I get to the ballpark early so I can look for Mike Z, and sure enough, it's him. He looks a lot more like his eighth-grade self than I do, what with all the gray hairs I have worked so hard to earn overtaking the black. We have a good visit after thirty-nine years of not seeing one another. Nice that baseball has allowed this chance meeting. Mike informs me that Baxter is a senior-laden team like Sandy Pines and that they actually have sixteen seniors on their team. *Yikes, that worries me some.*

Game time finally, and Danny White takes the mound on a blustery, chilly afternoon. The leadoff batter is Brad Ziniski, with whom Danny is familiar since they played on the same summer team last year. Mike related that they had been teammates during our pregame conversation. Brad rifles Danny's first offering of the game into center field for a solid single. Danny responds by striking out the number-two batter and then gets Brad with a pickoff move that results in a pitcher-to-first-to-second-base rundown and out number two. The next hitter singles, but Danny retires the following batter on a fly ball to Phil Tinsley in center field. No runs allowed equals a good start for Danny and the Panther defense.

Hunter is leading off for Sandy Pines and bests Brad's solid single leadoff with a big fly over the left field fence for a one to zero lead. Terry follows with a single, as does Woody. *That's a good start, son.* The next two hitters strike out, but Terry and Woody have moved to third and second on a double steal. Luke swings at strike three in the dirt, but the ball eludes the catcher, so Luke races to first, and Terry races home. The inning ends with the Panthers up two to zero. I'm good with that.

Danny is going strong on the mound today, and the Red Devils can muster only two hits through the fifth inning. Danny collects six more strikeouts over that span, giving him seven through five innings of shutout work.

The Panthers get singles from Bobby, Danny, and Terry but no runs in the bottom of the second. The bats are more run-productive for the home boys in the bottom of the third. Major leads off with a ringing double to the gap in left center, and Luke follows with a single that plates Major's courtesy runner. Pat sacrifice-bunts Luke to second, and a groundout by Phil gets Luke to third. Bobby spanks one to the shortstop, who misplays it, allowing Luke to score. After four complete, the score stands at four to zero, Sandy Pines.

No runs for the Panthers in the fifth, although Woody has another solid single.

The Red Devils reduce the deficit in the top of the sixth by scoring one run off a double and a single. Danny strikes out another hitter to end the top of the sixth. Then Danny helps himself in the bottom of the sixth by belting his first homer of the year over the left field fence. That's all the runs for the Panthers this inning, so we go to the top of the seventh with the Panthers again enjoying a four-run lead, five to one in this region opener.

Danny retires the first two batters on groundouts, and that brings Brad Z back to the plate. With the count one ball and two strikes, the next pitch either comes close to hitting the batter, or it does hit him. I have no idea from way down the left side bleachers, but Brad believes it hit him, and he heads for first. The home plate ump stops him and tells him to return to the batter's box. Brad pulls down his sock and points to where he says the ball hit him and continues on to first base. Much arguing ensues as the ump insists Brad return to bat, and the Baxter head coach pleads their cause to no avail.

Brad angrily returns to the batter's box, his mood obvious from his body language. He steps in, with his sock still down around his ankle, and after the count reaches three-two, he smashes the next pitch over the left field fence, retaining wall, windscreen fence, and onto Evergreen Boulevard—quite a punctuation mark for his argument. And now I'm wishing the ump had agreed with the hit-batsman plea.

Fortunately, the game ends two batters later with the Panthers on top five to two. Unfortunately, it appears there is some unsportsmanlike trash-talking taking place during the after-game handshake by the two teams at home plate. Nothing major occurs; boys will be boys.

Well, that's a good start to region play, and five and one overall ain't bad either.

Next game is away at Arlington. I hate that place. On the way home I tell my nerves to relax and Mort to shut up.

Chapter Twelve

Game seven is at Arlington, and it's a nasty, cold, six p.m. start with a gray sky spitting drizzle at us. Did I mention that I hate this place? It seems like we never do well here, whether it's a summer ball game or a JV high school game. And the real clincher is that this is the locale where I sort of fainted or collapsed or had some kind of "health episode" three years ago.

It was a very hot summer afternoon, and I had hit range balls at a nearby golf practice facility for about an hour before the game. Shortly after the game started, I felt quite woozy and tried to leave the stands, kind of weak, staggering down to the sidewalk behind a dugout. Of course, the other parents hurried over to see how I was; we're at the age where heart attack is the first concern. One of the moms had been a nurse, and she felt it was heat stroke or heat prostration or some kind of heat thing and had someone bring her a small sack of ice from the concession stand. She deposited the ice sack onto my crotch area, saying that was the quickest way to cool the blood. Since I was in no position to argue, I accepted the treatment.

Major Thomas's dad, John, gave me a ride home, where I watched the Major League All Star Game Home Run Derby. The only good thing about the incident was that I didn't have to watch our team lose another game at that field. I've wondered since my surgery if that episode didn't have something to do with my lung mass. Did I mention I hate this place?

Back to the present, and yes, the weather is a harbinger for the Panthers' fate versus the Knights.

It's a scoreless game until the Panthers break through in the top of the fourth with a run on two hits and a sacrifice bunt. Unfortunately, Phil can't stand the prosperity as the strike zone suddenly eludes him completely. The first three batters draw walks, and that chases Phil from the mound and brings on Mike Drew in relief from the bullpen. A slow roller to second gets the tying run home before a single plates the go-ahead run.

Although Arlington doesn't need any more offense, they score two in the bottom of the fifth and one more in the sixth to make the final margin five to one—*bad, guys.*

The Panthers finished with six hits and six strikeouts. They used four pitchers: Phil, Mike, Hank, and Pat. And so another—and hopefully the last—nasty night comes to an end at the home of the Knights. Did I mention I hate this place?

Panthers now stand at five and two overall and one and one in region play. I was hoping for better.

Chapter Thirteen

Tonight's game eight is to take place at Hightower, which is one of my favorite places to watch a game. We've never had much luck here, but it's a great situation for the spectators, with the field sitting down in a natural amphitheater setting. The Panthers may not get the game in because the weather is very iffy, and I'm worried the team's confidence is iffy also.

After the Arlington game, Woody told me that now he didn't think they were as good as they thought they were before the season began. For that particular game, I guess he's right. Six hits and six strikeouts—maybe that was just a darn good pitching job, but I know I expect this senior-dominant club to score more than one run in a game. These guys need to come out fighting tonight against Hightower, or I'm afraid they'll get down and just go through the motions until Coach Pat jerks them back to reality. They can't afford a letdown at the start of region play, and it's up to the captains—Danny, Major, and Woody—to keep their dobbers up and maintain a no-quit attitude. I hope I'm able to get that point across to Woody before the game. If not, then I'll point it out for the upcoming Florida tourney.

Speaking of the tourney, I saw a copy of Berkwood High's schedule, and they're going to Sarasota also. They are a real power in the metro area and have beaten our rival Northlake already this season. It would be great to play them in Florida and see how we stack up.

Woody seemed fairly receptive to my advice but didn't have a chance to put it into action since tonight's game has been rained out before the first pitch is thrown. Looks like the Panthers' next game will take place in Florida.

Chapter Fourteen

It's beautiful here in Florida, a little breezy, but very nice. My daughter, Kimberly, and I had a smooth ride down yesterday. She drove about three hours in the middle of the trip, which gave me a good break and made it a fairly easy ride. Although, I consider any ride to Florida a fairly easy ride. Jessica stayed home to take care of the family dog, Aztec. She didn't want to put him in the kennel, and we weren't sure if Kim was going or not up 'til the last minute. We're sharing a condo with the Christophers: Mack, Becky, and their younger son, David. I've always enjoyed watching the games with Mack and Becky, and this trip is a good chance to get to know them better.

There's a cookout at the pool area this first evening, and it feels great to be on a baseball trip again. We've made them in the past summers with many of these same families, and it's a lot of fun to be doing it again. It's also fun getting to know the families of the younger guys. Unfortunately, Woody doesn't share Kim's and my enthusiasm for this particular trip. I ask him how it's going, whether he's enjoying the trip, and he pulls no punches in letting me know how he feels.

"This totally stinks. I'd rather be in Panama City with Jack and Mike. They're chasing the honeys while I'm stuck here chasing ground balls!"

I steer him away from the others before answering. "You haven't played the first game yet, and you've already copped this rotten attitude. Heck, I thought this was gonna be a great baseball trip!"

"Maybe for you, but this ain't the part of Florida I want to be in. I need a break from baseball."

"A break? Shoot, the season's barely started; you don't need a break. If anything, you need to work harder!"

"Heck yes, I need a break. I need to be on the beach with the girls. You know, sun and fun for my spring vacation. I don't need to be cooped up with a bunch of ballplayers waiting to play four lousy ball games; there're plenty of games left in Atlanta!"

And then he informs me that at the eleven a.m. practice today he dogged it and got a good reaming from Coach.

I answer, "Well, for crying out loud, I really thought you were looking forward to this trip and these games, but what the heck do I know. It's too late to worry about Panama City now, so just put that out of your mind and concentrate on the here and now, on the baseball. Anybody can go at it half-hearted; we've traveled too far to take that kind of attitude."

I don't know if he's really that upset about not getting to go to Panama City, or if the pressure to perform brought on by the errors is getting to him. It's probably a combination of the two. Most problems seem to be a combination of things. Anyway, he seems better after letting some steam off. Hopefully he'll have a better outlook when the games begin. *Dang these teenagers and their dang hormones*, I think. *He needs to pay more attention to what his old man says and less to his instincts. I believe the beginning of Proverbs addresses that issue. I'll have to guide him to that passage.*

Chapter Fifteen

Well, here we go! It's time for the first game of the Sarasota Baseball Classic. I've borrowed an older recorder from a friend to start taping Woody for possible use in the recruiting process. It's big, one of the *shoulder* type, but on the good side, you can pop the VCR tape straight into the VCR for viewing. My buddy hasn't used the unit in quite a few years and doesn't know how good the battery is, but I've received operating instructions and am ready to shoot.

While recording Woody during infield warm-ups before the game, I see the old tentativeness has followed us to Florida, and he's having trouble handling routine grounders that he used to scoop up without any effort. Or at least, it seemed like it was effortless. I'm also concerned that filming him is putting even more pressure on him. However, I only intend to tape his at bats during the game. I ask him about the recorder, and he says it doesn't bother him at all, but unfortunately, he seems to be still sporting a *'tude*.

Game one versus the Port Orange Hurricanes could be titled 555 Miles to a Nightmare on Procter Street. Our first game is a five p.m. start and is the first of two games to be played on one of the local host high school team's fields, located on Procter Street.

The Panthers hit first and go in order on a groundout to short by Danny and infield pop-ups by Hunter and Terry. The Canes open their half of the first with a solid single off Danny. The number-two hitter draws a walk before a deep drive to center field is hauled in on a circus catch by Phil. Maybe they'll get outta this jam. The designated hitter bats next for the Canes and launches a shot to right that Hunter snags. *Whew, that was a bit of a rocket heading for the gap between right and center fields, but Hunter made a nice running catch.* Now there are two on and two out—nightmare time.

A slow roller to Woody at third and it's an instant replay of the first game of the season. The hopper eludes Woody like a frightened chipmunk, and the bases are loaded on the E5. *Dear God, this ain't fair. Please let us off this stinking hook!* But no, a single plates two runs—damage done. The next batter is hit by a pitch, putting men on first and second again. This is getting to be too much, and it's only the first inning! I'm feeling sick and angry at the same time—sick for Woody's inability to play up to his potential and angry at his attitude. *Geez, I hope this is one of those games that ends up totally different than the way it starts.*

Luckily, the next batter, the eighth Cane to hit in the bottom of the first, grounds out to Pat at shortstop to end the first. I'm churning inside, and knowing Woody's attitude before the game, I worry he'll have a major meltdown and get himself yanked out of the game. That might be the best thing for him in the long run, but I don't think I can deal with that kind of embarrassment on the first night this far from home.

Major leads off the second with a solid single, and when Woody steps to the plate, prayers for a redeeming shot race through my mind, but he pops up to the second baseman. *Shoot!* Pat attempts to bunt Major to second, but the pitcher throws to second base in time for the out there. With two out, Phil reaches first on a hit-by-pitch, but the threat dies with an inning-ending strikeout. Fortunately, Danny gets the Canes in order in their second at bat.

Both sides go one, two, three in the third. The Panthers go in order in the fourth inning as well. The Canes get two singles in the bottom of the fourth but no runs, and the game seems to be developing into a pitchers' duel. Jason gets a two-out single in the top of the fifth, but to no avail as no more hits follow. When the Panthers take the field for the bottom of the fifth, sophomore Joe James takes Woody's position at third. I don't know what happened, and I don't think I want to know. I'm sitting near the Sandy Pines dugout, and at least I haven't heard any loud crashes or screaming. *Surf's up* in the old belly for sure now. The Canes go in order, and Joe isn't tested at third.

The top of the order comes up for the Panthers, who trail two to zero in the sixth, and Danny leads off with a single. Terry puts down yet another good sacrifice bunt that moves Danny to second base. Hunter reaches base on an error by the second baseman. A walk to Major loads the bases and brings Joe out of the on-deck circle toward home plate. But Coach Pat reenters Woody to hit. Well, just what the Pelhams need, some massive *on-the-spot* pressure. Baseball can be too-darn-much like real life.

Woody responds with an RBI single—*thank you, Lord*—and the bases are still loaded with one out and one run in. Looks like we're in pretty good shape now; I know my stomach is in a lot better shape. It's a chance for a huge inning. But the Canes bring in a lefty to pitch, and he promptly strikes out the next two Panther batters to end the inning and quell the uprising. That's a big opportunity missed.

It gets worse as the Canes pad their lead with two runs in the bottom of the sixth on a walk, a sacrifice bunt attempt that's mishandled, another sac bunt, a sac fly, and a single. The Cane lefty continues his mastery of the Panthers in the *last-chance* top of the seventh with two more strikeouts and a pop-up to the first baseman. Game over—heck of a start.

Coach Pat gathers the team as always in the outfield and drops his pearls of wisdom on the players. I learn later that he challenges the players by questioning if they might be afraid to play the best they can; maybe they're afraid to contend and win the state championship. Two *players-only* meetings take place that night also. The first game was a disappointment in style and outcome, but maybe it will result in the team creating some good chemistry for the future. Can you tell I'm looking for the rainbow?

The next day brings a ten a.m. practice to further capture the boys' attention. There's no game this day, but there is another cookout on the pool deck that night. At the get-together, John Thomas, Major's dad, asks me if I've heard about what Woody did in the meeting on the field after the game. I say I haven't, and he tells me that after Coach Pat reamed them out and left the field, Woody kept them there and apologized for his attitude. John says he was impressed with Woody's willingness to be accountable. So am I. I guess at least one good thing has come out of last night's aggravation.

The Christophers are proving to be great condo-mates, and we're really enjoying each other's company—the first game's results notwithstanding. I'm surprised to find out in checking my scorebook that the Panthers generated only three hits in the first game loss. I suppose I was too focused on Woody's travails to realize the guys weren't hitting the ball very well.

Hopefully the bats will wake up for the next three games, or we came a long way to create some reverse momentum.

We will join the rest of the tournament's first-game losers in playing our remaining games at the Cincinnati Reds' training facility. No hope to play for the championship or face Berkwood since they won their first game. Well, let's see if the boys can win three now, and maybe we'll meet Berkwood later, back in Georgia.

Chapter Sixteen

Game two is versus the Orange Bay Sting Rays. Orange Bay is the current number-two-ranked 3A team in Florida. The Reds' training site is about an hour from our condo, and Kim and I ride with the Christophers. Today Mack wants to get there plenty early since his son, Allan, is pitching. I'm happy to oblige. I'd rather be there an hour early than five minutes late.

There are four fields here that radiate from the center like four slices of pie. There are no lights, no scoreboards, and no videotaping 'cause the battery has run down already; it's kaput! It lasted about five minutes the first game and didn't even make the first pitch for this game. Murphy strikes again. But the observation deck located in the center of the fields has an outlet, so I can run off the charger the next two games as long as I bring an extension cord.

We're the home team, and Allan starts the game off by striking out the Rays' leadoff hitter. *Super, Allan! Now just strike out the next twenty batters!* After a groundout, two reach base via a single and a walk. *Allan, were you not paying attention to my instructions?* This time Allan hears my plea and strikes out the next batter to end the threat and bring the good guys in to bat.

Danny leads off with a single, steals second, and advances

to third on a groundout. Now that's the way our turn at bat should start. Woody follows with a well-hit sacrifice fly to left field, and the Panthers lead one to zero at the end of one.

The Rays collect one hit in the top of the second but no runs as Allan strikes out two more batters to bring his K total to four after just two innings. *Maybe he is hearing me.* The Panthers strike for three more runs in the bottom of the second on singles by Bobby and Hunter, a triple by Pat, and a double by Allan. I'm sure Mack is all smiles, since his boy is playing a great game. I'm giving him space to focus on Allan's efforts without too many distractions, but I'm wishing the gosh-darn recorder battery was working so I could be taping some of big Al's exploits. The Panthers lead four to zero after two.

The Sting Rays get one run on three singles in the top of the third. Not bad, just one run on three hits. The Panthers are retired in order in the third inning and also in the fourth and fifth innings. The Florida sun is starting to heat up, and the action on the field is about to follow suit.

With one on and one out in the top of the fifth, the batter smacks one to Woody, and he boots another grounder to put runners on first and second. I might just hurl. But that runner is erased on a beautiful strike-'em-out, throw-'em-out double play to end the inning—just a little acid reflux to deal with. The error both worries and mystifies me, and I fear the misplays are in Woody's head for sure now, making him even more tentative. Isn't that just what we need?

Orange Bay scratches out a run in the top of the sixth on a single, a walk, and an error on the shortstop. *Oh heck, is it contagious?*

The score stands at four to two in favor of the Panthers when Woody leads off the bottom of the sixth with a single. That's good. But that dark cloud is still hanging over him, and he's picked off first; that's real bad. He's just not focused. Sandy Pines plates no runs in the sixth, and we go to the seventh still ahead four to two.

With two outs and the Panthers on the verge of victory, cruel fate almost unbelievably seeks out Woody and sends a grounder between his legs for yet another of the most embarrassing errors. *What the heck is going on?* I know it's got to be absolutely eating him up now, and it is so frustrating as a parent to be able to do nothing but sit and watch and suffer along with him. This trip is turning into a disaster. A long ball now, and the score is tied. I can hardly watch. But thank God, the inning ends as it began with a groundout to short, and the Panthers win four to two. *Whew!* Allan gives up eight hits but also Ks eight for a very strong outing.

As the undercurrent of nausea begins to fade, I focus on today's good. I'm happy for Mack and Becky. I'm happy that Woody hit well, and I'm happy for the win. But to heck with those *seeing-eye* ground balls.

Chapter Seventeen

Kim and I are getting to know the Christophers much better and enjoying the process quite a bit. Mack and Becky are both New Yorkers with quick wit and a readiness to laugh. Mack and I are swapping college stories, hopefully out of earshot of Kim, while she is being entertained by Becky's tales of Allan's and David's shenanigans. They're both smokers, as is Kim unfortunately, so that creates a bit of a bond also.

Mack seems to be enthralled with an electronic, handheld Yahtzee game, and I'm trying to figure out some magic words to help Woody pull out of his error funk. Mack and I are on the balcony of our second-story condo unit watching Coach Pat and Assistant Coach Edgar Lawrence fish in one of the large ponds located on the grounds. Pat is casting artificial bait, as is Edgar. They're catching a few small bass when Mack wonders out loud what they're fishing with. I can tell easily that it's plastic worms, and when I inform Mack, he is amazed that I know the answer.

In that New York tone, he hollers at Becky, "Steve knows everything!" and asks, "How did you know that? How did you know what bait they were using? I'm just amazed at how much you know!" I answer that it's not hard to tell; once you've seen it used, it's pretty obvious.

Mack adds another crack along the lines of, "Steve is the smartest person in the world!" as we continue to discuss the coaches' fishing. And I'm thinking, *Most of the time, I'm just wishing I knew* something, *let alone everything.*

This afternoon's game is against the Miami-Dade Lightning. We're running a little late, courtesy of Mack's quick nap that turned out not to be so quick when Becky supposedly didn't wake him up. I'm sure she woke him and he nodded back off. Becky is also sure and lets him know in no uncertain terms.

I get to the observation deck and hook up and plug in the video recorder to tape the warm-ups. As they're ending, I see Brian Smith, a sophomore who usually backs up shortstop, taking turns at third with Woody. Under the circumstances, this doesn't look good, and Woody's body language coming into the dugout area tells me he's not starting. And if I had to make a quick guess, I'd say he's not hitting either. That's just what I needed, a little something else to worry about. But once again I'm wrong, and he turns out to be the designated hitter for this game.

The Panthers are visitors for the game but waste a single and score none in the top of the first. Mike Drew is our starting pitcher, and he is having trouble with his breaking ball—trouble both with the amount of break and the ump's vision of the strike zone. At any rate, he surrenders singles to the first two batters and then walks the next man to load the bases. Coach Pat lets Mike face another batter, but the number-five hitter rips a solid single to left field that chases Mike out of the game. That brings Phil on in relief.

Since Woody isn't playing in the field, he's been warming Phil up in the bullpen, and I have been taping the warm-up session just because I've missed seeing Woody catch the last year and a half. I'm sure Woody's situation both in the present and the possibilities for the future would be much better if he were catching, but the team is better served with him playing third. Baseball is most definitely a team sport.

The first out in the bottom of the first comes on a caught-stealing. When the runner at first breaks for second, Major guns the ball to Pat, who's standing short of second base. The man on third breaks for home, thinking the throw is going all the way to second, and Pat rifles the ball back to Major at home for the put-out. Finally, there's something to cheer about.

Phil strikes out the next batter for out number two. Then after a walk, he gets the number-nine hitter to ground-out to short, ending the inning. The Lightning post four runs on four hits, two walks, and a hit batsman. The Panthers are in a hole early. Did I think this trip was gonna be fun?

Major leads off the second with a called third strike on a full count, and he is three steps toward first before he realizes the ump has called the pitch strike three.

Mack has had all he can take of the home plate ump's version of the strike zone and speaks for all the Panther faithful when he hollers out, "Aw, come on, Blue! What are you looking at? Why don't you just pick a score and let us know what it is?" You gotta love Mack.

Woody is up next, and I'm wondering how much not playing in the field will affect his confidence at the plate. He answers quickly by ripping the first pitch to left field for a single. Well, that's a welcome relief. But the Lightning turn their second twin killing in as many innings when a grounder off Pat's bat goes short-to-second-to-first to end the inning.

Miami-Dade plates one in the home second without a clean hit, thanks to a fly ball in the sun that's not caught, a wild pitch, and an infield groundout. The score now stands at five to zero, Lightning, after two, and things definitely ain't looking good. Somebody stop the madness.

The third starts well with a single by Bobby. Brian draws a walk, and then Billy Sims, another sophomore in the game in left field, reaches first when hit by a pitch, to load the bases. But our luck with the umps continues when Danny sends a grounder to short. The shortstop flips the ball to second for the out. Billy slides hard but seemingly cleanly into second, and there's no throw to first to try for the double play. A run has scored, and runners are at the corners with one out. But wait, the field ump has called runner's interference at second base, resulting in an automatic double play. And what's worse, it's a dead ball situation when the runner's interference occurs, so our runners have to return to third and second! No score and two outs with men on second and third.

In the heat of the moment, it sure seems that the Panthers are getting jobbed by the men in blue. Just to add insult to injury, Hunter is called out on strikes to end the inning. Sandy Pines trails five to zero after three when Phil faces the minimum in the bottom of the third. He gets a double play to erase a leadoff single and then a groundout to second to end the inning.

After two walks open the Panther fourth, Woody rips the first pitch he sees to deep left field, but the fence is way out there, and there's a strong wind blowing straight in from left. It's a long out, but if pulled just a little more, would have been a two-RBI, standup double—*if*. Pat hits next and grounds into a fielder's choice. We have runners at first and third with two out, and now the Lightning hurler loses all concept of the strike zone, hitting the next three batters in a row.

And I guess the fielders don't want the pitcher to suffer alone because the shortstop commits an error to keep the inning alive and the runs coming home. Then the pitcher takes back control of things, walking the next batter. This is the ninth and last batter he has faced this inning. The new hurler gets Luke to fly out to center on his second at bat of the inning for the third out, but the score is now tied five to five. Well, that was weird, but welcome.

The Lightning regains the lead six to five in the bottom of the fourth. A leadoff single is erased at second on a second-to-short fielder's choice. But the runner at first subsequently advances to second on a wild pitch and then to third on another wild pitch. After Phil Ks the next batter for out number two, the following hitter strokes a single to plate the go-ahead run.

Major opens the Panther fifth with a walk. Woody steps in next and fouls off an attempted bunt. He shows bunt again and then swings away when the first baseman and third baseman charge the plate. But he fouls this one off also. I wonder if Coach Pat will call for the sacrifice bunt again with two strikes on Woody. I know Woody is trying extra hard at the plate since that is the only place he can contribute in this game. Coach Pat does call for the sac bunt again, and Woody gets it down as pretty as you please to advance the runner to second. Pat and Bobby follow with back-to-back singles, and the Panthers tie the game at six. Things are looking up.

Phil Ks the first batter in the Lightning half of the fifth. The next hitter lines a shot that Bobby spears for out number two, a great grab when we really needed it. Phil walks the next man, and Coach Pat brings Pat in from shortstop to pitch. When Pat leaves shortstop, Brian moves from third to shortstop, and Woody comes in at third base. Pat can't find the strike zone, or at least this ump's strike zone, and walks the next two batters to load the bases with two outs. All three runners are on courtesy of a free pass, and this game has blossomed into a bona fide gut-churner. Pat induces a pop-up to short out of the next hitter to end the threat. *Whew, again.*

Our leadoff man, Danny, is the first batter in the top of the sixth, and he gets things off to a positive start with a single. Hunter singles next, and the Panthers get the go-ahead run when Major hits into a short to first fielder's choice that plates one. Woody bats next with Hunter at third and lines the first pitch toward left field. But the third sacker stabs out and up and snags the bullet for out number three! That was a solid slap by Woody, but tough luck on the good play by the third baseman. And that was his second hard-hit ball with nothing to show for it; that's baseball, but it's frustrating as all get out. However, the Panthers finally have a lead at seven to six.

Our nerves get a rest in the Lightning half of the sixth as they go in order. It must be catching because the Panthers go one, two, three in the top of the seventh.

Three more outs to get for an amazing and satisfying come-from-behind victory. The Panthers get the first out on a grounder to short. The next hitter reaches first via an error on the shortstop. So there's one out and one on when the next batter sends a grounder hopping toward Woody at third. Adrenaline explodes in my gut. *Oh shoot, why couldn't he have hit it to second instead?* Dread flushes through me, and I want to shut my eyes but don't. Woody plays the hop and makes the throw to first for out number two. *What were you worried about, oh ye of little faith?* Our first sacker scoops up a grounder off the bat of the following hitter and steps on the bag to end the game.

Sandy Pines prevails seven to six and is now two and one for the tourney with one game left. This game took me back to my days coaching nine- and ten-year-olds at Jones Park. There was enough ugly in this game for a whole season of high school baseball, most notably three hit batsmen in a row. But a win is a win no matter how improbable.

That night we get Woody and Allan to accompany us to

dinner at the Bradenton Ale House. We are not only celebrating a victory but also David's birthday. The parents are responsible for feeding the players tonight, and we feel lucky to have pried our sons away from the team card game for a meal with the family. The food is quite good and at good prices, nothing like we experienced the night before at a beachside eatery. That was a disappointment—expensive with lousy service. Of course, Woody has to get the car keys to manage his and Al's escape as soon as they've finished eating. But the rest of us enjoy our time and David's birthday giant fudge brownie sundae.

Back at the condo, I'm pondering leaving and remembering how I always hate to leave my sister's place at the beach. As I think back, I recall last summer's departure day as Jessica's sister, Monica, and her daughter and I worked together taking down our beach cabana shelter. And it reminds me of how much easier things get done through teamwork. Weird that I would think of that, but I hope the team is coming to understand the concept of true teamwork, and anyone can see it has been a bonding experience for them. I try not to dwell on how much teamwork it can take to overcome certain errors.

That night Mort wakes me in the middle of the night. Seems he's been picking at me regularly on the trip. While playing golf with the dads, he's asking, "Don't you want to enjoy this in the years ahead?" Sitting at the beach for a few minutes with Kim, he whispers, "Don't you want to share these times with Kim in the future?" This night I wake from a dream of Jess standing over me in my casket, crying and asking why. *Why* is still ringing in my head as I roll out of bed the next morning. Mort is really piling on here lately, and I'm beginning to think he's making some sense.

Chapter Eighteen

Well, here's the last game on the spring vacation trip to Florida. It's our third game at the Ed Smith Complex, and I guess you could say we're playing for the ESC Championship. The opponent today is Northeast Miami. The Sea Hawks remind me of the Tamiami team of Hispanic kids that knocked our twelve-year-old state champs out of region play in 1996. Heck, there may be some of those same kids on this team, just like we have some of our kids still playing together. It's unlikely but interesting to consider.

The Panthers are the home team, and senior Hank Jackson is on the mound to start the game. The leadoff hitter reaches first on a throwing error on the third baseman; it's not Woody; he is the DH again today. Maybe it's the fields here and not the third basemen—*get real.* Hey, I'm just trying not to worry too much, trying to enjoy this last game. The next batter grounds out, shortstop-to-first, so there's a runner at second with one out. Batter number three singles home a run and then steals second. The clean-up hitter also delivers an RBI single, and we're down by two with only one out in the top of the first. *Ho hum, what's new?* He also steals second on Luke, who's catching today. Major is playing first, but I think Luke is still feeling some of the effects of the fever he experienced soon after arriving in Florida. The number-five hitter draws a walk, but Hank gets out of the inning on consecutive fly balls to the outfield. The Panthers come to bat in the bottom of the first trailing by two.

Danny and Hunter put together back-to-back singles, and Woody bats third with men on first and third. I'm really hoping he has another good day at the plate. Of course, I'm still worried about his not playing in the field and trying not to panic. I rationalize that it's a combination of his play and a chance for some other kids to get playing time during the trip to Florida. Quite possibly, Coach is trying to take some pressure off Woody by not playing him in the field, give him a chance to breathe easy before returning to the region-six wars. Woody hits the second pitch he sees hard but on the ground and right at the shortstop. They turn the double play, short to second to first, but Danny scores from third. The inning ends on Major's fly ball to left field.

Hank is greeted in the top of the second with a leadoff single. The next Sea Hawk grounds out to short. Now the runner at first reaches third base on a balk and a wild pitch. It's back to the top of the order, and the leadoff man again reaches base on an error, scoring the runner from third. The next batter chases Hank with a single and brings Mike Drew in from the bullpen. I'm hoping Mike has better luck with this ump's strike zone than he did yesterday as a starter. Mike induces a double-play ball from the first man he faces, and it's three to one, Sea Hawks, at the end of one and a half innings.

The Panthers waste singles by Pat and Luke in their half of the second and go to the third inning still down by two runs.

The first Sea Hawk hitter reaches base on an error, but the next three are outs, and no damage is done.

Sandy Pines strikes back in the bottom of the third when

Woody comes through with an RBI double after a one-out single by Danny and a walk to Hunter. He hits the ball hard again with men on base and this time gets rewarded. But that's all the scoring the Panthers can muster this inning, and they go to the fourth trailing two to three.

Mike makes short work of the Sea Hawks in the fourth by striking out the first two hitters and then getting an inning-ending ground ball to short.

Sandy Pines fares much better in the home half of the fourth. Bobby starts things off with a single and is sacrifice-bunted to second by Phil.

Brian Smith draws the one-out walk to put runners at first and second. Danny is hit by a pitch to load the bases. Hunter and Woody follow with RBI singles, and then Major is hit by a pitch to again load the bases. This is good; this is very good. Unfortunately, the Panthers leave the bases loaded when a grounder to first is thrown home for the force-out there, and the next hitter strikes out. But Sandy Pines is finally ahead, leading five to three going into the sixth. *Gosh darn, that could have been so much better.*

The sixth starts well for the Panthers when the first man up grounds out. But after two errors and a single, Allan comes on to relieve Mike. After a sacrifice bunt, Allan walks a man to load the bases and then is called for a balk when he steps off the rubber and toward the runner from first, who is a third of the way to second base. I don't know what he did wrong, but the tying run comes home on the balk. The Sea Hawks are finally retired on a grounder to Allan, and this game is reaching the gut-bomber level now. You just know the last game would have to go this way!

Hunter opens the Sandy Pines sixth with a walk, and Woody sacrifice-bunts him to second. That's another good bunt for Woody, who hasn't been called on to bunt often. Major singles the go-ahead run home, and then the next two hitters are outs to end the inning. But hey, the Panthers lead six to five with three outs to get. *Come on guys; let's leave the sunshine state with a W.*

Northeast opens the seventh inning with a single. *Yipes!* The number-two batter lines out to short, and it turns into a double play when the runner at first goes too far toward second and is forced out on Pat's throw to first. That's two down and one more to go, and now comes the controversy. You can't have a tournament without a little controversy. It just so happens that ours comes in the final game.

It begins when the Sea Hawks dispute a called strike, and all their fans and players and coaches are yelling at the ump when Allan delivers the next pitch. The batter swings and misses; strike three and game over. But one Sea Hawk fan, probably the batter's father, continues to berate the umps in Spanish and English as they are leaving the field. He even comes over to the gate where they exit the playing surface to lambaste them some more. One of our moms is standing next to me on the observation deck while I'm taping the end of the game.

She is understandably displeased with the display of poor sportsmanship and hollers at the man, "What's the matter with you? It's only a game!" She's right, but I'm thinking, *Let's not draw any of that venom this way.* The man and his buddy look up and see I'm taping, and the buddy tries to get the man to calm down, but he is apparently proud to rant and rave and rattles off his name to the camera.

I take the camera off my shoulder, indicating I'm no longer taping as our mom continues to shout, "It's only a game!"

Then the man's buddy shouts back at us, "It is not just a game; it's not a game!" I'm baffled by that last statement and start down off the deck to get the heck outta there. Apparently that last salvo was the end because both sides are heading their opposite ways to the parking lot. So we finish as champs of the Ed Smith Complex with an exciting final victory that includes an unexpectedly exciting exit. *Take that, Mort.*

Chapter Nineteen

The ride home isn't as much of a downer as most return trips from Florida vacations. The season will swing into full region play on Monday, just two days away. I didn't get to see the match-up with Berkwood that I had hoped for, but they didn't make it to the championship game of the undefeated teams either. I think I heard they lost their third game in the tourney. So maybe neither of us is as good as I thought, but time will tell.

As Kim and I are talking during the ride home and I'm enjoying this time with her, the guilt begins to creep up inside me. Just a little at first, but then when I consciously realize it's there, it floods out all other emotions. As I glance over at Kim, I see the scar on her chin, and I'm reminded of the courage she displayed when she suffered that injury. It was the summer before her first year of high school, and while riding her horse bareback beside the road, the horse spooked and threw her. She was carrying a three-foot-long two by four to the barn, and when she hit the ground, the board stood on end, and her face hit the upturned end. It tore a four-inch gash across her chin and then broke her cheekbone.

The three hours in the operating room while the plastic surgeon repaired her injuries were three of the longest hours of our lives for Jess and me. It killed me inside to see her lying in that hospital bed in such pain and with all those stitches in her face. I was worried to the point of being ill about the emotional effect the facial injury would have on my adolescent daughter, about to enter the new and unknown world of high school. But she never let it get her down. She said the scar was a part of her, and she accepted it as such. I was and still am amazed by the level of courage she exhibited.

Am I lacking courage now? Am I cheating her? Am I cheating Woody? Am I cheating Jessica by not following up on my health as soon as possible? Am I just living my life, or what may be left of it, vicariously through my son? Am I unable to see the big picture of the future and what it can be? Since this may be Woody's last season in baseball, am I willing to risk it being my last season, period? That's just too many questions for this old man to figure out right now. What the hey, I had really hoped I wouldn't have any second thoughts about my decision, but eight years of Catholic school isn't going to let me get by totally guilt-free.

Everyone arrives back safely Saturday night, thankfully. When he gets to the house, Woody and I discuss the games and the trip, and he admits that he did have a good time after all. There was a lot of horsing around between the older and younger players, he says, but it was a good way to get to know them, and each other, better. I'm happy to hear that the trip was a success and that he didn't stay aggravated over not being in Panama City. Sometimes kids manage to mature a little bit in spite of themselves.

Sunday afternoon I get Woody to let me hit him grounders at the high school field. I'm hoping the practice will boost his confidence, but at any rate we can get him some more reps to take his mind out of the equation and get him to trust his reactions. I know he has excellent hand-eye coordination and exceptional reactions, but he's got to quit thinking about it and just play.

He misses a few and loses his temper and says he can't do it. He says he doesn't care; he's not going to play at the next level, and he's accepted it, so why can't I? Well, there it is. He's been trying to prove to himself that he's good enough to play in college, and the pressure is preventing him from playing his best even at this level. He says he's sorry he has disappointed me and let me down. Well that's a nice kick in the teeth. My perceived expectations for him are just adding to the pressure—the last thing I, or any father, want to happen. I tell Woody he hasn't disappointed me and it doesn't matter if he plays in college, and it doesn't matter to me. I just want him to be the best he can be now, at this level. I tell him I know he can dang well catch grounders and remind him that he had only two errors all last season. I tell him we both know he can play third, we just have to get him out of this funk, and that I don't want him to let this beat him. I tell him to trust his eyes and hands, take his brain out of the process, no more thinking, and no more internal pressure.

He snags a few and then makes a really good quick grab of a short-hopper. "Luck!" he shouts.

I shout back, "You had to think to say that—no thinking!"

I hit him more grounders, and he looks smooth, not tentative. After a while, he asks how long we're going to keep this up, and I tell him as long as he wants and remind him that the harder he works, the luckier he'll get. Woody hollers back that he wants to get ten in a row without missing, and now the pressure's on me too. I've got to hit decent grounders that are reachable but not easy. He hasn't missed any through eight tries and asks how many that makes. I tell him, "No thinking. I'll stop when you reach ten." Woody snags the next two, and we're headed for home.

I decide to have a little sit-down with Woody before we exit the field and steer him into the home dugout, out of the sun. He's not adverse to the idea, and I dive right in as we settle in on the pines.

"So, bud, I'm sorry to hear I've been putting undue pressure on you about playing in college. It was never my intention. I just want you to have the most success and fun you can in your senior season. No need to worry what comes after that right now."

"It's not really you, Dad. I just don't think I'm good enough. I'm stinking it up in the field. I haven't hit any home runs. I feel like I'm flaming out in my last year."

"Well, your coaches know you've got good enough skills behind the plate for the next level—especially Coach Lawrence. When Kim and I had dinner with him and a bunch of other parents in Sarasota, he was talking about the Central Georgia coach being his old roommate and how he wanted to get you over there as a catcher. He can get you hooked up."

"I'll believe it when I see it," Woody answers.

"Talking about catching reminds me of my favorite catcher, Yogi," I say.

Woody rolls his eyes and sighs. "I know, Dad. 'It ain't over 'til it's over.'"

"Well, it's true, and years before he made that quote famous as the Mets manager, he proved it to me personally."

"Oh, he did, did he?" Woody adds with more than a little disbelief in his voice.

"He did, indeed. It was my twelfth or thirteenth birthday, 1961 or 1962, can't remember which. I collected baseball cards; they were a penny apiece and came with a flat, thin piece of bubble gum wrapped up in each card. Wow, it's far out to think of a penny buying anything now, let alone a card and a piece of gum. Anyway, I wanted Yogi's card so bad that when my cousin John gave me a buck for my birthday present—"

"Wow, a whole buck!" Woody interrupts.

"Yes, impudent youth, a whole buck! And it was worth something back then, namely a box of one hundred baseball cards. That's how they sold them, an open box of a hundred that you fished around in to pick out your selections. But I took my buck and bought an unopened box of one hundred, sure I could get one Yogi card out of that hundred.

"Your Uncle John and I rushed my box back from the drugstore to the little house we lived in on Roswell Road in Sandy Springs, brimming with anticipation. We sat down on the floor in the small living room and began to open each card individually. There were some good ones: Sandy Kofax, Don Drysdale of the LA Dodgers, Warren Spahn, and Eddie Mathews of the then Milwaukee Braves, and lots of Yanks—Whitey Ford, Bobby Richardson, Roger Maris, and even Mickey Mantle.

"Halfway through the box and the stack of bubble gum was climbing like a pink skyscraper in our tiny den. And still no Yogi. I wasn't really worried yet; there was at least half a box to go. Well, the pink skyscrapers, we had two now—fifty-five pieces was as high as we could go in a stack—continued to grow, and the paper wrappers piled up but still no Yogi. With twenty cards left, I began to worry. When we got to the final ten and started the countdown, I was really worried. When we got to the last two, I figured *no way*. I was really bumming out; I figured I'd wasted that whole dollar. When John opened the next to last card, and it was my second Ernie Banks, I figured *game over*. I might even have whispered "shoot" or something else. And then I opened the very last of the one hundred, and there was Yogi Berra's beautiful mug smiling up at me!"

"No way, Pops. You're making this up. No way, man!" Woody says.

"Way, dude. I ain't lying. The very last one. It wasn't over 'til it was over."

"No way," Woody says.

"We'll call your Uncle John when we get home; he'll tell ya. I'm sure he remembers. It was awesome, and it's true."

Woody brings us back to the present. "Anyway, if I'm dreaming, I'm dreaming about pro ball, getting paid to play, and I realize now that that ain't happening. So what's the point in playing a little college ball if it's not taking me to the next level?"

"Well, son, there are a lot of advantages to playing in college. You can make a lot of good contacts for the future, and you've got built-in buddies with the team, and that's a good thing when you're out on your own for the first time. It's kinda like a fraternity; you've got older guys to clue you in on professors and classes, and let's face it, even though it ain't right, you'll probably get preferential treatment to some degree as an athlete. Heck, you've unfortunately tried to take advantage of that to some degree already with your goofing off in at least one class this year."

Woody gives a little grin and says, "Yeah, I guess so."

"Well, kid, you might as well go all out and let the chips fall where they may. I know it's hard to think about giving it your all, busting your butt on every play, and still coming up short. I think it's human nature to hold back a little so we might still be able to wonder if we could have made it if we had gone all out. I think I probably did that some when I walked on to try and play football at Tech. But trust me; it's better to leave it all on the field. Besides, you'll have more fun now, and who knows how good you'll turn out to be if you don't hold yourself back. And most importantly, your teammates deserve your best effort. This is a team sport, and taking the emphasis off you and putting it on the team might be just what the doctor ordered. Anyway, it's not life and death; it's not war. You oughta be able to get a grin out of it no matter what, right?"

And then I hold my closed left hand out to him and pop it open, revealing the smiley face I've drawn in the palm. Only this is a mean, frowning face with its tongue sticking out; figured he needed a change of pace. He grins and giggles a little as he shakes his head. But as always, the smiley face in the hand is a success.

For a while, it looked like this outing was going to be a disaster, but in the end I think it turned out well. I tell him that I bet he starts at third tomorrow versus Nelton, but he guarantees he won't. We'll see. Nelton is another power in our region. The game is at their place, and I'm thinking Coach Pat will want his most experienced players on the diamond.

Back at home that night, John confirms my Yogi baseball card tale to Woody on the phone. It was way too good a story to go without validation.

Chapter Twenty

Whoa Nellie, this is huge, game eight of the regular season at Nelton. This is the team to beat in Region Six. Woody had a huge day here last year, even got his picture on the cover of the local paper making a play in the field. Big picture it was, about eight inches by four inches, and in color too. That game was on a Friday, and on Saturday morning, while I was walking down to pick up the paper in the driveway, our next-door neighbor hollered to me about seeing Woody's picture in the paper. He didn't elaborate, so I thought it was probably some random picture of students at the high school doing something or other. Well, I found the sports page as I was walking back to the house, and there was that big color photo on the front page. I was in kind of a daze when I spotted it because it was April 1, and my brain was racing, trying to figure out if this was some sort of April fool's joke, and if so, how did someone get a photo in the newspaper. But it was for real. He had a bases-loaded double, which resulted in three RBIs and some other timely hits that day. I'm hoping he'll have another big game today. And oh yeah, I was right. Woody is starting at third.

Danny is our leadoff hitter to begin the game, and he starts things off with a walk, but Hunter follows with a K. Woody hits next and gets behind, no balls and two strikes. He battles and gets the count to three balls and two strikes after fouling off four or five strikes. It's a good duel between Woody and the Nelton hurler and one Woody finally wins with a solid liner into left field for a single. Major and Terry follow with singles, and the Panthers score two in the top of the first. *Very good start, the kind that allows my gut to settle into the game, and I appreciate that, fellas.*

Allan is on the mound for Sandy Pines, and he gets the Lions' leadoff hitter to fly out to left field. The next batter smacks a grounder toward third; *oh shucks, the gut is instantly unsettled!* But Woody comes up cleanly with it and makes a strong throw to first for the second out. There was never a doubt in my mind! Thank goodness he got a chance early in the game, and it wasn't one of those frightened chipmunk hoppers. However, the next two hitters bang out singles, and then Allan walks the following batter to load the bases, yuck-ola! *Just had to make it interesting*, I think. But he induces a grounder to short from the next batter, and the force-out at second ends the inning, *whew.*

Sandy Pines gets another run in the second when Allan draws a walk with one out and Hunter singles home the courtesy runner, who has moved up to second when an attempted pickoff at first goes wild and wide right. Most pickoff attempts in high school baseball seem to be high-risk, low-reward chances. We'll take 'em any way we can get 'em.

The three to zero lead disappears in the bottom of the second on a solo homer and four consecutive singles, and the Panthers trail three to four going to the top of the third. *Well, that smooth sailing didn't last very long, did it? Here's hoping for some more excitement on our side.*

Woody leads off the third and reaches first when he's hit by a pitch. Major bats next and draws a walk before Terry puts down another good sacrifice bunt toward third and reaches first on the third sacker's throwing error. Bobby hits a sacrifice fly to left, and Pat and Allan follow with singles to make the score six to four in favor of the Panthers after two and a half. *This game is fun again!*

The Lions open their half of the third with a single, then Al comes back to strike out the next batter. The next two hitters go down, courtesy of Woody, the first on a liner to third, and the next and third out of the inning on a grounder to third and the throw-out to first. Woody looks to have his confidence back; maybe he likes this park. Like I said before, he had a big day here last year. At any rate, it's so far, so good today.

In the top of the fourth, Hunter starts things off with a single. Woody follows with a walk—*nice going, kid*—before Major is caught looking at strike number three for out number one. Terry singles Hunter home and Woody to third. The next batter fails to make contact on a suicide-squeeze bunt, and Woody is out number two in the ensuing rundown between home and third, *fiddlesticks!* Phil goes down swinging for out number three, but Sandy Pines now leads seven to four. And that will have to hold up as the Panthers go hitless and scoreless the rest of the way.

The Lions strand one runner in the bottom of the fourth and two more in the fifth and then go one, two, three in the sixth. So we go to the seventh and final inning still up by three, *thank you very much.*

Nelton opens the bottom of the seventh with two consecutive walks, *look out!* The following hitter singles home one run, but a great relay throw from Hunter to Terry to Major cuts down the second runner at home for out number one; *great teamwork.* Allan Ks the next batter and then walks the number-nine hitter. Look out again, two outs, two on, and ahead by two runs with the leadoff man coming up to bat! My gut feels like this is the Cuban missile crisis or something. Not to worry, Al induces a grounder to short, which Pat grabs and flips to Bobby at second for the force-out and a Panthers victory.

And it's a big win in a lot of ways. The team really wanted and needed to beat Nelton, and they got the job done. The last time they faced these guys was in the state playoffs last year, and Nelton took two games to eliminate the Panthers and end their season. Not to mention, the guys did it in their fifth game in seven days and after a long drive home from Florida just a couple of days removed. I know this is a very satisfying win for the team, and it's a great way to get back into action after spring break. Things are looking good.

Chapter Twenty-One

No rest for the weary. It's another day and another game. Today the Panthers are making up the game rained out just before the Florida trip, taking on the Hightower Tigers at their place. As I mentioned earlier, this is one of my favorite places to watch a game. I have to admit that I am expecting a win. Hightower's record, both overall and in the region, isn't very impressive, and with the Panthers just having beaten Nelton, my expectations are high.

But maybe the boys were worn out. After the game, Woody said he felt exhausted, and he looked tired out there. Or maybe it's just a bad-luck day. Sandy Pines gets ten hits but leaves nine men on base in losing three to seven. Danny gets the loss on the mound, but Phil had the hard luck of facing the Tigers' big gun with the bases loaded. And the University of South Carolina signee didn't disappoint the home crowd, blasting the second pitch from Phil way over the center field fence for a grand slam and the winning margin. The Tigers managed only seven hits but got them at the right time to secure the victory; it seems to happen that way a lot in baseball. Hunter, Pat, and Bobby each collect two hits in the loss.

And I'm tired too. The knowledge I'm carrying alone and Mort's hammering away are really beginning to wear me down.

One minute I tell myself, *You're fine; probably just a bad X-ray*, and the next minute Mort chimes in with, *Yeah, just like the one that found your first tumor*. I guess it's dawning on me that the meaning of my life is tied irrevocably to the lives of my family. I guess I am being selfish in the long run. Someday these games will be ancient memories. I'll drive by Sandy Pines and think, *It's been six or seven years since Woody played here*. The same way I used to think, *Kim and Woody will be going to school here in a few years* when I drove by in the past.

Time marches on, and I'm realizing I can't freeze or prolong the here and now no matter how bad I want to. It's time to find out. I've heard something about a new test that can tell if you have any cancer in your body, so I'm going to check with the doc tomorrow to see if that is something that would be available to me.

Chapter Twenty-Two

A third game in three days. That's especially taxing on your pitching staff. The Panthers are hosting the Fielding Flyers today in another crucial region game. This is a game the Panthers need and should win, but then I figured they should have won yesterday against Hightower. I don't want to make that same big fat mistake today. At least Sandy Pines is finally playing at home again. It's been six games and two weeks since the Panthers have been able to battle it out on their home turf.

And I'm probably feeling even better than the team since the doc gave me the good news today that I can have one of those new tests. But that thought is temporarily forced to the back of my mind when Major's dad tells me before the game that there's a parents' meeting after the game. When I ask him what for, he says Coach Pat wants to address the changes in the starting lineup for today's game. *What's up?* My stomach does a back flip as I think, *Now what the heck has happened? Maybe Woody isn't starting due to his first pitch groundout with the bases loaded last game.* Projection can be so much fun.

But no, Woody is starting. However, two starters are missing from the lineup. Now I really wonder what's up.

Pat starts on the mound, and the Flyer leadoff hitter lays down a good bunt toward third. Another back flip for the old stomach, but Woody charges, comes up cleanly with the ball, and guns down the runner with a strong throw to first, *whew*. I'm still nervous, but he seems to be back in the fielding groove. The next two batters go in order, so Pat gets them one, two, three in the first.

The Flyers score three in the top of the second on a double followed by three consecutive singles. But the Panthers answer back with two runs on a single by designated hitter Luke Williams and two Flyer errors. *That's better, but let's get the lead, boys.*

Fielding adds to their lead in the third when the lead-off batter reaches second on a throwing error and is singled home. The Panthers are down two to four when they come to bat in the bottom of the third. *Can't we just win every game ten or fifteen to nothing?*

Woody opens the home half of the third with a double to the gap between center and right fields—*nice*. The next two hitters go down on a fly ball to left and a groundout to short. The count reaches no balls and two strikes on the following hitter, and Coach Pat sends Woody on an attempted steal of third, or it's a hit and run. At any rate, Woody's thrown out at third to end the inning, and my stomach does about a half-gainer as the adrenaline spews freely. It's still two to four—bad guys.

Mike Drew takes the mound for the Panthers in the top of the fourth and shuts down the Flyers. In fact, he shuts them down the rest of the way, allowing no hits, striking out three, and walking two.

The fireworks erupt for the home team in the bottom of the fourth as the first nine batters not only reach base but score, and the Panthers lead eleven to four. *I just needed to be a little more patient; good things come to those who wait.*

Highlights include doubles by Pat, Woody, Major, and Terry. The first out of the inning doesn't come until Luke grounds out to second in his second at bat of the inning. The Flyers use three relief pitchers in inning number four.

The home boys end it in the sixth when Luke draws a walk and Bobby and Billy single to load the bases. Hunter steps up and promptly sends a blast high and deep off the Evergreen Boulevard fence for a walk-off grand slam! That's some *big fly*, baby. It's a great win, and the Panthers are now three and two in the region and ten and four overall. It ain't fifteen to zero, but it's almost that good. It was totally important for the team to grab momentum back and not go on a two-game losing streak at this stage of the season. There's a huge game coming up on Monday against the number-one team in the region. And I've got a big date myself the day after tomorrow at Northside Hospital for my cancer scan. I haven't heard from Mort lately.

After the game at the parents' meeting, Coach Pat explains that he's having some problems with some of the seniors. He says he may lose some battles, but he will win the war. Further, he's trying to make his players into better men and get them ready for college ball, not just win baseball games. He also says he's not afraid to lose a game to set things right. He may not be afraid to lose a game, but I think I am. He says this team has more talent than even they know and can stand some people sitting out. And if he sits them out a game, it doesn't mean he loves them any less or that they won't start the next game. But if they make the mistake again, they'll sit again.

Coach Pat makes sense, but I never really discovered what the problem was with the two players who sat out, and I guess it's a good thing it stayed in-house, among the team.

At home that night, Woody says there was a scout from

Jenkins-Ball that was paying a lot of attention to him during the game. Kimberly says Coach Pat shouldn't tell them scouts are going to be there before the game, and Woody tells her he didn't. Mike Drew told him. Mike knows they're scouts because they are looking at him and are probably going to make him a scholarship offer.

The Panthers have five more games before the final four seeded region games.

Five wins would be just what the doctor ordered. Did I say *doctor*? I must have something on my mind.

Chapter Twenty-Three

Friday comes and with it a trip to the hospital for my scan. No pressure, just a check to see how the old bod's holding up. There's nothing to be nervous about, right? Yeah, right. Pulling into the hospital parking lot from Peachtree Dunwoody Road starts the memories flowing. But strangely, the first are of arriving here for the births of our two children. They were quite different.

First there was the panic-stricken rush when Jess's water broke with Kimberly—panic-stricken for me anyway. We arrive with expectations of a momentary birth and then endure a fourteen-hour wait. I'm so nervous I can't sit still, and the nurse has to turn off the sound of the fetal monitor because I can't stand to listen to a heartbeat. It totally gives me the willies. After hours of coffee and nerves, the time finally arrives for the trip to the delivery room. I have to wear a gown, a head cover kind of a like a shower cap, a mask, and shoe covers that go over each shoe and stay shut around your ankle with an elastic strap. I'm as nervous as I can possibly be, can't think straight, rushing and fumbling with gown buttons when the nurse comes to get me. The grin on her face quickly turns to giggles as she tells me I've got one of my shoe covers on my head instead of my cap. She gets me squared away, and in the delivery room I'm hyperventilating so fast, I just about inhale and swallow my mask. But I don't pass out, and my first look at my baby daughter is just about the most wonderful thing I've ever experienced. I never thought a baby could be that beautiful.

By contrast, Woody's birth seemed quite calm and routine; we were veterans then. But seeing my infant son for the first time was an equally overwhelming moment.

No thoughts of my cancer surgery invade my mind until I've walked halfway across the parking lot. I approach the hospital entrance seemingly in slow motion, and as I reach for the door, a vivid and frightful picture flashes to mind. The picture is from the movie *Saving Private Ryan*. I'm in a Normandy-landing boat, looking at the front panel that's about to be lowered for landing on the beach. I'm queasy in the belly, near ready to hurl, and weak in the knees. But for me it's total nerves and not a combination of seasickness and nerves. What's waiting for me when the ramp drops? A bullet or life?

And if it's life, am I going to be severely wounded again? Am I going back to nowhere-ville with my life in the hands of the masked man with the knife and the poison man with his hands on the controls of the limbo me? I sure don't want to take that bullet now. Hot dog, I'm having a surgery flashback as I wait for the doc. But I've calmed down some. It's weird, but I'm not nearly as nervous as when Woody's facing a two-strike count with the tying run on second and two outs.

Now I'm recalling lying in the hospital bed last time, a chunk of my lung hacked out, a chest tube jammed in my side, and my mind dulled by pain. I remember wondering how awful it would have been to be in that condition on the battlefield. What kind of horrible situation would that be, maybe lying on the beach at Normandy with an eight-millimeter slug in my lung and my buddies lying dead or dying around me. Or maybe it's the Battle of the Bulge, and I've been blown into a foxhole of mud and icy puddles with a chunk of shrapnel in my lung, feeling nothing but cold numbness and frigid fear. Or better yet, maybe it's World War I, and the wound in my lung is from the hideous saw-tooth bayonet. I'm lying there in a crater in no man's land, wondering if I'm dying, wondering if the mustard gas has abated, and maybe even hoping the end will come soon.

Where the heck did that trip come from? Anyway, it makes me realize that facing surgery and recovery in a climate-controlled hospital room doesn't seem so bad after all.

The ramp drops, the procedure proceeds, and for now what waits for me is life. I'm clean, no more CA right now—at least not now. What an incredible load has been lifted, what a weight off my heart! I can hardly believe I've been this fortunate. What an awesome moment in time this is, especially since I've been trying to live in the moment. Obviously, I haven't always been successful, but I've been trying. And I think I might have just had a vision of Mort as a butterfly, flitting out of sight.

But all is not well. Turns out the hospital has called my home phone number for health insurance information instead of calling me at work, as I, of course, instructed them to do. Why won't health providers ever call my work number? Now I'm totally busted, and the avalanche of guilt that Jessica lets loose on me is gigantic and deserved, I guess. I believe her temper can be as hot as her hair is red. When I get home, it goes something like this:

"What's going on, Steve? The hospital called. I know you're having some kind of test without telling me, again! This is so unfair. What in the world are you thinking? You tried to hide that first bad X-ray and CT scan from me before the surgery, and now you're doing it again! Am I supposed to be scared to death by the hospital out of the blue instead of you having the decency to include me in our life situations?"

"Sorry, sorry, sorry; it's okay. I'm okay. I didn't want to worry you or the kids. There was a spot on my lung X-ray during my physical."

Jess attacks even harder now as I cringe under the withering and probably deserved assault. "This has been going on since December? I can't believe it! And you're just now getting checked out. Dear God, help me! I'm married to a total freaking idiot!"

"I'm sorry. I wanted to wait 'til Woody's season was over but decided I'd better go ahead. I didn't want to mess him up."

"Oh, so you think dying after the baseball season wouldn't mess him up? Lord, help me. You just didn't want surgery to mess up your watching his games, did you? Men are so insane about sports. I don't think I can believe this!"

"Well, it's his senior year, his last season, and he's got a lot of pressure on him with college coming up. I didn't want to make it worse. I know it was stupid, and talking about it now makes my choice sound really, really stupid. I figured a couple months wouldn't hurt, but the guilt and worry got to me; I heard about a scan that can detect any cancer in your body, and I had it done and I'm clean. Isn't that the main thing? I was okay all along."

After a long, silent stare, Jess finishes me off with, "I'm glad you're not gonna die, but I could kill you just the same!" And then she embraces me with a mighty python hug and a "you're such a gigantic nut, but I love you anyway" whisper in my ear. We head out for a celebratory dinner before the kids get home because Jess agrees it's best to keep my "self-serving, self-centered, secret condition, and selfish conniving" from the kids. No reason to saddle them with this info since it's now in the past, albeit the very recent past. Tonight I thank God for all my blessings, paramount among them my family and the health to enjoy them and that most wonderful gift: *time*.

On Saturday I have a blast pitching whiffle balls to Woody in the backyard. I even dare give him a golf tip about firing the hip and hope it helps and doesn't screw up his other swing thoughts and mechanics.

On Sunday Danny calls Woody to catch for him and hit in the indoor facility at school. Woody comes back saying the catching felt good; I like to hear that. He also says he had his most solid contact with a wooden bat yet while hitting, another nugget of good news.

Monday morning I grab the local paper as usual and check the sports section. The region standings are on the front page along with an accompanying article. Fulton, today's opponent, is number one in the region with no losses. Sandy Pines is listed in the number-five slot with two region losses, *ugh*. Northlake and Nelton each have two losses also but have four wins to Sandy Pines's three. Hammond is second with a record of five and one. *Well, fiddlesticks, we're not in as good of shape as I thought.* Furthermore, Fulton is ranked second in the state and Hammond fifth. This is a pivotal week for the Panthers, facing both these highly ranked teams with Ardmore sandwiched in between. This could turn out to be a huge, huge week. This is what you play for; adrenaline pumps, start your engines!

Chapter Twenty-Four

Fulton is located about halfway home from work, and I arrive just before the game is about to start but barely have enough time to get the video recorder ready to go. This is another great place to watch and tape, with rows of ledges cut into the hillside above the field on the third base side. And it's the best day yet to watch a game for me since I don't have the cancer cloud hanging over me. Maybe Mort will show up to give me an "Atta-boy!"

Unfortunately, Jessica and Kimberly fall prey once again to my directions and don't arrive until the third inning. What I didn't realize in instructing them on getting to the game from home is that the name of the key road involved changes between the school's location and their exit off Highway 400. So they continued north and stopped to ask for directions when they feared they were about to go out of Georgia into North Carolina. Hard as I try, I don't seem to be able to give good or even adequate directions. I know how to get there; I just don't know how to get someone else there.

Danny leads it off with a groundout back to the pitcher. But red-hot Hunter bats next and starts a succession of three singles in a row. Major and Woody add the other two hits. Before the dust settles, the Panthers plate five in the top of the first. That's a great beginning against this formidable opponent. You know me; I'm hoping for fifteen to zero.

Allan takes the mound for Sandy Pines and gives up no hits and no runs in the bottom of the first.

After two singles and a walk, the Bears bring on a new pitcher to face Woody, and he greets him with a long drive to center field that's run down for out number one. Naturally, the wind is blowing in today. Pat adds a two-out single after a walk to Luke, and the Panthers score three more in the second to make it eight to zero. Okay, sixteen to zero after four will work.

Fulton manages a two-out hit but nothing more in their half of the second.

Phil leads off the third with an infield hit and eventually scores on a skyscraper sacrifice fly to center field off the bat of Major. It's now nine to zero after two and a half innings. The run machine has slowed, but no complaints from the peanut gallery.

Allan gets the Bears one, two, three in the bottom of the third, and then the Panthers get one more in the fourth.

Allan records two walks and three strikeouts in the bottom of the fourth. Sandy Pines leads ten to zero after four. *Who's your daddy?*

Hunter gets his third single of the game with one out in the top of the fifth. Woody steps in with two out but never gets a swing because Hunter is caught stealing on the first pitch to end the Panthers' fifth. The guys are now just three outs away from a ten-to-zero win against the number-two team in the state, via the ten-run mercy rule after five innings. Things are definitely looking up.

But the Bears respond in the bottom of the fifth. After a leadoff single, the next batter grounds to third. Woody fields the ball cleanly, but his throw to second to start a potential double play sails wide right and into right field, *ugh*. Now, with two on, Allan strikes out the next batter for out number one. My gut's churning like a blender set to puree, and I'm sure Woody's is too.

The next man grounds to the shortstop, whose only play is to first. The next batter singles before Allan gets the third out on his second K of the inning and his fifth in the last two innings. It's now ten to two going into the sixth.

Woody leads off the Panther sixth with another long fly ball out to center field. Danny's dad kids me that Woody's "warning track power" isn't quite enough to get the ball over the fence today. I'm not amused. Luke manages a two-out double, and Pat is walked intentionally before Bobby grounds out to end the inning.

Allan runs out of gas in the Bear sixth. The leadoff man draws a walk, and after a hard hit fly to right brings the first out of the inning, Coach Pat brings Mike Drew on in relief. Allan has thrown about 110 pitches by now, and I kid his dad, Mack, after the game that Woody's error in the fifth was intentional to give Allan a chance at more strikeouts. The first hitter Mike faces rips a triple, scoring another run. We go to the seventh up ten to three.

After a bases-loaded walk to Major in the top of the seventh, Woody bangs out a single, and the Panthers lead thirteen to three going into the bottom of the final inning. I'm liking this a lot.

With one out, Mike gives up a run in the bottom of the seventh. Phil comes on to pitch and gets the final two outs, securing a big, big win for the Panthers. And a very nice start to this week, I might add.

Next up is a home contest against Ardmore on Wednesday.

Chapter Twenty-Five

Wednesday at home versus the Ardmore Arrows. Well, the Panthers handled Goliath on Monday, and today they get David. Ardmore is winless in region play and in last place in the region standings. A perfect stumbling block sandwiched between games against the number-one and number two-teams. I wasn't aware until I read it in the paper today that they were winless in the region, and I hope the boys don't know it. This is a massively critical week in the season and really sets the tone for state playoff possibilities.

Driving up to the field, I notice that the big American flag at the Arby's on Evergreen Boulevard is standing straight and stiff to the east, meaning the wind is blowing out at the field. I arrive quite early to deliver a long-sleeved jersey to Woody; it's a little chilly as well as windy. The players are in the outfield stretching when I enter the dugout to find Woody's bat bag and leave the jersey. As I'm leaving the dugout, Coach Pat is coming back after talking to the Ardmore coach.

I ask Coach Pat, "You think you can keep that long-ball wind out of their minds?"

He grins and says he hopes so. I'm thinking that's two distractions for the guys: a team that's winless in the region and a strong wind blowing *out* that tempts home run swings.

Phil is on the mound for the Panthers and gives up one run on a sacrifice fly in the first, *not delightful*. The Panthers answer quickly with four runs in the bottom of the inning, *sweet*. The highlight is a mammoth two-run blast by Major that lands on Evergreen Boulevard and takes one giant bounce before disappearing. I'm hoping that shot won't tempt all the Panther hitters to swing for the fences. Woody and Hunter add singles in the inning.

No runs tally for either the Arrows or Panthers in the next four innings, so the score is still four to one entering the sixth.

In the top of the sixth, Mike Drew comes on in relief of Phil after two singles and a walk load the bases. Mike gives up a run-scoring single to the first batter he faces, and Coach Pat immediately brings Allan to the mound to try and quell the uprising. Now there is one run in and the bases loaded with two outs as the count reaches two balls and two strikes, and the tension mounts to that gut-twisting level.

This has gotta be super tough on Allan, pitching now on one day's rest after throwing more than a hundred pitches against the number-two team in the state. The bases are loaded, nowhere to put the hitter, and it's all on Allan at this moment in time. And Allan answers the call with a rally-killing strikeout! It's a huge moment and a huge result, and the crowd roars its approval. As my gut and I bet, a couple dozen others momentarily relax.

The Panthers fail to score in the sixth, so we go to the seventh with the score four to two.

In the top of the seventh, an infield single with one out and two consecutive walks load the bases for the Arrows. *Here we go.* A grounder to short nets out number two at second but no double play, and a run scores. Now the score is four to three with two out and a man on third. *Pass the antacid quickly, please.* The next hitter delivers an RBI single, and the game is tied; *look out, David is twirling his sling.* Allan roars back to strike out the following batter for out number three. We go to the bottom of the seventh needing a run to win, and we need it this inning. We don't want Allan to have to throw another pitch, and we need Danny and Pat for the next big game tomorrow against Hammond. As I pace the bleachers, I'm thinking out loud. "Forget about that wind blowing out, guys, and string a couple of hits together to end this thing."

With one out in the top of the seventh, Major reaches first on a walk, and yes, I was hoping he'd drop another bomb on Evergreen, against my advice. Brian Smith enters the game as a courtesy runner for Major and is safe on a steal of second when the second baseman drops the ball. So now Woody comes to bat with the potential winning run in scoring position. I'm wishing and hoping, and Major's dad, John, says to me, "Woody is going to go yard and win this thing right now." And when Woody connects with the next pitch, John and I are both hollering. It's a high blast toward right center, but it's too high, and the right fielder hauls it in for out number two, *gosh darn it!* But the fly ball is deep to the outfield; Brian tags up and makes it to third, ninety feet away from a victory.

John says, "That's big. Anything can happen; a wild pitch can win it now." Ardmore brings in a new pitcher, and John's prediction comes true. A wild pitch goes to the backstop, and Brian goes home! Panthers win five to four. That's a close one and another very big win. The team dodges the letdown bullet with the third big game of the week coming up on Friday at Hammond.

Chapter Twenty-Six

Here we are at Hammond for the third big game of the week. It's also a chance for redemption for blowing that three-run lead when the Panthers and the Lancers met in our second game of the season. This game is away for Sandy Pines, but I don't really mind. This park seems to be to Woody's liking; he has played well here every time we've been at this field. He had an especially stellar doubleheader in a tournament here last year in fall ball. Woody had four doubles, two homers, and two singles in twelve trips to the plate. I've been hoping for that kind of production to return this spring; maybe it will start today. Perhaps this place will be magic for him again, and he'll begin a strong finish to his final high school season here and now. He could sure use a couple of dingers to get the power numbers started.

The sun is way bright today and pretty much directly in my eyes since I've moved past the visitor's dugout and down along the wooden fence on the left field line. No fence to videotape through, but old sol is tough to look into. I want to get some good tape of Woody and his grade-school buddies in this big region battle, and down here offers the best visitor view.

Danny gets the call as our starter today, and he is well rested. Hammond sends the same pitcher we faced in the previous game to the mound, and the Panthers had some success against him then.

When Woody comes to bat in the top of the first, there are men on first and third with one out. Unfortunately, he told me before the game that he felt weak and like he was going to yak, so I'm not as hopeful as I had been before we spoke. But he hammers the first pitch, only it's right at the shortstop. Woody is only two steps toward first as the shortstop flips to second for the first out of the six-to-four-to-three twin killing. No reward for Woody on a hard-hit ball, and no runs for the Panthers in the top of the first.

The Lancers' division-one-signed leadoff man starts the game off for them with a home run over the center field fence. *Well, that's certainly not good.* But it's the fourth or fifth time this season that he's done that. Danny gets a fly ball out to center sandwiched between two strikeouts for a strong finish to the bottom of the first.

Both teams go quietly in the second, but the Panthers score two in the third on singles by Phil and Major and a solid line-drive double by Woody. I guess he likes this place even when nauseous. Panthers lead two to one after three and a half innings. That glare in my eyes doesn't seem quite so annoying with a one-run lead.

The score remains the same when Woody leads off the sixth with a single and Danny follows with a double to put men at first and third with no outs. And here's a chance for a big inning, maybe even a knockout punch. Pat lifts a fly to right field, and Woody tags up and just beats the throw home for a three-to-one lead. Bobby hits another fly, this time to center, and Danny tags and scores. It's four to one, Panthers, going to the bottom of the sixth, just six more outs to vindication. No knockout punch, but it's a nice lead.

Ah, but it's the sixth inning, and the Lancers are at the top of their order. Their leadoff man draws a walk—never a good start to an inning. And it gets much worse from there. The number-two man singles, then a double and a triple follow. It's like a snowball rolling downhill. The triple possibly could have been caught, but our left fielder battled the sun in his eyes unsuccessfully and never put a glove on the ball; *dang that bright sun*. The next man doubles, and the score is knotted at four with a runner on second and no outs. After a fly ball out, the next batter singles, and that brings Mike Drew to the mound from the bullpen. The following two hitters single, and then there's a walk before the Panthers finally record out number two on a grounder to short. The snowball is now about the size of Stone Mountain.

After Mike falls behind two balls and no strikes to the Lancers' number-three hitter, Coach Pat decides to give Woody a chance on the mound. He warmed up a few times during the Florida trip but never got to pitch. I guess Coach figures the damage is done with the score now ten to four in favor of Hammond, and this is a good chance to let Woody sling a few. He's coming on with two balls already on the hitter, which makes his first appearance a little more difficult. Woody pitches well. The batter fouls back a couple before Woody throws ball three for a full count. Woody delivers a good fastball that's called ball four, but he thinks he has struck out the batter.

Coach Pat can see Woody is a little miffed and hollers, "Don't worry about it, Woody! He just hasn't seen one that quick before!" Our side gets a good chuckle out of that one, and Woody induces a soft liner from the next hitter to end the inning. The Panthers come to bat for the last time, trailing by six runs. Hammond has flipped the game on Sandy Pines, scoring nine runs on seven hits in the bottom of the sixth. That stinking sixth once again seems to be the Panthers' jinxed inning.

No rally today for the Panthers as the last out comes with Woody standing in the on-deck circle. What a revolting development this is. Sandy Pines goes from *almost* in great shape in the region to tied for third—stink, stank, stunk! Southpark and then major rival Northlake come calling next week before the final four seeded region games.

Dang it. I didn't want it to be like this. I had really hoped for a triumphant final season for these seniors, but now they will have to scrap like the dickens. Oh well, maybe that's a better way to get into State, fighting and clawing all the way, with every inning of every game counting. That is, if they *can* get into State.

Mack Christopher and I go to Northlake to watch them take on Fulton the next night, and it's the quickest game either of us can remember seeing. A sophomore pitcher gets the win, two to zero for Northlake, and we figure the Panthers will probably see him next Wednesday. But first things first, Southpark will be rolling in on Monday afternoon.

And Saturday night is prom night, so I get to repeat both my *drinking* and *sex* talks to Woody. The drinking talk is much more personally painful.

Saturday morning I catch Woody alone, having his usual late breakfast—it's almost noon—and pull up a chair.

"Woody, you remember that night you spent out with a few of the guys a couple of months ago?"

"You mean the campfire cookout?" Woody answers back a little sheepishly.

"That's the one," I reply.

"Oh, come on, Dad. Don't give me the drinking or the drinking and driving lecture now. It's too early."

"It's never too early," I reply and then steam ahead. "I'm thankful you had your first experience with the power of alcohol in a relatively safe and friendly environment. Camping out after one of the guy's girlfriends took all your car keys and left you out in the woods at least showed some common sense."

"Yeah, but that ground was still awfully hard to sleep on," Woody answers.

"That night you got a taste, literally, of how alcohol can get control of your body, and you probably got an idea of what it can do to your brain too," I continue.

"Yeah, yeah, I know how bad it can be and how dangerous it is," he shoots back.

"Well, son, I'm gonna remind you of why you've never seen me without a mustache," I begin.

"No need, Dad. I'm well aware of the dangers of drinking and driving, and we've got a limo tonight anyway," Woody responds.

"I know you've got the limo. You and a couple of your teammates and your dates, right?"

Woody grunts an affirmative and nods with his head down in that *Oh no, am I gonna have to listen to this* teenage way.

I push ahead. "But I want to explain something about the night I messed up my face, besides the complete insanity of driving into that telephone pole. I obviously drank too much. My two fraternity brothers that were still up with me shooting pool after the party knew I'd had too much. They'd been drinking too but not as bad as me. And then I decided to drive home. I wanted to sleep in my own bed. Why, I have no idea. No one was at home. My folks were in Texas. But the alcohol was in charge now, and it wanted to drive the twenty miles home from Tech in the wee hours.

"My two fraternity brothers knew I shouldn't drive, so they tried to get my keys from me, chased me out of the house and two or three times around it, through the bushes and trees, and down the back steps, all in the pitch dark. They couldn't catch me, so we all figured I ought to be able to drive since I had eluded them and not broken my neck or a leg in the process. Obviously the booze had clouded their judgment some too. So I took off, fell asleep, and smashed head-on into a telephone pole on the wrong side of the road. I was driving in the oncoming lane for who knows how long. The people that stopped to help me, if they'd been coming in the opposite direction a minute or two earlier, I might have killed them. I thank God every day that I didn't hit anyone that night, especially those two. The point is that the alcohol controlled me, made me think I should be able to drive. It took over my decision-making ability, and that's what it can do. It can take over whether you give it permission to or not. And it can destroy your ability to make a logical or even sane judgment about anything, Woody. Anything. There's a saying about drinking that I heard once and still remember. It's short, but the words can be brutally accurate:

> First the man drinks the wine,
> Then the wine drinks the wine,
> Then the wine drinks the man.

That's what happened to me that night, Woody. And I hope and pray it never happens to you."

"It won't, Dad; we're not even planning on doing a bunch of drinking. But I won't let that happen to me, ever."

"Well, you better be planning on doing no drinking since it's illegal at your age. But later, when you are legal, remember that saying and stop before the wine begins to drink the wine."

"I will, Dad," Woody promises, hoping the lecture is over, but no such luck.

"And on the subject of sex," I begin.

Woody grunts "Oh no" and slumps back in his chair overdramatically.

"All I'm gonna say is that it's nature tricking you into the propagation of the race. Nature turns the hormones loose in you to try and shove you into procreation, just like the birds and the bees. I'll give you one simple rule: Don't have sex with anybody you don't want to have a child with 'cause it can and it does happen. No prevention is 100 percent. I know the truly dangerous health risks have been made obvious to you kids; don't ever forget them. And especially don't forget nature's hoped-for outcome: sex equals children. Only abstinence is 100 percent effective against that outcome."

A beleaguered Woody attempts to bring the lecture to an end with a quick "amen" as he rapidly pushes away from the table and heads for the sink with his plate.

But I press on, unabated. "I know I've told you before that the other side of the person coin from the flesh—the sex side—is the spirit." Woody speeds up his cleaning activities at the sink in hopes of a quick getaway. "The time that sex is right is the time when those two sides blend together in love and the commitment of marriage." Woody is hotfooting it down the hall now, making a break for the shower and a hoped-for end to the sermon. My raised voice chases after him. "That's when it's real; that's when it's right, when the two sides of each person are in harmony and the two individuals are joined together completely."

I've had to raise my voice even more at the end as Woody has closed the bathroom door, and he fires back, "Amen again, brother!"

I'm not really sure I'm getting through to him. I'm going to redirect him to that passage in Proverbs.

Chapter Twenty-Seven

The Southpark Spartans are about midway in the region standings, I think. At any rate they are ranked below Sandy Pines, and the Panthers really need to bounce back after the Hammond fiasco. The next game after Southpark, against Northlake, is huge, and I hope the kids aren't looking past the Spartans 'cause it's definitely crunch time now.

Phil is on the mound today, and he needs a good, long outing. A complete game would be perfect, allowing Coach Pat to save the rest of the staff for Northlake.

And Phil does the job. He gives up only two hits and strikes out eight, a great effort when they really, really needed it. The Panthers win four to zero. Sandy Pines gets one run in each of the first four innings for the final margin. Major and Pat record singles in the first for the first run. In the second, the Panthers get no hits but a run after a two-out walk, a passed ball, and a shortstop error. The run in the third is a result of hits by Danny and Luke, and a hit by Bobby in the fourth brings home another runner who was put aboard via the free-pass walk. Luckily, Woody's bat wasn't needed as he came away with two Ks. The good news is that sandwiched in between the two strikeouts was a good sacrifice bunt that helped get the third run around and eventually home in the third inning.

Next up is just the biggest game of these kids' high school careers—so far—coming against their archrival, the Northlake Hornets. At least it's a home game for the Panthers. I've got a two-day inspection just across the border in Alabama—typical—but should get through by noon on game day and be able to get to the field early. It's good I can get there early because the Pelhams and Michaelsons have concession-stand duty for the big game. Brother, isn't that another typical coincidence: cooking duty for the biggest game of the year.

Tuesday night in my motel room, I write Woody a note about tomorrow's game.

I want to let him know how much I think he is capable of and also let him know that even if this is the biggest game of his career, it's still a game, and games are for fun. I haven't decided whether to give it to him when I get home Wednesday afternoon. But when he comes home after school and says, "It's the biggest game of my life," I give him the note.

It's kind of neat how things work out sometimes. After he has left for the field, I see the note on the floor of the kids' bathroom. *That's great, my deep inspirational thoughts turned into john-reading material.* Oh well, we all just do the best we can. At any rate, I hope it helped give him some perspective.

As I prepare to head up to the field and begin my grilling duties, the ramifications of this game strike me again: win and the Panthers are in second place in the region for the final four game seeding; lose and they are in sixth. The whole season and post-season could be determined by this game. Maybe it's a good thing the typical SNAFU (Situation Normal All Fouled Up) has occurred with me having to work concessions for this game. Maybe it's best that I won't be able to follow every pitch and sweat out every play. Still, my stomach does a little half flip when I back the truck out of the driveway and head for the school.

Chapter Twenty-Eight

Wow, what great weather for a ball game. It's perfect. Wish I could enjoy the sights and sounds of this intense rivalry game. And it carries so much significance this time around. Ah, but duty calls, and I start grilling hotdogs and hamburgers as soon as I arrive. One of the other dads, who opened the stand, has already cooked one load. Jessica is inside the concession stand, which is located behind home plate, but the portable gas grill is back from the field about twenty yards and halfway between the home grandstands and the concession stand. Of course, the restrooms are on this side of the concession stand building also, so there's another flow of traffic I'll have to try and see through during the game.

Kimberly arrives just before game time with the video recorder and my scorebook. Bless her heart, she's going to try and keep the video and written record for me this game. Turns out the big video cam and the weak batteries are too much hassle, so she opts to do her best with the scorebook only. So during the game she's hollering down from the grandstands, asking questions about scoring plays I can't see as I flip burgers, stand on my tiptoes, and crane my neck trying to catch a glimpse of the action. I'm sure it is quite a comical scene to someone who's not tied up in nervous knots trying to do three things at once.

Jason's mom shows up to work with Jessica in the concession stand, but his dad apparently has to work late, so I'll be cooking alone. Since this is our big rival from three miles away and the biggest game of the year so far for both teams, this will be the biggest home crowd and the busiest concession-stand business of the season—naturally.

Allan is on the mound along with his undefeated record, and I can tell from the crowd reaction that he's greeted by back-to-back singles to start the game. I'm not disappointed to miss that. After one out, a fly ball to the outfield, I think, the bases get loaded due to a walk, I think. I'm flipping burgers through the thick grill smoke when something happens. I can't tell what the heck it is, and then something else happens, and then the inning is over. I don't know what transpired, but the scoreboard reads one run for the visitors when the Panthers come to bat.

And the Panthers go down one, two, three in their half of the first with Hunter and Major both striking out. From the little I can see while making like a Burger King trainee, this pitcher looks good, *hot diggity dog*. I'm thinking we're in real trouble really early because I think they've got a run.

Al gets the Hornets one, two, three in the second, but then the Panthers only send four batters to the plate in their half of the second. Woody leads off by looking at a called third strike. Don't you know I'd be able to stick my head between spectators like a sawed-off giraffe just in time to see that for myself! My gut somersaults as I head back to the grill and realize that that's three strikeouts in his last four at bats! *Oh no*, I'm thinking, *is he going into some kind of hideous, dad-tor-*

turing slump at the most important time of the season? I pray not; that's too horrid for even a Pelham to have to endure.

As I send another batch of grilled cow to the concession stand, I hear that Terry has also struck out to end the second inning. That's four strikeouts in the first six outs. *Ouch!* But I gotta get back to cooking, and luckily I'm too busy to spin completely into a nervous git right now.

There are no real threats mounted by either team in the third inning, but Hunter strikes out again. Bobby also strikes out in the third. Those are our two hottest hitters, and one of them has K'd twice. *Who the heck is pitching for the Hornets?*

Al gets Northlake one, two, three again in the top of the fourth. Woody leads off the bottom of the fourth for Sandy Pines. I hear him announced over the loudspeakers but am busy at the grill and can't get a look. I hear a loud crack of the bat, and the home crowd cheers, so I know it's a hit. I rush up to the viewing area next to the concession stand, and Danny's dad tells me he doubled. *Good for him.* Boy, is that ever a load off. Woody scores eventually on an error on the shortstop after reaching third on a fielder's choice. Bobby manages a two-out single with a man who has walked on second, and the Panthers get two in the fourth. *Hot diggity dog, for real!* We're up two to one.

Both sides go one, two, three in the fifth. Then comes the good old sixth.

Al strikes out the leadoff hitter for out number one. Next man up smacks a double and then two passed balls or wild pitches bring home a run. I don't know if they're wild pitches or passed balls since I can't see, but a run scores from second without the aid of a hit ball. And now the game is tied, and I can't see squat! The next two batters go down on a groundout to second and a fly out to right field. As the inning ends, one of the Hammond players, who has shown up to watch our game since his is over, comes by. I recognize it's one of Woody's best buds from grammar school and ask him how he thinks the game is going so far for Sandy Pines. He says it looks like our guys are doing good, being up two to one. I tell him I thought the score was tied, and he says, "No, Panthers are up two to one." I tell him thanks as he heads off and sneak a quick peek at the scoreboard, and sure enough, it's two to one. Danny's dad confirms that the run posted in the first inning was the scoreboard operator's error. But lucky Steve, today's reluctant grill master, had no way of knowing. So we're up two to one and coming to bat in the bottom of the sixth. What a goofy game this has been for me.

I get to watch Woody lead off the Panther sixth. Cooking is pretty much over now. He rips a liner toward the gap in right center field, and it looks like another double. But the right fielder races over, dives, and snags the ball just before it hits the grass. He slides along on his belly with his glove in the air, and Woody is robbed again. That's baseball, but it's a lot easier to take with a one-run lead. The next two hitters make outs also, so we go to the last inning still leading two to one.

I am able to watch this last part of the game since things are winding down concession-wise. The first Hornet batter lofts a bloop fly ball to right field, and Hunter comes racing in at full speed. He dives at the last second and makes a great catch for out number one and most importantly, keeps the possible tying run off base. *Go ahead and flip-flop, stomach; just two more outs to go.* The next man grounds out to Bobby at second base; one more to go. The third batter of the inning is also the third out of the inning and the final out of the game on a grounder back to Al that he tosses to first to end it.

So it was a great, great game that I didn't get to see. Heck,

I didn't even know what the real score was until the game was almost over! But hey, all's well that ends well. And on a personal note, it was also great to see Woody hit the ball hard twice after that first strikeout. Man, maybe I really am glad I was grilling and not able to watch and sweat bullets the whole time.

The next day we find out that Sandy Pines will play Ardmore, Southpark, Baxter, and Arlington in the final four seeded games. The Panthers have beaten three of the four already this season, and the feeling is that if they go three and one in these games, they're a lock for the state tournament. But this is like a new very short season, with some teams fighting to make State and others fighting to stop them. Nothing is gonna come easy, and the Panthers will have to play their very best to get those three wins.

Chapter Twenty-Nine

Well, it's time for the *final four* region games. Twelve days ago these guys from Ardmore forced us to score in the bottom of the seventh for the win. Hope it's easier this time around, but a win is a win, and as usual, we'll take 'em any way we can get 'em. *What's with all this "we" stuff?* I've got to cut back on the vicarious-living thing.

Danny's on the mound today for this home game, and he gets off to a bit of a rocky start in the first. A walk follows the leadoff short-to-first groundout, and that runner eventually scores after a rushed attempt at a double play results in an error. Then a slow roller to second brings the runner home. The Panthers are down one run when they come to bat in the bottom of the first—typical.

Major and Woody single back to back after two outs, but the threat dies before a run can score.

Danny gives up no hits or walks through the next four innings, although one man reaches first via catcher interference. Danny also records five strikeouts over these four innings; *very nice indeed.*

The Panthers get the offense in gear in the bottom of the second. Terry leads off with a solo homer, his second of the season, and a great time for it. With the score knotted at one, Bobby, Phil, and Hunter string singles together, and the Panthers lead two to one after two.

Woody and Pat single back to back with one out, and a walk to Terry loads the bases in the bottom of the third. But the bases are left loaded after a fly out and a groundout end the home half. We missed a great chance for a cushion there.

Phil singles to start the Panther fourth, and Major's two-out double eventually plates him after a sac bunt by Hunter moved him to second. Sandy Pines leads three to one after four and also after five as the Panthers go one, two, three in the fifth.

That brings us to the always-chaotic sixth. Danny has pitched quite well; in fact, he has a no-hitter through five complete. But that ends quickly as the first batter in the sixth singles. A double, a single, a groundout, and another single, and Danny's gone and Allan's in. Big Al also gives up a hit before getting out of the inning, but the Panthers now trail three to four! It could have been worse. The first man on base luckily was the first out at home when he tried to score on a wild pitch. But Major and Danny's hustle prevented that. However, another wild pitch or passed ball, again I don't know which it was, scored a run. There was another catcher's interference that allowed a man to reach first. I don't understand what's going on with that; we haven't had any other catcher's interference calls all season long. Maybe these guys are too far back in the batter's box. At any rate, the inning ends with men on first and third as well as the three that scored.

The Panthers' bats answer quickly in the bottom of the sixth. Allan leads off with a single and is sacrifice-bunted to second by Phil. Hunter singles to tie the score, and a new pitcher comes on for the Arrows. Danny greets him with a single. Major steps up with two on and one out. The count goes full, and then Major swats ball four, a high one, down the third base line for a two-run double. Now that's much better than a walk, ain't it? Panthers lead six to four when the inning ends, and Ardmore comes up for one last shot.

The first two batters go quietly on groundouts. But then back-to-back doubles make the score six to five with two out and a man on second. *All right, already. We don't need this much drama.* Thankfully the next man flies out, and the Panthers have a six-to-five win and maintain the number-two spot in the region. Since the top four teams in the final region standings will make State, the Panthers are still in excellent shape. Southpark comes calling on Monday.

Chapter Thirty

Monday is finally here, after what seemed like a never-ending weekend, and it's time to take on the Southpark Spartans again. My cousin John, whom I went to Florida with in March, is here for the game, as is an old friend from way back who has kept up with Woody's baseball through phone conversations and faxes from my office. They get their money's worth.

This is a game I'm thinking Sandy Pines should win easily; Northlake routed this bunch on Monday. But I should know better than to let my great expectations cloud my judgment. I'm expecting to see Allan on the mound today and then again for the last game on Friday at Arlington. We pretty much have to win two of the last three to make State, and I'm figuring Coach Pat wants his best pitcher in two of the games, right? Wrong. Once again I prove to myself that I don't know diddly. Phil is the starting pitcher today. I guess Coach wants Allan to beat Baxter and then be rested for the first game of State.

At any rate, Phil is greeted with a game-opening single; that's a kick in the teeth. The number-two hitter goes one better and doubles to drive in a run. We're barely in our seats and already down one to zero! The third batter reaches base on a shortstop error, *ugh*. Now there are men on first and third and no outs with one run already in. The clean-up hitter pops up to short center field, too short for the runner at third to tag up and score; *finally some good news.* Phil Ks the next batter, and things look better but still scary. The following batter grounds to short, and the inning ends on a force-out at second. *Whew, it could have been worse, but it was sure bad enough for the first half of the first inning.*

Seems the Panthers' bats are wide awake also. Hunter, Danny, Major, and Woody all single consecutively. The score's tied, bases loaded, and nobody's out; now that looks a whole lot better, a whole lot better! Terry steps up looking to do some damage but pops up to the catcher for the first out. Turns out looks ain't everything, especially concerning potential runs. After the pop-up, a double play ends the inning with the bases still loaded. *Well, spit!* The score stays tied.

The Spartans open the top of the second inning with a single, but no further damage is done. However, the second out comes on a long, line-drive blast to left field, where a fleet freshman up from the JV team hauls it in for a great catch. Coach Pat sure had him in at the right time.

The Panthers ease ahead in the bottom of the second when Bobby leads off and reaches second on a double-shortstop error. The fielder mishandles the grounder and throws the ball away at first. Bobby then reaches third on a wild pitch, and Phil brings him home with a sacrifice fly to right field. *Thanks much, Spartans.* Panthers lead two to one.

Naturally Southpark comes back in the top of the third to tie things up at two to two. The first man up reaches first on a shortstop error. Phil strikes out the next batter for out number one but then surrenders back-to-back singles, and the game is tied. Another E6 loads the bases before a comebacker to Phil allows him to throw home to force the lead runner. It's a great play as the blast rips the glove off the lefty's hand, but he manages to pounce on the ball and fire it home. Bases are still loaded with two outs when another grounder is rifled toward short. But this time our shortstop is up to the challenge and comes up clean with the ball and fires to first to end the Spartans' third.

The Panthers go one, two, three in their half, so it's two to two after three.

Southpark pushes across a run after two out in the top of the fourth to go up three to two. And it's not a cheap tally either, coming on a single followed by a triple.

The Panthers strike back in the bottom of the inning, courtesy of a walk to Bobby and Phil's first homer of the season. Now there's a case of a pitcher really helping himself at the plate. Good guys are up four to three after four. A lead at the halfway point is always good.

Phil works to only three batters in the top of the fifth, more good.

The Spartans bring on a new, slow-throwing junk baller in the fifth, and he's quite effective: three batters, three pop-up outs.

Danny takes the mound in the top of the sixth and opens with a strikeout. The next hitter blasts a long shot to center field, and even though it's just a long out, it's still a little disturbing to see the ninth man in the order stroke one like that. After a walk to the following batter, the inning ends on a grounder back to Danny—no crazy sixth this time around.

The Panthers go quietly again with a pop-up and two fly outs to right field. This Spartan hurler is in complete control so far. It's still four to three, good guys, going to the final inning. Hang on to your hats.

The Spartan seventh opens with a strikeout, and then the bottom drops out. A hit batter is followed by a single and a double, and it's tied up with men on second and third and only one out.

I'm glad for the company of my two buds to discuss the revolting happenings. Talking keeps me from thinking too much, and hence, worrying too much.

Now the snafu explodes with another of those critical passed ball/wild pitches—I don't know which. But the runner on third races for home as Major retrieves the ball at the backstop, turns, and throws to Danny, who is late getting to home. The runner is safe, but Danny fails to grab Major's slightly high throw, and the ball scoots through the infield and rolls to the outfield, allowing the other runner to score as well! I'm stunned and angry and agitated. There are some hideous goings on out on the field, and Sandy Pines is now down four to six.

Danny manages to regroup and strike out the current batter, but then two singles and a walk load the bases. This is going from bad to worse, and I didn't think that was possible. The ninth batter of the inning cracks one sharply toward the gap between short and second; I might faint, but Pat snares it and fires to first to end the disastrous Spartan seventh. Seems the disastrous sixth waited until the seventh today.

I've got a really, really bad feeling now; it seems like this might be the beginning of the end. We lose tonight and then to Baxter or Arlington, and we're out of it. Season over, high school baseball over, and me wondering what the heck happened! Good grief, I'm a major-league worrywart.

Down by two runs, Allan leads off the home half of the seventh with a strikeout. He's trying to work a walk. Panthers need base runners, and he takes some pitches he might have swung at otherwise. Our leadoff man, Hunter, follows with a fly ball out to right field. Well, I can feel the noose tightening.

What a horrible way to lose out. Danny works for a walk and gets the count full. This next pitch could be the last one. And the next pitch is the last one, at least for that baseball.

Danny smashes the delivery with a mighty grunt, and the ball rockets over the right field fence! It's five to six, and the Panthers are still alive. Major steps in but quickly gets in the hole—no balls and two strikes. Then the Spartans' pitcher makes what seems like a good, strategic pitch, but it's right down Major's alley. He throws a high fastball looking for the batter to chase it for a game-ending strike three. But Major doesn't chase this one; he catches it, big time. It's just where he likes it, and Major deposits it over the left field fence, and we're tied six to six. That's incredible! The Panthers haven't hit two home runs in a single game this year, let alone back to back and with two outs in the last inning. And that makes three homers in the game. Sometimes Yogi's wisdom is overwhelming; truly, "It ain't over 'til it's over."

Now Woody steps in, and we all know how bad he wants to make it three in a row and win the game. While I'm busy praying and hoping, the first pitch is outside for a ball. I'm guessing Woody is taking 'til there's a strike called, and I'm right. The next pitch is a strike in the ideal spot, almost right down the middle, but Woody takes it, and the count is even at one ball and one strike. Another ball makes it two and one, and then Woody takes a rip and fouls it straight back; *shoot, he just barely missed that one!* I know that's it for the home-run swings; he has to go into the two-strike, defensive-swing mode now. But Woody shows uncommon patience and draws the walk. The potential winning run is on first.

A new pitcher is brought in to face Terry. When the count reaches no balls and two strikes, Terry fouls off two in a row with Woody running. Woody isn't running when

Terry grounds to short. It looks like a force at second to end the inning, but the shortstop bobbles the ball, and no play is made. That potential winning run is now at second. Coach Pat calls time and sends speedy sophomore James Johnson in to pinch run for Woody at second base. If the next batter can deliver a hit, there's a good chance that speed will produce the winning run from second. You can tell the Spartan pitcher is feeling the pressure, and Pat works the count to three balls and one strike before drawing the walk.

The bases are now loaded for Bobby, the winning run just ninety feet away. Baseball is one crazy freaking game. With the pitcher struggling and Bobby's small strike zone, you figure there's a good chance for another walk. But the first pitch is strike one, naturally. As the tension mounts and more stomachs churn than just mine in this improbable comeback, Bobby works the count to three balls and two strikes. And then here it comes, the game-deciding pitch—*ball four*.

Panthers win! Holy cow! How crazy is this, and how wrong was my gut feeling? Down by two runs and down to their last out, these guys win with back-to-back homers and then a bases-loaded walk. Unbelievable. Maybe this team is bulletproof; maybe this is a team of destiny. We'll find out soon enough.

Next up is Wednesday's match-up at Baxter. And I learn from Tuesday's paper that Baxter lost to Hammond in extra innings, on an error no less, last night. A close loss to a team tied for number one in our region, coupled with the fact that this next game is Baxter's final game of the year, and I'm guessing the Red Devils will be loose and anxious to end on a winning note.

Chapter Thirty-One

Baxter is located between my office and home, but I'm still a little late arriving this afternoon due to some typical metro Atlanta traffic problems. Why won't that dadgum traffic behave? I hear them announcing the lineups over the loudspeakers as I'm walking from the parking lot, so I haven't missed anything yet.

It's a good thing I'm no later because the action starts immediately for the Panthers. Hunter leads off with a home run on a three-ball, two-strike count; can't beat that for a start. Danny is hit by a pitch and then reaches second on a throwing error by the catcher on an attempted pickoff. Major gets in the hole zero and two but comes through with an RBI single. So it's two to zero, Panthers, with a man on first and no outs.

Woody steps in, and with the count two balls and one strike, he gets one he likes and smacks it high toward right center field. Major's dad is standing next to me and hollers, "Get outta here!" at the crack of the bat. I have to look away from the video camera to follow the ball, and I see it soar over the fence. *Home freaking run*! Hot dog, that's a two-run shot! Man, I've been waiting all season to see that. But I do have enough composure to get back on the video and pick up Woody rounding first. He gets around the bases quickly;

no real home-run trot as he comes around and gets a quick congratulatory shake from Coach Pat at third. That's a great moment for Woody. The home run is the most rewarding moment in baseball, I think. And isn't it cool that you can record it and watch it as soon as you get home? And Woody can keep it to show to his grandkids if he wants. I'm enough of a simpleton to still be amazed by videotape instant replay. How does that happen? I can rewind the tape in the video cam and watch it between innings; no developing at the drugstore, no waving the Polaroid in the air, waiting for the image to appear. How the heck *does* that happen?

The fireworks are over for the Panthers in the first as the next three batters are outs. But that's a great first at bat; four runs and two homers; looks excellent so far.

Allan takes the mound to face the Red Devils, and that makes the four-to-zero lead look even better since he's still undefeated this season. However, the warm fuzzies are gone after four consecutive singles make the score four to two.

But things are going really well today for the Panthers as they get two in the second and then six more in a huge fifth inning to lead twelve to five after five. This is a lot more like my ideal game than that last one.

Baxter starts the sixth with back-to-back singles—dang sixth inning again. Mike comes on in relief of Al, and he shuts them down with no further damage.

Danny leads off the seventh with a home run over the fence in right field, his second seventh-inning homer in two games. That's all the fireworks the Panthers can muster, so Baxter comes up for possibly the last time in their season, and some of the players' careers, trailing five to thirteen.

Mike strikes out the first batter. The leadoff man is up next, and on the second called strike he says something, but he hasn't turned toward the ump or appear to be angry. The ump is on edge, having tossed the Baxter head coach earlier. He's also had numerous conversations about the crowd with the home team coaches. The ump immediately tosses the batter out of the game, causing more uproar from the home team's dugout and the home crowd. The replacement hitter rips a shot down the third base line for a double, and I'm beginning to wonder if this game is ever gonna end. The next hitter takes a called third strike, turns, and puts his hand on the ump's shoulder and says something to him. He's promptly thrown out also, and more delays follow as the ump explains his move to the coaches. Finally the next batter is settling into the batter's box when another derogatory shout aimed at the home plate ump comes from the crowd. That's it. The ump calls the game, and I can't blame him a bit. In the end, it's a lopsided and valuable win for the Panthers.

As the parents are waiting around for the players to come by on the way to their bus, someone gets a call on their cell phone, and we learn that Hammond has lost to Southpark. *Holy mackerel!* Seven and a half innings ago, I was afraid Sandy Pines wouldn't even make the state tourney, and now they're in first place in the region. What a wild finish to the regular season. If the Panthers beat Arlington on Monday, they will finish number one; if they lose, Northlake finishes in first. That's two huge reasons to go out and win.

We also hear that Fulton has beat Nelton, so Nelton is out unless Hightower beats Hammond on Monday. And if they do lose, Hammond will have gone from first place in the region to out of the state tourney in two games. This is one tough region, brother. The Panthers' record now stands at ten and three in the region and seventeen and five overall.

And Woody finally has his first home run, the long ball at

last. Right now, I admit it; I'm beginning to fantasize about him stringing a bunch together, hopefully in the state tourney. An old man can dream, can't he?

Chapter Thirty-Two

Well, here we go, one last time at the Knights' castle. And wouldn't you know it; it's cold and windy with the east wind blowing directly into the visitors' faces. This is a nice park, but I hate playing here. Still, it's kinda sad to realize that I'll probably never see another game contested on this field. And that realization is an uninvited reminder that the season, and with it high school baseball, is winding down.

The Knight pitcher is that slow-as-molasses, lefty, junk-ball thrower I watched against Fulton here last week. Woody comes to bat in the top of the first with two on and one out, and I'm wondering if he can do anything with this junk baller. He usually has trouble with these types of pitchers. Woody's true to form and manages only a two-strike slow bouncer to third that does at least move the runners up a base each. But the inning ends before the runners advance any farther. Maybe next time.

Danny takes the hill for the Panthers. Scary if you're superstitious since he lost here earlier this season. He's greeted with a ringing triple, not a good thing. The number-two hitter singles to plate the first run of the game. Danny comes back to strike out the next man and then gets a grounder from the clean-up hitter that comes back to him and turns it into a one-to-six-to-three double play—coulda been worse.

Andrew Smith draws a one-out walk in the top of the second for Sandy Pines. Jason moves him to second with a groundout to shortstop, and Terry singles Andrew home with the first of his four hits. It's a tied game after one and a half.

Arlington starts their half of the second with a walk. But after a fly out, Danny picks this man off first for out number two. The next man hits a comeback grounder to Danny, and the inning ends with the teams still tied. I think I can stand it as long as we don't get behind.

The Panthers score one on a wild pitch with the bases loaded in the top of the third to take the lead but could have, and probably should have, done a lot more damage. *Come on fellas, can't you make it easy on an old man one time?*

The Knights send eight batters to the plate and score three in the home half of the inning. Knights lead four to two after three, and here we go again. I don't like this one bit, no sir, not one bit.

In the fourth the Panthers score runs on a wild pitch, a hit batsman with the bases loaded, a walk with the bases loaded, and an infield error. So Sandy Pines leads six to four at the halfway point of the game; that's much better. But still, that's the second time they could have blown this game wide open.

Mike comes in to pitch and Ks the leadoff man to open the Knight fourth, and it's a good omen as they go down without mounting a threat.

The Panthers add two more in the fifth on doubles by Terry and Major. Phil and Hunter had walks in between. Woody reached first base on a hit-by-pitch. It's eight to four, good guys, after four and a half; it's getting even better.

The Knights go one, two, three in the bottom of the fifth,

and the Panthers add three in the sixth to go up eleven to four. Bobby, Phil, Terry, and Major single while Danny draws a walk and Woody reaches base on another hit by a pitch. A seven-run lead is a good thing with six outs left to get. Looks like they're trying to make it easy on this old man after all.

Wouldn't you know it? Arlington gets two back in the bottom of the sixth off a walk, a hit, and a couple of errors, *ouch*.

But the Panthers make it twelve to six on Terry's two-out double in the top of the seventh. Now it's a six-run lead, and just three more outs to go. *Let it be over, Yogi.*

Allan comes on to pitch the bottom of the seventh and gets the job done. The leadoff man hits a sky-high pop-up that Woody takes for out number one. The next batter singles before Allan strikes out the following hitter. The game ends on a fly ball out to right field, and the 2002 Sandy Pines Panthers are the Region Six 5A champs! It's a beautiful thing, and it makes it even sweeter to have done it here at the Knights' castle, where nothing good ever seemed to happen for us. I'm drained but excited.

The team forms up in the foul area in short right field for a champs team picture before the cupcakes and other goodies arrive to celebrate Terry's birthday. And he had a great one, getting four hits in the region championship clincher. Later, Coach Pat gets a Gatorade shower in the dugout, but I don't think he minds.

Now it's three days off until the Panthers host the number-four team from Region Five 5A, the Greenwood Vipers, in the first round of the playoffs. It is here, senior year state tournament play; how far can they go? I'm mighty proud of this team, of these guys. There were points in the season when things didn't look good at all, but they never gave up. They battled hard, and in the end won the region by finishing strong; no faint hearts here. I can't think of a better way to enter the playoffs. After all the years of watching Coach Pat's Sandy Pines teams compete in the state tourney, it's our turn now. Well, at least it's Woody's and the rest of the guys' turn. I know it will seem like it passes in the blink of an eye, no matter how far they go. And I can hardly wait for it to start.

But now it's time to enjoy what's been accomplished so far. Region champs and a Friday night to celebrate, that's a nice combination. Jessica and I are going to meet Mack and Becky at a local bar and grill to reminisce and enjoy the kids' championship season. The guys are heading out to celebrate on their own, most probably ending up and spending the night at one of the teammates' houses. I'd love to have them at our place, but it's just too small.

Before Woody heads out, I decide to give him some more anti-drinking advice; maybe I'm pushing too hard, but I don't think so. I can't help worrying about these kids and alcohol. I didn't really drink in high school—maybe once my senior year and then some beer on graduation night. It's a lot different now; the opportunities and the temptations are much more numerous for this generation. It would be nice if parents could stay in the present and not project what might or could happen. That's hard to do, but it's our job to try and teach our kids from our experiences. And if we've made mistakes and suffered the consequences, it's natural to want to protect our kids from suffering the same results. So I corner Woody in his room after he's cleaned up and about to leave.

"You guys have a lot to be proud of, a lot to celebrate tonight. I know I'm really proud of you, proud of all the players. I just hope you'll all keep your wits about you and stay the heck away from the booze."

"Come on, Dad. I'm not gonna screw up now that we're in

State. I remember the 'wine drinks the wine' speech; I don't need to hear it again," Woody counters.

"I'm not gonna give you that one."

"I really need to get going; the guys will be waiting," Woody answers with a hint of agitation.

"This won't take long," I say as I sit down on his bed and then dive in. "You never knew my dad; he died in 1977. He had a heart attack when he was visiting my sister in Arkansas. It was a serious heart attack, and he was no spring chicken; he was seventy-eight years old. Your mom and I went out and visited him in the hospital, and of course hoped and prayed he'd recover and get to come home. But his heart had suffered a lot of damage. He went home to my sister's house for a couple of days but had to go back into the hospital. It had been about three or four weeks since his heart attack, and every single time the phone rang I was afraid it was gonna be the news that he was gone. I was enduring a lot of stress, a ton of worry. And each ring of the phone was like a huge surge of electricity to my jangled nerves. Then your mom and I decided to get away for a weekend. We hooked up with some good friends, a fraternity brother and his wife, and headed out of town to an away Georgia Tech football game."

It was plain to see that Woody was getting very antsy, but I pressed on. "We met at a TGI Friday's for lunch before heading out. I was knocking back the Heinekens, knowing I didn't have to drive and relying on the alcohol to try and relieve the stress."

At this point Woody simply flat out revolts and says, "I'm sorry, Dad, but I've got to go," as he heads out of the room and disappears down the hall with, "We'll finish this tomorrow. I promise, tomorrow," shouted back over his shoulder.

I let him go, but I'm wondering what that was: total disrespect or just teenage impatience? I'm a little miffed but realize this tale was going to take a lot longer than I first imagined. But still, I wonder why my advice doesn't mean any more to him?

Woody gives his mom a quick hug and kiss, and then he's out the door with a parting, "I love you, guys."

Well, kiss my foot, I think as I waffle between angry disappointment at Woody's bolting in the middle of my sermon and proud joy at what he and the team have accomplished. I promise myself we will finish tomorrow; I will have my say.

But for now I can enjoy the kids' region championship and more importantly, my clean bill of health. Thinking back, I'm not really sure that I wasn't using the baseball season as an excuse to stick my head in the sand concerning my health. Perhaps I just didn't want to know if cancer was stalking me again and this time maybe had me square in its sights. I spent a lot of time carrying that fear, but thank God it turned out to be only that: fear.

And the region championship, how great is that? Eleven years since Woody started playing ball at Jones Park, and nine or ten since Danny began causing havoc on the base paths there; eight years since Woody's all-star team won the GRPA North Georgia championship in Dalton; six years since Danny, Major, Bobby, and Woody won a state championship. Six years, that's a long time in the life of an eighteen-year-old, but seems like just a few blinks of the eye to me. And it's been six years since Sandy Pines won State. It goes without saying that I hope it's their turn again.

But I think the most important thing to me is not necessarily to win State but to get there, to play in the finals. That would be awesome. I know high school baseball isn't very big except to the players and their family and friends. And I know in a few years, memories of this playoff season will fade. But for now, for us, it's excitement at its best.

Tomorrow does indeed bring a perfect environment for me to complete my tale, since Woody is in obvious hangover purgatory. He arrives home about noon with that squinty-eyed, head-tilted-forward pose of a man with hammers banging around in his head. As he shuffles through the door, I greet him with, "Well, good morning, or should I say good afternoon," a little louder than necessary for effect.

"Oh, Dad, not now; can't talk, need Coke to drink and cold water on my face," Woody pleads as he heads to the kitchen.

"Oh, yes indeed, right now," I shoot back in a raised voice with the appropriate level of anger.

"Oh, God, please help me," Woody moans prayerfully as he splashes water in his face.

"I was hoping last night to steer you away from this state you've put yourself in," I say, expecting full well that my speech would have had about as much effect as a single drop of rain plopping down in the middle of the Sahara Desert. "So now you get to hear it with M80s going off in your skull and that giant nausea snake writhing around in your belly," I add.

"Oh, God," Woody responds with his head hanging over the sink, droplets of water sliding down off his eyebrows, nose, and chin and free-falling into the sink below.

"Maybe this is your last time to imbibe too much, but the odds are that the wine will drink the wine, and then the man, again," I say.

Woody pulls a can of Coke from the fridge, holds it to his neck for a few moments, pops the top, and then brings it to his lips and tilts his head back, grimacing in hangover head pain as he pulls hard and swallows several times.

"Let's go out back on the deck in case you blow chunks," I say as I steer him in that direction.

"Help me, Lord," escapes in less than a whisper from Woody's lips.

"Now where were we?" I begin as Woody shields his eyes from the bright spring sun and chugs the rest of his Coke. "Oh yeah, I was drinking heavy at Friday's, trying to escape the fear and stress of my father's heart attack. I was preparing for a trip with my wife and friends that would take me far, with the help of alcohol, far away from the reality of my dad's grave condition. And drink I did.

"We drove a couple of hours, into South Carolina, drinking and playing word games like twenty questions. Then we stopped to get a room at a Holiday Inn before continuing on to the stadium for the seven-thirty-p.m. kickoff. My buddy was a scotch drinker, and he had bought a couple pints of Johnny Walker Red on the way out of town. He couldn't drink since he was driving, but the gals and I had been drinking wine during the drive. Bet you'd like a big slug of dry wine right now, wouldn't you, Woody!" I jab and then regret as he lurches for the railing and spews over it and down onto the grass below.

I head to the kitchen for a wet hand towel and fill a big plastic stadium cup full of ice and water and bring them to my self-betrayed son.

"Clean up, have a swig and a seat," I say as low groans come back to me from the Woodster.

"Anyway," I begin again, "after we check in and put our bags in the room, my buddy pulls the car over next to the dumpster, and I start grabbing all the McDonald's bags and other trash and pitch them in. It strikes me as strange that I hear what sounds like bottles hit the metal bottom of the empty dumpster. But I'm not thinking too clearly now and hop back in the car, and we head for the stadium. As we head down the interstate, my buddy Mike says, 'Hey, Steve, open up one of those bottles of Scotch.' I look around and say, 'What bottles of Scotch?' And then I remember the sounds of bottles hitting the bottom of the dumpster. 'Uh oh,' I say to Mike. 'I think I tossed them into the dumpster with the trash.'

"Mike just says, 'Oh,' takes the next exit, and returns to our motel, more tickled at my dopey move than angry about it. Naturally, I get to do the dumpster diving; luckily it was empty except for our contributions. I find the two pints; one was unscathed while the other had just had the neck broken off. But it was almost upright and not much had spilled out. So we head back down the highway with me taking large sips of scotch out of the broken neck of a pint of Johnny Walker Red. If that's not the wine drinking the wine, then I don't know what is."

I think Woody's listening but shoot a quick "are you paying attention" his way.

And he replies, "Yes, broken bottle of scotch."

I continue. "I drink 'til we get to the stadium parking lot, and then Mike joins in and tries to catch up. We're early enough to polish off the scotch before kickoff, so we're feeling no pain when the game starts."

"May I be excused to lie down?" Woody interrupts.

"No, sir," I shoot back before continuing.

"Tech is playing pretty poorly, and I'm letting them have it, playing the boozed-up critical fan to the hilt. I guess if we had been in the opponents' section, I might have been viewed as a comical aside to the contest. But we were in a small section of Tech fans since I bought the tickets at Tech.

"Well, a guy in front of me gets tired of my mouth and starts making comments back over his shoulder, loud enough so I can hear."

"This is getting better; did you punch his lights out?" Woody pipes up as his interest level rises.

"I was toasted enough that I just started getting worse to aggravate him more. I flat out didn't care. That is, the *wine me* didn't care. I was getting relief from my stress, and now I was getting mean. This guy finally stands up, turns around, and yells at me to shut up and let them watch the game in peace. I just tell him to shut his mouth and sit his butt down so I can see the game. His girl—wife or girlfriend, I don't know which—tugs on him and gets him to sit down. Our two wives are on me quietly to cool it, but I look at Mike, and I can tell he's ready to back me if I want to jump in. The booze has turned the fear and dread and stress into pure anger now, raw, white-hot, *I want to kick some butt, I want to do serious damage* anger.

"So I begin again, doing my best with my mouth to get him to start the fight. I want him to make the first move, jump, and shove me, or even throw a punch; I don't care. I just want him to go first. And I know that, in my condition, once he starts it, I'm gonna mess him up bad. He's younger and stocky, but it doesn't matter to me because I've got gravity in my favor since I'm a row above him. And even if he throws a damaging first shot, I know I won't really feel it. I know I'll come hard and dirty, and I will inflict serious pain and damage because the burning rage that's flowing through me now is in control, and what little is left of my rational mind is switched off."

Woody is in rapt concentration now.

"Something exciting happens on the field for Tech, and the guy jumps up to cheer with most of the rest of our section. And I decide, *This is it; no more waiting. I'm gonna drill him right no*w. So I jump to my feet, flaming with rage to do the deed. But as soon as I get upright, in a millisecond, the rage, the anger, the desire for violence flows out of me. It's gone;

it's gone in a flash, like someone pulled a plug. I drop back into my seat bewildered and spent, like my body is totally drained. It's like I was on the edge of a cliff, teetering, about to go over, wanting to go over, and someone or something pulled me back."

Woody says, "I thought I was gonna hear about a whale of a rumble, a beat-down for the Pelham history book! And nothing happened the rest of the game?"

"No, I went from a raging lunatic to a monk with a vow of silence. And I found out why when I got home the next day. We got up and left the Holiday Inn, Mike and I all hung over, and came straight back to Atlanta. Your mom and I got our car at Mike and Cindy's and drove directly home. When we walked in the door, the phone started ringing. I answered it, and it was my Aunt Jane, and she gave me the awful news that we had lost my dad the previous night. Of course, I was stunned, and she added that my mom and my sister and brother-in-law were driving to Atlanta now and would probably be at my parents' house shortly. Your mom and I got right back in the car and drove to my parents.' We pulled in the carport and got out of the car, and they pulled up right behind us."

"Holy cow," escapes from Woody as he is understandably wrapped up in the story now.

"If I had gotten in that fight the night before, it would have been devastating for my mother, my family. I might have been in jail or the hospital instead of embracing and comforting my mother. I'm betting I would have had a messed-up face at the least and would not have arrived there in time, at that moment, for my mom. I'm telling you, Woody, that night it took some sort of miraculous event, some sort of spiritual intervention from the Almighty through my dad's spirit or an angel or some other heavenly force to completely alter my mindset and actions instantaneously. It took something miraculous to overcome the wine drinking the man that night. Miraculous occurrences are very few and very far between, son, so you see I'm trying to guide you away from putting yourself in need of one. You cannot trust alcohol consumption to be rational any time, but especially when you're young; far better to avoid it completely than have it destroy your life or, God forbid, someone else's life."

"I hear you, Dad," Woody says. But the look in his eighteen-year-old eyes says, "That'll never happen to me."

The story had come to an end, and now it was time to lay down the law.

"Well, you know the deal about drinking and driving. I believe you when you say you haven't, but if you do, the truck's gone. I'll sell it the next day for whatever I can get for it. And if I find out you've been drinking again at all, the truck is off limits until you go off to college. You can get your buds to drive you around."

I guess the hangover pain and the natural rebellion of the teen male combined to create an outburst from Woody. "Just because you let alcohol get the better of you, it doesn't mean I'm going to! I'm not that stupid!"

My responding outburst was instant. "Well, ain't that special! You know, sharing humiliating experiences from my past isn't my idea of a good time. But I'm willing to do it to try and help you avoid making the same mistakes. Apparently, though, you're too smart to need any advice!"

"I'm sorry, Dad, I just feel so rotten now, and I don't plan on screwing up. Plus, I don't think I'll ever drink again. I didn't mean what I said; I'm just too messed up right now for any more lecturing," Woody answers.

"Okay, I'll finish up by asking you to try and understand why the government wants you in the army at age eighteen and doesn't want you drinking until you're twenty-one. Same reason. It's because eighteen-year-old males think they're invincible and immortal. That's a good attitude for warriors if you're the general but a recipe for disaster for drunken teenagers and their parents."

"Okay, okay," Woody moans as he shields the bright sunlight from his eyes with his hand and shuffles back inside.

He'll understand someday, if he has kids of his own, what it's like to fear for your children's safety and their decision-making abilities. I remember my mother saying, "You'll understand when you have children." I had no idea on earth what she was talking about, absolutely none. I only knew about how what I did affected me and couldn't figure why in the world it had any effect on her. I know now that if I'd never had Kim and Woody, I still wouldn't know what she meant.

The next day, when Woody and I are calmer and he's feeling much better and even a little human, we talk for a short time again on the deck. He comes to me as I'm watching the birds twitter in and out of the feeders while a slight breeze ruffles the leaves. He asks me about the miraculous moment that stopped my fight at the football game.

"Why do you think that happened for you that day, Dad, at the football game?"

"I don't really know, Woody, but I've always tried to include the Almighty in my daily life. I try to remain connected to the spiritual, though not always successfully. But I don't let that lack of success prevent me from continuing to try. I believe spirituality has to have regular exercise, like any other aspect of life. Your muscles, your hand-eye coordination, your brain power through your studies in school, these all need exercise to grow. So does the spirit. You need to be open to and connected to the spirit to feel it, and that connection comes through things like prayer, church, the Scriptures, and charitable deeds to name a few. It's like you have to *boot up* your own personal connection to the spiritual Internet. You have to initiate and maintain your daily involvement with God and his gift of the spirit.

"Sometimes that spirit is like the light breeze we feel now and see rustling the leaves on the cherry tree. And sometimes it can blow through like a hurricane, like it did to me that night. Like the wind, you can't see it, but you can feel it, and you can see its effect in yourself and in others. I don't exactly know why it happened for me that night, and I'm certainly not saying I earned that moment or deserved it in any way. I could never earn something of that spiritual magnitude. No, son, I don't know how it happened for me that night, but I am forever grateful that it did."

Woody seems a little baffled, but hopefully he'll connect it together someday.

After he heads back indoors, my thoughts drift back to parochial school and the Sisters of Mercy who taught me at Our Lady of the Assumption School. I wish we could have afforded to send Kim and Woody to Catholic school. There's something about having religion as a subject in school, just like English or math, that helps make it an everyday thing. And being taught by those nuns in those black-and-white habits with those giant rosary beads for belts was like being taught by God's handpicked instructors, another daily reminder that God was involved in our lives.

Chapter Thirty-Three

Well, this is it. State begins tonight, and I'm as excited as a six-year-old on Christmas morning. I'm taking a half day off to be sure I'm not rushed and not late; can't trust Atlanta traffic on a day that's this important.

I went to North Bowen last evening for their state playoff doubleheader versus Fulton. North Bowen is in the other 5A region in our county, and a couple of their players were on our summer traveling teams up until sophomore year in high school. I know and like their parents and enjoy watching the kids play ball. I was hoping they could pull it off against Fulton but recalled that Fulton was ranked in the top two in the state earlier in the season. Phil and Danny's parents showed up for the game also, and Major's mom made it for the second game. His dad was out of town or would have been there too.

Fulton won the first game eight to five, and unfortunately one of our guys gave up two two-run homers and was tagged with the loss. North Bowen was ahead in game two six to three when I left, with Fulton coming to bat in the bottom of the seventh. I told my fellow parents that I didn't want to see it if Fulton came back, and I wanted to beat the traffic. As I was walking to the parking lot, I heard the crack of a bat and loud cheering, and it sounded like it was coming from the Fulton side of the stands. As I reached my truck, I heard more cheering, and as I drove out I got a glimpse of the scoreboard and saw that there were no outs yet.

When I got home, Jessica told me that Danny's mom called and said Fulton won seven to six. Ugh, it's over for North Bowen just like that; season terminated! I felt a lot of disappointment for them and hoped we wouldn't suffer the same fate. The kids fight all season to get to the playoffs, and then it's over in one evening's doubleheader, ouch with a capital O.

I didn't sleep too well last night, baseball nerves. I guess I'm wondering again if I have been aiming at this time since way back in 1996 when Sandy Pines won State and our twelve-year-old team from Jones Park also won State. Maybe, probably. It's really a neat part of life, having coached some of these kids when they were nine, ten, eleven, and twelve years old. And then following them constantly for these past seasons brings us to this final juncture. Years later, these will just be distant memories. But now I'm thinking how grateful I am that my past surgery was successful and this year's scare was only a scare. Heck, we ought to thank the good Lord every day that our family is well, that nobody is in the hospital or sick with a serious illness. There ought to be a lot of thanksgiving prayer in our lives, including recognizing that simply being alive is a beautiful thing and special times like these should be appreciated to the max. It's been a great run, and if we lose, it shouldn't take away from our memories, but I don't think we're going to lose.

I check out the local morning paper to read the pregame coverage for tonight's twin bill against Greenwood. Three key players are listed for each team, and I'm excited to see that Woody is one of the three for Sandy Pines, along with Hunter and Major. Although Woody has only one home run, he is near the top in RBIs and batting average for the Panthers. I know this little bit of press will pump him up too. The writer picks Sandy Pines to take the series in two games; let's hope he's right.

Chapter Thirty-Four

**State: Round One, Game One
versus Greenwood Vipers**

I'm at the field early as planned. I even have some warm-up music for when the teams are taking pregame practice. After listening to the same old tunes all season, I'm looking for some more upbeat-type sounds. So I bring REO Speedwagon's "Roll with the Changes" and some other lively rock and roll classic tunes to liven things up a bit; at least they'll liven *me* up. The girl handling the music is also happy for something new and takes my selections eagerly.

It could not possibly be a better Friday afternoon for baseball with a clear, sunny sky and a delightful spring temperature. I'm still pinching myself; it's hard to believe it's really here, playoff time. I just hope Woody and the rest of his teammates aren't as nervous as I am.

Game one is all I could hope for, a total shellacking. Allan throws a two-hit, seven-strikeout and shutout gem! The Panthers collect twelve hits and eleven runs in the five-inning whitewash, and that's with no hits in the first inning. You couldn't do much more offensively in a ten-run, rule-shortened game. Greenwood saved their ace pitcher for game two, and the pitchers they use in game one are totally overmatched. Hunter goes three for four with a triple, a single, and a double. Danny goes two for three with a walk-off homer in the bottom of the fifth. Woody goes two for three with two doubles; Bobby goes two for three with a single and a double, and Allan helps himself with a sacrifice fly and a double. It's no contest. And that's the way I like 'em: nail-biters with thrilling, come-from-behind victories are only great after the fact. In the playoffs especially, I prefer the never-in-doubt, ahead-all-the-way routes. But that's just me.

State: Round One, Game Two versus Greenwood Vipers

Sandy Pines bats as visitor in the nightcap. Danny is up second and records a one-out single but is erased in a six-to-four-to-three double play off Major's bat. So the Panthers send the minimum to the plate in their half of the first. Phil is on the mound for the Panthers, and after surrendering a leadoff walk, he battles back to strike out the next two hitters. The clean-up hitter delivers a run-scoring single, and the Vipers lead one to zero at the end of one. There's that leadoff walk coming back to haunt the pitcher and his team again. And the Panthers won't be in control all the way from the beginning in this one.

Woody leads off the Panther second with a single and is sac-bunted to second by Terry, who always seems to get the job done on the sacrifice bunt. But two groundouts leave Woody stranded at second and Sandy Pines still trailing by one after two at bats. It's worrisome, but there's certainly no need to panic yet.

Phil records two more Ks and one walk in a scoreless bottom of the second; that's better.

In the top of the third after singles by Pat and Hunter and a walk to Danny, Major delivers a sacrifice fly. Woody then belts a two-RBI single, and the Panthers lead three to one after two and a half innings. *Way to go Woody and Pat and Hunter and Danny and Major*; hey, I know it's a team sport.

But the Vipers answer back with four in the bottom of the third. They collect the four runs on four singles after a leadoff double and two throwing errors on one play. The score stands at three to five in favor of the Vipers after three. It's anything but comfortable to be trailing again, but we still have four at bats. Trailing by two now would be excruciating if the Panthers had lost the first game and were facing elimination. A first-round scenario like that would really have me sweating bullets.

Allan, who is designated hitter tonight, opens the fateful fourth with a single. Bobby follows with an infield single off the pitcher's glove before Pat flies out to center field. Mike Drew, who came on to pitch in the third, attempts a sac bunt, but the catcher pounces on the ball and throws to third to force the lead runner. Two on, two out, and Hunter comes to the plate. I'm thinking, *Hunter's due for a long ball*, but he falls behind in the count, one ball and two strikes. And then, sure enough, he blasts the next pitch over the right center field fence and Sandy Pines leads six to five. How about that? A positive premonition that proves true—extremely rare, and at times even thought to be extinct. I'll have to work on conjuring up a few more of those.

Danny delivers a single, and Major follows with a towering bomb onto Evergreen Boulevard that chases the Greenwood ace and makes the score eight to five, Panthers. There ain't anything better than home-team homers. Woody greets the new pitcher with a hard-hit ball to third. The third sacker can't handle it, and Woody reaches first. Terry is the ninth batter of the inning, and he rips a shot over the left field fence for another two-run dinger and a ten-to-five lead. Now there's a power surge for ya: three two-out homers in one inning! I could get used to this.

With the Vipers down by five, Mike walks the first two batters in the bottom of the fourth without throwing a strike; *well, spit*. And as usual, the walks come back to haunt him as the Vipers plate two to cut the margin to ten to seven after four.

No runs are scored by either team in the fifth, although Greenwood gets singles from their first two batters. That brings Pat on to pitch in relief of Mike. He gets a grounder to short for out number one and a fly out to center field for out number two. During the next hitter's at bat, the runner at first breaks for second, and Major throws to Bobby at second. Then the runner at third breaks for home, and Bobby throws home in time for out number three and no damage done. That's gotta be demoralizing for the Vipers, making the third out at home.

The Panthers look to add to their lead in the top of the sixth. Major opens the inning with a fly out to left. Woody hits another hard one at the third baseman and reaches first again on an error. Terry doubles, and then the center fielder misplays Allan's deep fly ball, allowing Woody to score and Terry to reach third. The next hitter puts down a squeeze bunt that the pitcher can't field cleanly, and another run scores on the error. Brian Smith, who's in at shortstop, singles after a groundout by Pat, and Sandy Pines leads fourteen to seven after five and a half. I'm breathing pretty easy now; a seven-run lead can do that, but as Yogi said, "It ain't over 'til it's over."

The Vipers get a two-out single but no runs in the sixth. It's a very good thing to escape the sixth with no catastrophes.

Danny pops out to the shortstop to start the seventh, and then Major follows with another Evergreen-Boulevard missile to push the score to fifteen to seven. It's really good to see our guys hit the long ball, but I'm wondering if maybe Major should save some for the next opponent. Woody hammers his third shot in a row at the third sacker, and this time is awarded a hit. Unfortunately for Woody, the throw gets by the first baseman, and the first base coach sends him to second with a "go, go, go." But then the coach sees the catcher has hustled down the first base line and is retrieving the ball and now hollers, "Back, back, back." Woody turns back and dives for first base but is tagged out for out number two. A pop-up to short ends the Panther seventh. An eight-run lead in the last inning should be enough to keep the Pepto on the shelf.

It's the Vipers' last chance, trailing by eight. With two outs and the first-round sweep only one out away, Pat gives up a single and two walks to load the bases. Of course I'm thinking, *Come on guys; let's get this thing over with.* And accommodatingly, the next hitter grounds to Terry at first to end the game and the series.

The Panthers have administered a two-game whirlwind beating to the Vipers. They belted out twelve hits, including six doubles, one triple, and one home run in the first game that was cut short at five innings. In the second game, they hammered out thirteen hits, including four home runs. That makes five home runs in two games. Let me repeat: there ain't anything better than home-team homers! They outscored the Vipers twenty-six to seven in the two-game sweep. That's more than impressive, but I'm sure the pickings won't be so easy from here on out.

Two days later, the local paper informs me that our next opponent is the Sebastian Wolves, who played in the same region with Berkwood and two other strong teams. The Wolves finished second in the region by going an impressive fifteen and three after a one and nine record in their first ten games. They are a young team, having graduated eleven seniors last year, just as Sandy Pines will this year. Their eleven took the Wolves to the state quarterfinals last year, where they were ousted by our rival, Northlake.

Speaking of Northlake, the Hornets were knocked out of this year's tourney last night in a two-game sweep at the hands of Berkwood. The way the state tournament brackets are set up, it was possible that the Panthers and the Hornets could have once again met in the finals for the state championship, but not now. That chance for déjà vu is gone. Coach Pat states that he's impressed by Sebastian's second-place finish in region eight. He also allows that to get through the state playoffs, a team is probably going to have to go through region eight. Well, here we go.

Chapter Thirty-Five

**State: Round Two, Game One
versus Sebastian Wolves**

It's Tuesday afternoon and another beautiful day at the old ballpark. However, the sun will be bright and hot on the home crowd grandstands. In fact, it's so hot in our stands that after I turn over my CDs to the music gal in the scorers' spaces above the concession stand, I decide to watch the first few innings from the enemy side. It's in the shade and affords a front view of right-handed hitters, of which Woody is one, for videotaping purposes. Jess and Kim won't come over for the start, but I'm guessing the heat will bring at least Jess later.

It's strange walking behind the first base line dugout and down that side to the far bleachers. It's strange but a little familiar, since this was the home dugout and fan side when Sandy Pines won state against Northlake in 1996. I can still vividly recall sitting with Kim and Coach Pat's daughter, Beth Ann, in these stands as they shook their cans filled with coins as noisemakers and shouted frantically, as only young girls can, six years ago. I'm not sure why the Panthers changed dugouts, but I've heard that the first-base-side dugout is colder in cold-weather days at the opening of the season. Also, there is an outlet in the third-base dugout for use of a space heater during those cold days. I guess it makes sense, but doggone if I don't prefer this side. The view's better, and it's so much more pleasant in the shade. There aren't any Sebastian fans in this section of the stands; they are all situated in the stands between the concession stand and the visitor dugout. I can videotape over the fence and get some much closer shots than from our side.

Again Allan takes his unbeaten record to the mound today and starts strong, striking out the Wolves' leadoff hitter. Unfortunately things change quickly as the next two batters record cheap singles. The following batter draws a walk, and the bases are juiced. *What the heck, I'm positive this isn't how the game's supposed to start.* Allan takes the pressure and Ks the next hitter. One more out to get, and we escape this snafu. And the Panthers do escape this time, getting a fielder's choice grounder to Pat at short, and he flips it to Bobby at second to end the unpleasantness. *Whew, that's too close for comfort.*

Hunter starts the Sandy Pines half of the first with a fly ball out to right field. Danny gets things rolling next with a solid single. Major flies out to center field, so Woody steps in with a man on and two outs. Woody comes through, delivering a ringing shot to the left field corner for an RBI double. Terry next rips a single that scores Woody, but he's thrown out at second trying to stretch the hit into a double. Two runs after two outs is totally acceptable. Of course, I would have liked more.

Al is greeted in the top of the second with another single. But that runner is cut down at second when the next hitter bounces into a short-to-second-fielder's-choice for out number one. Al can't stand the prosperity and walks the next batter; one out, runners at first and second. The Wolves' leadoff hitter steps in for the second time and promptly delivers a run-scoring single, *spit!* Now there are men on first and third and one run in with only one out. The first swirl of adrenaline has jetted into my stomach. Is Al still wearing his escape-artist garb? Yes, the next batter lines a shot back to Al, who snags it and throws to first to double the runner there. Panthers still lead two to one. Before Sandy Pines' first batter steps in, Jessica joins me in the shade as I expected she would. I guess since we're ahead, it's okay to be on this side for now.

Allan helps himself by drawing a walk on four straight balls to open the Panther second. Bobby sacrifices the courtesy runner to second with a bunt, and Pat singles to put runners at first and third with one out. Our ninth batter, the designated hitter, steps up to the plate next. Coach Pat signals for the suicide-squeeze bunt, but the hitter lunges at and misses the curve ball delivered by the Wolves' hurler. The runner coming home from third slams on the breaks about ten feet from home and tries to turn and run back to third. But he's a dead duck for the tag out, and Coach Pat is fuming mad. Our batter is understandably shaken and eventually strikes out to end the inning. We've missed a golden scoring opportunity, and the Wolves seem to have seized the momentum. Adrenaline swirl number two is launched.

Sebastian records their fifth hit, a single, but scores no runs in the top of the third.

Hunter opens the Sandy Pines at bat with another fly out to right field. Danny follows with his second single, but Major grounds into a second-to-shortstop force-out of Danny. Woody steps in with two out and delivers a swinging bunt and reaches first. The catcher's throw appears to pull the first baseman off the bag, but through a dad's eyes it looks like a bang-bang play anyway, and I score it a hit. I find out later that the official scorekeeper scored it an E2, but I had a better view since it happened right in front of me. Terry comes to bat with men on first and second, works the count full, and then takes a hack at a high one and strikes out to end the inning. It's still Panthers two to one after three complete.

The Wolves come out ripping in the top of the fourth with two doubles sandwiched around a strikeout. After the fourth batter of the inning flies out to center field, the next hitter singles to give the Wolves a three-to-two lead. Al Ks the following man to end the threat, but the Wolves are hitting the ball hard as well as having the lead. Things are getting *scary*.

The Panthers answer back in the bottom of the fourth. Bobby gets the ball rolling with a one-out single. With Pat at bat, Bobby gets the steal sign and takes off for second on the attempted steal. It's a close play as the second sacker takes the throw from the catcher and Bobby slides headfirst in a cloud of dust. The second baseman has his glove, with the ball supposedly in it, under Bobby, who has his hand on the base. The ump watches as the fielder reaches around Bobby with his bare hand, roots around, and comes out with the ball in his bare right hand. He holds it up to the ump, who inexplicably signals *out*! How the ump believes that ball wasn't out of the glove under Bobby I'll never know. But Coach Pat doesn't protest too strongly, so I guess it's just more twilight zone on the base paths for the Panthers today.

Pat walks on four straight pitches; it would have been nice to have known that ahead of time. Junior pitcher Paul Purser bats for Smith as the DH, making the game even more weird. Paul is up from the JV, and I don't know if he's ever had an at bat in the last three years, but he must have shown something in batting practice since joining the varsity for the playoffs. And sure enough, Coach Pat's pulled the right string, and Paul delivers a solid single. There are two on and two out, and we're back to the top of the order. You can't hold Hunter down for long, and this time the mutton-chopped right fielder delivers an RBI double to tie the game. *Now, that's better.* But the inning ends on Danny's pop-up out to second. At least we're tied, but this doesn't feel comfortable.

The Wolves open the fifth with a walk. Al had a three-and-two count but lost him. I hate to say it, but this doesn't look like Al's day. The next man lays down a sacrifice bunt and moves the runner to second. Al gets a fly ball out to center field from the following batter for out number two. Maybe he can get out of this yet. But no, a single plates the go-ahead run, and the next man hits one by Terry at first. I see Terry indicate that he never saw the ball, and after the game we learn that the pep signs that are across the bottom of the home stands are keeping Terry and Bobby from being able to see the ball come off the bat. The signs are taken down between games.

Now it's men on first and third with two outs, and we're already down a run. The next batter hits a grounder to short, and Pat fields it nicely, close to second base, and it appears the inning will end. But for some reason the throw to Bobby at second is rushed and low, and everybody is safe as run number five scores for Sebastian. The nerves are starting to rev up now. The inning does finally end when the next batter pops out to Al, but momentum has definitely swung to the Wolves. Jessica and I decide to move back to our side; maybe we can bring *Mo* along with us. And besides, it appears that it really has been bad karma to watch from the enemy's side. The Panthers are now down three to five.

Sandy Pines has Major, Woody, and Terry as the first three batters in the bottom of the fifth, so maybe the Panthers can answer. Major hits a swinging bunt and is thrown out. Woody strikes out on a high pitch with a two-ball, two-strike count, and Terry flies out to center field; *Oh, Mommy,* what a bad, bad time to go one, two, three. More *Mo* to Sebastian and that old nemesis, doubt, has wiggled into my psyche, not to mention queasiness into my belly. The beginning-of-the-end fear is beginning to grow.

Al walks the leadoff hitter in the top of the sixth; oh no, it's the *sixth,* and that's the end of the night for him. Mike comes in and Ks the first two men he faces. This is good; this is definitely good. But, uh-oh, the next batter singles, and runners are on the corners now. In my gut this now feels like bad things, really bad things. Coach Pat pulls Mike and inserts Pat from shortstop; he's pulling all the strings, hoping to get out of the inning before more damage is done. But Pat uncorks a wild pitch and run number six rushes home. *Holy frijoles, we're coming apart at the seams!* Pat composes himself and strikes out the following batter to end the inning. But the Panthers and the Panther fans are reeling with the Wolves now up by three runs.

Bobby manages a one-out single before Pat flies out to center. Paul Purser reaches first after being hit by a pitch, so we have runners on first and second and Hunter coming to bat. Maybe we do still have a chance, maybe; but Hunter grounds out to third.

The Wolves do no more damage in the top of the seventh, but there's a big-enough mountain to climb already.

The weirdness continues in the bottom of the seventh for Sandy Pines. Danny leads off and Ks on a pitch that hits him in the right shoulder. Why would Danny swing at a pitch that was on its way to hitting him? He goes down in the dirt, and I'm thinking, *Oh, no*! *He's our pitcher for game two.* Danny gets up with the trainer and heads to the dugout okay—I hope. Major draws a walk, and Woody is hit by a pitch before Terry flies out to right. Now it's two on but two out, and the chances are running out as my gut churns like a merry-go-round. The next batter is hit by a pitch, so now the bases are loaded for Bobby. Maybe, just maybe, they can do it. With a count of one ball and two strikes, Bobby pops out to the first baseman in foul territory to end the game.

Is this the beginning of the end? Sebastian has saved their ace for game two, so you know it won't be easy for the Panthers.

I take some stuff to the truck in the parking lot between games, mostly just to walk while I worry and project unhappy things. On the way back to the field, I meet young John Thomas on his way to the parking lot. He lets me know that he believes the guys will get this second game. I mention that they are going to have to play like his '94 Sandy Pines team that came back from the brink of elimination at Chastain and went on to play for the state championship at Bates. He says they will, and he says it with a good deal of confidence. I certainly hope he's right. At least his attitude has helped rekindle some hope for Mister Glass Half-Empty. And I figure since he's closer to their age, he probably knows their mindset better than I do.

As I reenter the park, I'm thinking, *If you can't be happy for what you do have, then maybe you should be happy for what you don't have.* Immediately I'm happy for something I don't have: cancer. And that makes me happy for what I do have: a clean bill of health and at least one more game for the Panthers to get back in this thing!

State: Round Two, Game Two
versus Sebastian Wolves

Well, here it is; backs against the wall; win or the season is history. I have to go back to my home spot down the left field line; gotta be able to pace. I can't take the pressure-cooker atmosphere of the big stands between the Panther dugout and home plate.

The Panthers bat as visitors in the second game, and Hunter opens the game with a walk on four straight balls. Danny hits next and sends Hunter to third with a single. But Major is caught looking for strike three on a count of one ball and two strikes, *rat spit!* Another hit, and we could've really been rolling early. Woody steps in as I attempt to take deep, slow breaths. "Come on, buddy, keep it going." The first pitch to Woody dives into the dirt. It skips past the catcher, and Hunter comes home on the wild pitch. "Good job, Woody, way to scare the pitcher into a dirt ball," I joke to myself. The count reaches three balls and two strikes, and my breaths are now rapid and shallow. On the payoff pitch, Woody hammers a double into the left field corner to plate Danny.

Panthers lead two to zero, and Woody is on second with only one out. This is a good start so far, but we could sure use some more. The good ends with strikeouts by the next two hitters, the first looking and the second swinging. But still, that's not bad at all after one at bat. I'm proud and happy for Woody. Tonight he's really hitting well, and we need that.

Danny's on the mound, and he gets the Wolf leadoff hitter on a groundout to second. Unfortunately, the good start is followed by back-to-back singles, and the lead is quickly cut to two to one. A walk puts men at first and second now with one out, and it's *uh-oh* time already. A grounder to second results in out number two, but now there are men on second and third. My stomach is doing barrel rolls as Danny comes on strong and strikes out the next batter on three straight pitches. *That's the way to do it, guys!* Sandy Pines escapes the first inning with the lead.

The Panthers get a runner to first when Pat reaches base on a shortstop error with two outs. *Come on, fellas! Make 'em pay,* I plead in my head as I pace the bleachers. But Hunter is caught looking for out number three, and that's the end of the threat for Sandy Pines.

The Wolves get a leadoff single in the bottom of the second, and then Danny retires the next three hitters on two Ks followed by a grounder back to him.

Danny starts the third off with a single, and Major reaches base when he's hit by a pitch. The pacing ceases and rapid breaths are back as Woody steps in with men on first and second and no outs. John Thomas wonders out loud if Coach will have Woody bunt to move the runners up a base. It seems like a good idea to put runners on second and third with one out. But Coach lets Woody swing away, and he rips the first pitch right at the third sacker. The infielder knocks the ball down, picks it up, and steps on third base to force Danny before firing to first to nip Woody by a step for the double play, *ugh*! Terry follows with a groundout to end an inning that looked to have excellent possibilities a short time ago. My twisting gut reminds me to hope that that missed opportunity doesn't come back to haunt us.

The Wolves surge ahead in the bottom of the third. The leadoff hitter singles, and then two consecutive errors in the middle infield allow the tying run to score, also putting men on first and third with no outs. A sacrifice fly to right field from the next batter scores the go-ahead run. *Oh no*! The following hitter singles to put men on first and third with only one out, and that *this-could-be-the-end* fear erupts in my mind again, flooding all corners with dread. Danny induces a comeback grounder to himself, checks the runner at third, and throws to first for out number two. That's better, but we are still in a heck of a jam and don't want to get down by more than a run at this juncture. The next batter rockets a grounder to third, and the dreaded demons flame ever higher inside my skull. Woody smoothly fields the shot and rifles a throw to first for the out to end the inning and the damage.

Sandy Pines' half of the fourth goes quickly. A walk and three groundouts are all the Panthers can muster. I take a deep breath and swallow hard; we're down one at the halfway point.

Sebastian does more damage in the bottom of the fourth, scoring one run on a walk followed by a single, a fielder's choice, and another single. When the inning ends on a groundout to third—Woody's much calmer than his old man tonight—the Panthers trail two to four with three more at bats to go. That's nine outs, and a lot can still happen with nine outs to go, but I'd be breathing a lot easier if we were the ones ahead by two at this point in the game. Those nine outs could be the last nine of the season.

Hunter opens the top of the fifth with a fly out to center field. Danny draws a walk, and Major reaches base on a shortstop error; men on first and second for Woody. I tell myself that he can do it, he's hot, he's hitting the ball hard, but I'm praying double speed at the same time. And Woody delivers a solid RBI single that scores Danny and cuts the Wolves' lead to one run!

"Atta boy, son. You're really pulling your weight tonight," I whisper. With men now on first and second and only one out, I'm hoping for a big inning. But the hopes die quickly when the next two hitters make outs on a pop-up to short and a strikeout to end the inning and strand the possible tying and go-ahead runs. It could have been better, but at least the lead is down to one run with two at bats to go.

Mike Drew comes in to pitch in the bottom of the fifth, and

he retires three in a row after the first batter singles. *That's excellent, absolutely super work when we needed it. Great job, Mike.*

Unfortunately, the Wolves' pitcher goes Mike one better in the top of the sixth. He Ks the first batter he faces and gets the next two on infield groundouts. Sandy Pines must hold the Wolves scoreless in the bottom of the sixth—yes, the *sixth*. It could be getting close to *over* time, as in the season and high school careers. The senior parents all have to be feeling it. I know I am.

Mike holds the Wolves back in the bottom of the sixth with some fine help from Woody, Major, and Pat. The first Sebastian batter grounds one sharply to third, and my stomach leapfrogs into my throat. No problem. Woody snags it and fires to first for out number one. The next man draws a walk, and my stomach nosedives to around my knees. *Come on, guys.* The third hitter of the inning rifles another grounder at Woody. He drops down to one knee, takes the ball off his chest, and then grabs it up and whips a bullet to second to force the lead runner.

"Atta boy!" I holler as Bobby's dad shouts, "Great play, Woody!"

Major's dad and older brother, as well as Bobby's dad and Mack and I, are all pacing, worrying, and cheering in the left field foul line bleachers. The third out comes when the runner at first is cut down trying to steal second. Major makes a strong throw, and Pat makes a good sweep tag. The play brings the cheering crowd to its feet, pumps up the players, and helps create a much-needed momentum surge as the players huddle up before their last at bats.

The team is definitely fired up, but I'm beginning to approach hyperventilation. I learn later from Kim that Jessica is beginning to tear up, and two other moms are also starting to cry. Probably the rest of the senior moms are reaching for hankies as well. We know that it can all be over in just three more outs. Eight, nine, ten years of playing against and with each other, all the spring breaks and summers traveling together, all this camaraderie could end in a matter of minutes. *Settle down, innards, here we go. It's crunch time.*

I turn to Mack and blurt out, "If they pull this out, I'll play a "Roll with the Changes" air guitar solo on top of the home dugout next game."

And Mack, as nervous and worried as I am, answers back, "And I'll play air drums right up there with you."

We have our leadoff hitter, Hunter, up first in the top of the seventh, and you can't ask for much more. Hunter draws a walk, putting the potential tying run on first and raising the hopes of the home crowd. Now the crowd is buzzing, ready for the big play that will get us back in this thing. Danny steps in and shows bunt once or twice, but then the count reaches two strikes on questionable called strikes that draw the ire of the panicky home crowd. I figure he'll be swinging away. Wrong.

Danny drops down a near-perfect bunt toward the third base line. The pitcher and third sacker charge, but the catcher gets to the ball first, his back to first base as he grabs it. He turns and fires to first. But the hurried throw sails over the first baseman's reaching mitt and takes off down the first base foul line toward right field.

Pandemonium breaks loose! The crowd screams with one voice. Hunter races toward third and Danny to second. The right fielder retrieves the ball but makes a bad throw as Hunter rounds third. The ball skids across the infield and to the fence next to the Panther dugout as Hunter sprints home with the tying run! It's totally chaotic on the home side now. Screams of relief, joy, and expectation roll out of the stands and dugout as Danny stands at second with the score tied and no outs.

Major steps up to the plate and drops a sac bunt down the first base line. It's perfect; the first baseman comes in and fields it as Danny races to third. Major heads for first, but after the first baseman grabs the ball, he stops and starts back-pedaling to delay the put-out. As he backs up, the first baseman comes forward, and the home plate ump calls Major out. Major has done his job, and the go-ahead run is on third with one out and Woody coming to bat. The excitement is cascading out of the stands as a group of students start a "Woody, Woody, Woody" chant and others join in.

Bobby's dad is next to me hollering, "Watch the pitch in the dirt. Look for the pitch in the dirt!"

He's hoping for one past the catcher to score Danny from third. And me, I'm pretty much in total hyperventilation mode now, wondering if I can maintain consciousness.

I bring the video camera up to my shoulder and frame Woody at the plate in the viewfinder. After I line up the shot, I lift my head to watch while holding the camera steady. Woody just crushes the first pitch. He really murders it, but he's a little ahead of it, and his hooking line drive is headed directly for me. I drop behind the fence, and the other dads duck and scatter as the ball ricochets off the pipe on top of the fence and rockets past us like a rifle shot. The crowd starts the "Woody" chant back up as we dads scramble back to our viewing spots, and I'm thinking, *My own son almost knocked my teeth out*! The crowd continues the chant until the pitcher delivers the pitch. Woody rips at the next pitch, and you can hear the loud crack of the bat on the ball throughout the suddenly silent park.

As the ball rockets toward right center field, I hear young

John Thomas shouting, "Oh, there it goes!" over the instant roar of the crowd in the stands.

I forget the camera and just follow the flight of the ball with my naked eyes as I yell, "Get, get, get!"

So many thoughts flash in my mind. *The runner is going to score even if it's caught. It might be a home run. They're not going to catch it,* and I holler, "Get outta here!" The crowd has reached another level of roaring as the ball hits the base of the fence in right center, and Woody pulls up at second with the biggest RBI of his life! This is incredible excitement for our team and fans, but I'm sure no one is more excited than me, probably not even Woody. Not many parents are fortunate enough to experience this kind of thrill with and for their children. How great is it to be alive right now?

As I watch Woody, obviously excited and fired up at second base, I hear young John Thomas say, "Way to go, Woody Pelham!" and I'm reminded of his confident words between games.

How fitting that I should be standing with him when the Panthers grab the lead.

We do have the lead, but more runs would be wonderful. Terry bats next as the crowd tries to settle down, and he is issued an intentional walk to set up the possible double play. The strategy works for the most part as the next batter hits a grounder to third, and the force-out there makes out number two. Still men on first and second, but Al also grounds out, and the Panther seventh is history. But what splendid history it is; Panthers lead five to four. We still need three more outs to force a deciding game three tomorrow, just three more outs.

Mike gets the first batter on a strikeout, and the crowd is roaring again. The next batter grounds one toward the hole between short and second, but Pat races over, scoops it up, and makes a strong throw to first. It's a bang-bang play, and the ump calls the runner safe. I scream my disapproval, as does the rest of the crowd. It looked to me like the ump made the call before either the ball or the runner got to first, but the call is safe. The next batter puts down a sacrifice bunt that moves the runner to second. Now the potential tying run is at second with two away and just one more out to get.

And Mike brings the screaming crowd to its feet by striking out the next hitter. What a celebration on the field and in the stands. The Panthers are back from the brink to play another day. I couldn't have come up with a more dramatic, gut-wrenching, nail-biting, and emotion-drenched game if I was making this journal up! I couldn't imagine this game in my wildest dreams.

Chapter Thirty-Six

The morning's local sports page headlines read: "Fighting to Survive." And the opening line of the article states, "Woody Pelham wasn't quite ready to see his senior baseball season come to an end."

Good for him, Woody gets his five seconds of fame. The article even has a quote from Woody, as well as describing his heroics. Seeing the term *heroics* associated with a baseball game, and my son in particular, is a little unsettling to me. I holler at Jess, who's pouring me a cup of coffee.

"They're calling Woody a hero in the paper; that doesn't sound right to me, calling a high school baseball player a hero. Anyway, it's a team sport; one player didn't win the game."

"Oh, don't make a big deal out of it. Writers like to spice up their stories. I kinda like it," she replies.

"I guess I just think of heroes as soldiers or firefighters or cops, people who put their lives on the line and lose them sometimes. I don't want their sacrifices diminished by putting ball players in the same category."

"That's not what the writer's doing; he's just saying on the level of this high school playoff game, there were athletic heroics involved. Don't spoil it for Woody; let him enjoy his moment in the sun."

"Yeah, I guess you're right. I just hope his head doesn't get too big for his ball cap."

And then from somewhere deep in my aging memory bank, a thought flickers to the surface.

"Hey, hon, do you remember that little girl who was injured during that heavy snowfall some years back? I think her name is Elizabeth Johnson."

"Yes, I do. I think she was eight or nine, and she stepped on a downed power line. It was an awful tragedy."

"Yeah, it was. She lost both of her legs. I don't think I'll ever forget that. I remember thinking how something as beautiful and peaceful-looking as that snowfall had caused something so horrible."

"Well, why in the world did you think of that now?"

"Baseball heroes, we were talking about baseball heroes. I guess it triggered the memory of an article in a sports magazine that mentioned that little girl's story and Dale Murphy. You remember him playing for the Braves?"

"Of course."

"Well, in the article about Dale Murphy, there was the story of Elizabeth Johnson being at a Braves home game. I'm sure it was a special deal for her, and I don't recall how long after the accident it was; maybe a year or so, maybe less. Anyway, Dale was talking to her, or maybe it was her nurse, or maybe they just got a message to him; I can't remember which. But the thing was, she or the nurse asked Dale to hit a home run for her."

"Did he hit one for her?"

"No, he hit two. And my throat's lumping up again just talking about it. I don't remember anything on the local news or in the Atlanta papers about it when it happened, but it was in that article."

"So I guess ball players can be heroes," Jess says.
"Yeah, I guess they can."

Of course, a copy of today's article is arriving by noon via fax at any and all available relatives' locations. It's a very happy day in the Pelham family circle, but the evening will bring the third and deciding game.

State: Round Two, Game Three versus Sebastian Wolves

Yet again it's another great day for a ball game; the weather has definitely been doing its part. The Panthers start things off by losing the coin toss to decide home team and will bat as visitors. We've got Phil on the mound tonight, and he's capable of a good outing against this or any club. And you might say he's due for an extended outing, five good innings minimum. Mike and Pat can probably go for short stints, but a complete game from Phil would be great.

Of course, I'm back down in the left field bleachers again with the other guys from last night. I'm guessing that everybody on our side is attempting to sit in exactly the same spots they were in when the second game ended. There is a little bit of superstition to be found around ballparks.

The atmosphere is a little sedated. I think the Wolves and their fans are still stunned from last night's loss, and the Panthers and their fans are still pinching themselves to be sure it really happened.

The Wolves' starting pitcher takes the mound, and he appears young, thin, and smallish. He's a freshman lefty and doesn't seem to be throwing very hard during warm-ups. Hunter steps in and smacks a two-ball, no-strike pitch into right field for a leadoff single. Danny bats next and works the count to two balls and one strike when the ump calls a strike that looks low to me.

I turn and holler to Phil, who's warming up behind us, that "he likes 'em low."

There, I've made my contribution. Danny grounds one to short that is flipped to second to force Hunter. Major launches a high, deep shot to dead center. I turn to watch the center fielder settle under the ball on the warning track, and as the ball drops toward him, I turn away. Then I hear shouts and see the field ump signal safe. The center fielder just flat dropped the ball. Now men are on first and second with one out for Woody. Woody hits the first pitch hard but right at the shortstop. He fields the grounder and flips to second for the force-out, making it two down with men on first and third. Terry takes a ball and then hits one toward the second sacker who fields it cleanly but makes a throwing error, and a run scores. With men on second and third, the designated hitter strikes out on three pitches. That's an ugly ending, but the Panthers get one run, anyway.

Phil starts off like a Cy Young award winner, striking out the side in the bottom of the first. It doesn't get any better than that, and the Panthers manage to carry last night's momentum through the first inning of tonight's game. That's very good for the nerves department.

In the second inning, Sandy Pines gets hits from Pat and Hunter but no runs. Sebastian manages a two-out double, but Phil closes the door on that threat with another K.

The Panthers open the third with a double from Major. Woody hits another one hard but again right at the shortstop, and he's thrown out at first while the courtesy runner advances to third. At least he's still hitting the ball hard. Terry grounds to short also, but the run scores on the play. We go to the bottom of the third up two to zero. That's okay. That's pretty good. I'd rather have seven or eight or a hundred, but we're okay for now.

Again the Wolves get a base runner aboard with two outs but no harm as a fly ball to Hunter in right field ends the inning.

Bobby leads off the Panther fourth with another ground-out to short. That first out is followed by three successive walks. With the bases loaded, Danny steps in and delivers a double that plates three. *Now you're rolling, boys.* Major draws the fourth walk of the inning before Woody drills another one right at the shortstop. The force-out is made at second, but at least a run scores. Terry goes down swinging for out number three, but the Panthers have a semi-comfortable lead of six to zero after four and a half innings. Much better than last night, much, much, much better.

Things continue to improve when Phil carves out the heart of the Wolves' lineup, striking out the number-three man in the lineup and the clean-up hitter for the first two outs of the inning. He induces a ground ball from the next hitter to short for out number three, and Sebastian goes down one, two, three in the fourth.

In the top of the fifth, three consecutive singles from Bobby, Pat, and Jason chase the Wolves' starter. Hunter greets the new pitcher with another single. Danny walks ahead of a sac fly from Major. Woody rips a line shot at the third sacker that pops out of his glove, which was raised in defense. Woody reaches first on the error, and then Terry chases the reliever with an RBI double. Yes indeed, this is more like what I had in mind! The next pitcher gets the tenth batter of the inning for out number three, but the Panthers have added five runs to up their tally to eleven. Since it's now eleven to zero, if the

Panthers can get three outs before the Wolves can score two, they advance via the ten-run rule.

Phil makes short work of the Wolves in the bottom of the fifth with three groundouts in a row, and it's over. The senior-laden Panthers, behind their senior left-hander, have swamped the Wolves, who were forced to start a freshman pitcher. Phil finishes with seven strikeouts, no walks, and one hit in the mercy-rule shortened game. That's a heck of a performance just when the Panthers needed it. It's not another scintillating, emotion-filled, come-from-behind-win, but in my book it's just what the doctor ordered. A series win over a team that had you with one foot in the grave is hard to beat.

And now it's time for Mack and me to own up to our pledges before the Panther comeback victory in game two.

The other dads who were out in the left field bleachers and heard us have made arrangements for our performance. They clear it with Coach Pat and escort us toward the home dugout after the visitor crowd has filed out, and it's just friendlies in the stands. Word has spread in those home stands, and most, including the students (maybe especially the students), are staying behind to witness the middle-aged rockers' performance. They put a chair up on top for Mack to sit in at his air drums and another for me as John Thomas informs me that I'm expected to do the organ solo also! They've even got a stand-up mic, unplugged thank goodness, up there to lend authenticity.

As I head up the stepladder to the roof of the dugout, John hands me an old electric guitar (no strings, luckily) someone has lent him to help humiliate me further in my performance. I've put on my goofy "I'm crazy about those Panthers" baseball cap that has two bills sticking out at forty-five-degree angles to each other. I've got it on backwards. I might as well look as ridiculous as I'm gonna be acting. Yeah, right. I'm thinking this could really be embarrassing, but the crowd seems to be in a good mood what with the relief of winning game three and advancing. They even seem to be up for the concert, or the humiliation, and start staccato-clapping as we're getting to our spots on the top of the dugout.

Mack played some drums with a group in college, so at least he's kinda for real. Plus, Mack and I are really too old to get embarrassed, so we decide what the heck, lets have a good time and just let it rip. And let it rip we do. Since the mic is up there and the crowd's urging us on, I go ahead and lip sync as well as air guitar from the beginning of "Roll with the Changes." Heck, we even get the crowd to sing along with the chorus. I gotta say, it's a bit of a rush leading even just a hundred or so people into the chorus of a rock and roll ditty.

As the rousing grand finale concludes, I realize I've never had so much fun making an idiot out of myself in my entire life. In fact, Woody tells me at the field that we were not too embarrassing and he actually got a kick out of it.

But Woody seems a little less excited than I had expected when he finally arrives home.

"So bud, on to the quarterfinals, the *elite eight*," I greet him.

"Yep, we're still playing."

"I thought you'd be more up after the win tonight. You guys aren't worrying about Bates already, are ya?"

"No, it's just beginning to sink in that the season is almost over; we may have only two games left. And I missed another chance tonight to impress the scouts. Time's running out. I need more hits and some home runs quick, but it doesn't look like that's gonna happen. I'm beginning to think there's no use in trying anymore. I'm not gonna be playing in college, so why not just accept it?"

"Whoa, Nellie! You've got the cart about a half mile ahead of the horse here, partner. You guys have a great chance to keep going, even to get to the finals. That's the most important thing. You're a very, very good team that doesn't quit, and you're still playing because you don't quit. No matter the final outcome, you don't ever quit, as a team or as an individual. That's how you guys got this far. Whatever happens in your individual future is in the future. But you don't quit trying your hardest when you're part of a team and that team needs your best. That shouldn't even enter your mind now."

I pause for a response that doesn't come and then continue.

"I don't want to preach at you, Woody, but the Pelhams are not quitters; they're fighters. My mother, your Nana, fought right up to the end and then some. You know she died of a brain tumor when you were five, but I've never told you about the day she died. I'm not trying to be over dramatic, but facts are facts, and you need to know the facts. It was your mom's birthday, and I took a day off to spend some time with her and to visit my mother in the nursing home. I knew the time was dwindling down to the day when the tumor would shut down her breathing. When I arrived at the nursing home, she was in the Chain-Stokes stage. That's usually close to the end when breathing becomes rapid and shallow. The nurse told me the end could be coming or she might go back to normal breathing and rebound for hours or even a day or so. I didn't know what to do, whether to go call my sister or just stay with her. Since I didn't want her to be alone, I stayed beside her bed, keeping her hand in mine. Her eyes remained closed, but I'm sure she knew I was there.

"After a while, I don't know how long, her breathing slowed way down and became very labored, as if each breath was a huge struggle. I felt she was slipping away and feared that her next breath would be her last. And then she did stop breathing. I waited for the next breath, but it didn't come. So I leaned forward and kissed her on the forehead and said goodbye. And then my tears came. After a while, as I wept beside her bed, she suddenly inhaled and began to take slow, labored breaths again. It seemed like it had been at least a minute, maybe it was less, but she seemed to be gone, and she had fought back. A few minutes later her brother—my uncle—and my aunt arrived with another couple who were old friends. And shortly, my cousin John and his wife also arrived. I was no longer alone, and my aunt was beside me when my mother passed a few minutes later.

"I'm sure that some people might say her passing and then her regaining breath after stopping was just a function of the tumor. But I know my mother was one heck of a fighter, and I truly believe she refused to leave me alone. She refused to quit even at death's door. And because she didn't, I had love and consolation beside me at that devastating moment instead of solitary grief. Like I said, I'm not trying to be dramatic. I know baseball and death aren't comparable. But son, you have to make a practice of not quitting, not giving up in all things, large or small, if you want that quality to be there for the biggest things."

"Holy cow, Dad, that's way, way heavy, and kind of scary. Another miracle when Nana died, just like when your dad died. You must be Saint Stephen or something."

"You know I'm no saint, Woody. You've ridden with me in rush-hour traffic before. And I'm not saying what happened with Nana was miraculous or anything like what happened when my dad died. That was an outside influence exerted on me; this was my mother's inner strength refusing to give up, refusing to leave me alone in my grief. Her actions most probably were aided by her spiritual life, but the bottom line of this experience is not ever giving up. This was a huge event in my life and something I felt you needed to know about, and now seemed as good a time as any to share it with you.

"Look, Woody, I've had a terrific time watching you play ball these four years of high school and all the years before. It's been great, nerve racking at times, but great. I feel very fortunate to have had this experience, but when it's over, I'll still have a lot of great memories. Whether you have two, four, or six or more games left, don't worry about what's next. Just play hard and never give up. That's the best way to enjoy your last high school season. You know that cartoon of the crane starting to swallow a frog? And the frog has his hand squeezing the crane's neck so the bird can't keep swallowing him? That's the point. You never give up; you never stop trying. Take it one game, one play, one at bat at a time. Don't worry about what comes after. There's time enough for that later."

"Ok, Dad. I can do that. And thanks for telling me about Nana. I know that wasn't easy."

Woody heads for bed, and I'm hoping I didn't put a bummer on the night's victory.

Later as I'm brushing my teeth, my thoughts drift back to Mack's and my performance at the ballpark. With a smile, I realize you're never too old to have fun at your own expense. And I hope the headlines the next day won't read, "Two Geezers Rock the House at Sandy Pines Field."

Now it's on the road to Bates High School, located an hour south of Macon, and the scene of the 1994 state finals heartbreak for the Sandy Pines Panthers.

Chapter Thirty-Seven

The Bates series begins on Saturday with a doubleheader. Of special note, the Barons are winners of their last twenty-two games. That's awfully strong, twenty-two in a row. Those of us who attended or know the story of the 1994 state finals are eager for Sandy Pines to get back there and even the score. But it appears obvious that that won't be an easy task.

An article in the local paper on Friday recounts Sandy Pines's ability to come back from the brink of elimination. They pulled it off to win crucial playoff games in the championship run of 1996 and runner-up finishes of '94 and '99. Some of those comeback victories came with two outs in the last inning, with the team down one or even two runs. Woody gets some more ink for capping the latest seventh inning rally with his double in Tuesday's win over Sebastian.

The story of the Sandy Pines win in the state semifinals in 1994 brings back some vivid memories. The Panthers were trailing two to four in the bottom of the seventh, having already lost game one. There was one man on and two outs when a single put two runners on. Major's older brother, John, batted next and drew a walk to load the bases. As I'm reading the article, I can see the situation as if it was yesterday.

The Panthers were playing another metro-Atlanta area

team, so Woody and I were there. The field was below the surrounding area, which included the football practice field. Spring football was going on, and when the practice ended, the entire team lined up along the left field line higher ground behind our visitor stands. It added to the intensity of the moment with all these football players standing behind and above us cheering their team on. I might even say that it felt a bit intimidating. Woody and Major were sitting on top of a small building behind the Panther dugout with an excellent view of the proceedings.

With the bases now loaded and the football team rooting for the final, game-ending and series-clinching out, the next Panther batter delivered a grounder that hopped through the third baseman's legs, drove in two runs, and tied the game at four. Right now I hate to think of a ball going between a third baseman's legs, even in past tense. Later in the inning, another walk with the bases loaded scored the winning run for Sandy Pines. They won the next day and went on to face Bates in the state finals.

Saturday morning's paper carries the story of that 1994 state championship match-up. The first game lasted seventeen innings, more than twice the normal length of a high school game. The starting pitcher for Sandy Pines later became the St. Louis Cardinals number-one draft pick in the 1997 major league draft. And he was one of four pitchers who combined for fifty-four strikeouts in that marathon—fifty-four strikeouts! Each team posted one run in the first inning before going scoreless for the next fifteen. The Panthers finally scored one in the top of the seventeenth, but the Barons broke their hearts with a two-out, two-run homer in the bottom of the seventeenth.

I remember that night well because I was coaching at Jones Park, where we had a game, or Woody and I probably would have been at the Panther/Baron doubleheader. Phil Allen was on our team, and he was and still is a neighbor of the Thomases. The Allens were planning to go to the third and deciding game on Saturday, as were Woody and I, if the teams split the Friday doubleheader. Our game at Jones Park went late, until after ten p.m., so Phil's mom said she would call the Thomases' cell phone when she got home from our game. When Woody and I got home, I called her, and she said the game was still going on, tied in the fifteenth inning. So we knew there would be at least one game on Saturday. She called me later with the bad news about the loss and the start time for Saturday's first game.

In the morning, Woody and I took off on the ride I figured would take three hours. But I miscalculated, and when we exited off interstate, we were already late and still had thirty minutes more to go. We were on a busy four-lane road and approaching a traffic light as I was trying to read the street sign. Woody suddenly hollered, "Dad!" I looked back to the road and saw an old couple ahead of us stopping on a dime for a light that had just turned yellow. I slammed on the brakes, but we were seemingly already on top of their car, and as the adrenaline surged, I can't be sure that some profanity didn't escape my lips.

It was one of those occasions where time seems to go in super-slow motion, and I just waited for the impact. Somehow we didn't hit them as our van skidded to a stop and rocked forward. I expected to at least bump them on the final surge, but we didn't, and it seemed we were above their trunk looking down on the top of their car. I couldn't believe we hadn't hit them and told Woody our guardian angels must have held us back, and we probably came within an inch of their bumper. He just asked me if I had said what he thought I had said—oops.

We finally got to the game, and Sandy Pines was already trailing zero to five in the bottom of the third inning. I thought we had driven a long way and almost wrecked just to see the Panthers get routed. But the boys battled back to tie and then lead the game by the bottom of the fifth, with the Panthers batting as the home team. There was a loud, overflowing home crowd, and it turned into a very exciting game that the Barons finally won eight to seven to clinch the state championship. It was a heart-breaking series for Sandy Pines, and I really felt for the kids and Coach Pat and his family.

Together, the Barons and the Panthers have a combined eight state finals appearances in the last thirteen years. And now Coach Pat and a new band of Panthers are venturing back to Bates to face a Baron team that has won twenty-two straight games. I seem to remember thinking in 1994 that Woody and I might be back there someday, but nah, I'm probably just imagining it. At any rate, it should be one doozy of a series.

Chapter Thirty-Eight

The Christophers are riding with us today, and Jessica and I are looking forward to their company. We're at the Sandy Pines parking lot at ten thirty a.m. for the planned rendezvous, but they're running a little late.

As they are getting out of their van, Mack hollers to me. "Are you nervous, Steve? I'm nervous as all get out!"

He proves how nervous a minute later, after he gets a page. He tries to call the number repeatedly on his cell phone but can't make it work.

He thinks the battery must be dead and shouts at Becky. "Becky, why won't this thing work?"

The page has come from his work, and he finally realizes he's dialing area code 770 instead of 404.

He makes the call, and it confirms that he's picking someone up at the airport on Monday and driving to Birmingham. He won't be able to make Monday's deciding game if there is one, so he's hoping for a Sandy Pines sweep. Their son, Allan, is the starting pitcher in game one, so they are indeed even more nervous than Jessica and I.

Jagged nerves aside, it's a fun ride down. We play the handheld electronic version of Who Wants to Be a Millionaire!—*we* being Becky, their younger son, David, Jess, and me. Mack's playing electronic Yahtzee again, just like in Florida. I think he's too uptight to think about Millionaire questions. I tell him if we win the million before we get to our exit, we'll win both the games.

My needle works, and Mack responds with a logical, "The two things are totally unrelated, Steve!"

"I guess, but don't worry 'cause yesterday I heard 'Maggie May' by Rod Stewart, and that's a lucky song."

I tell him that my roommate and I heard it once before a big football win at Tech in the early seventies, so we both hope to hear it before any big game. He howls his disapproval as we continue down the highway, striving desperately to win the million and so guarantee victory for the Panthers.

We hit the game-site exit without winning the million, but I'm still not as worried as Mack. Since we're early, as planned, we swing by the team's motel, which is just off the exit road. As we roll into the parking lot, I see some parents visiting in the pool area. We park, and Coach Pat is coming across the lot in uniform to put some paperwork in the team van that's parked next to me. Becky asks if the boys behaved last night, and Pat says they didn't have any choice since he had them in their rooms at ten thirty p.m.

We walk with John Thomas to Major and Woody's room, and Mike Drew is there also, playing video games. I can't help but wonder what time all the video-game-playing ended last night. It's time for them to start getting into their uniforms, so after we say our hellos and use the restroom, we meet back at the van. Mack's ready to get to the field, but the rest of us want to get something to eat. He says okay, but we decide it will be smarter to go find the field first and then grab a bite.

I recognize the intersection where I almost rear-ended the car in '94 when Woody and I came down for the finals.

Jessica gets out the directions and says the school and field are on Cole Road. I was thinking and saying it was on this main drag, which isn't Cole Road. Luckily she wises me up, since the next light is Cole, and we make a left, and the school is down the road about a half mile on the left. Another example of the over-fifty fading memory. Mack's not ready to take up his position behind home plate yet, so we head out to get some lunch.

The closest place we can find is a Popeye's fried chicken joint. It's just fast food, and Mack's still nervous as all get out as we're standing in line reading the menu board. Mack looks at the fried goodies behind the glass and asks, "Are those clam strips? I want clam strips."

I'm about to say, "No, those are crawdads," when Becky grabs my arm to stop me and whispers, "He won't know the difference," and she orders them for him.

Becky's almost as nervous as Mack and just wants him to eat without a lot of discussion. We get our orders and sit down to eat.

Mack takes a bite out of his "clam strip" and grimaces and says, "What's this? This isn't clam strips."

I can't help laughing and tell him they're crawdads as Becky tries to drown me out with, "They're practically the same thing; eat!"

But Mack will have none of it. "These are awful. I can't eat these."

He eats his French fries as Jessica takes a bite of a crawdad and says, "They're not too awful."

She offers to trade her chicken sandwich, but Mack declines, saying he's too nervous to eat much anyway. Mack and Becky are really a hoot, and David's needles are goosing his dad's nerves up another notch much of the time. It reminds me of the Florida trip, and I'm missing Kim. She couldn't get any coworker to trade days with her, so she couldn't be here today. But I'm happy that Jessica could make the trip this time.

Chapter Thirty-Nine

State: Quarterfinals, Game One versus Bates Barons

Well, here we are, back at Bates, but this time for the quarterfinals instead of the finals. There are nice aluminum bleachers behind the home plate area, an area I could not get close to eight years ago. A small section on the third base side is marked "Visitor." Coach Pat's wife, Sarah, is in the stands behind home plate and hollers for us to come join her. We do, and it's a much better view; you can't see all of left field from the official visitor section. We know how these fans are from our '94 visit and wonder if they'll try to move us out and into visitor-ville once the place starts filling up. They don't, but some Baron adult fans do mix in with us. It's not packed like '94, but I tell Jess that's probably because this is the quarterfinals and that was the finals, the championship series. And who knows, maybe after twenty-two straight wins, the fans are expecting a win and not worrying about being here at the start of game one.

It's time for the first pitch, so here we go, guts churning and burning.

Hunter opens the series by drawing a walk on a three-ball, two-strike count. The Baron pitcher is a junk baller, and he Ks

Danny next with some good benders. The forty to fifty Bates students behind home plate roar their Step Cheer after the strikeout. They holler "step" on each one of Danny's footfalls back to the dugout and then a hateful "Sit down!" when he enters the dugout. That's some pretty inhospitable behavior. They even have a poster inviting fans to join the Step Club. These fans really love it when Major follows Danny with another strikeout and they can perform their cheer again. Woody bats next and misses badly with his first cut, and I'm thinking, *Uh-oh, three Ks in a row would be a lot of momentum for the Barons*. But he does make contact on a one-ball, two-strike pitch, hitting a weak pop-up to the first baseman. So the Panthers take the field after a very inauspicious offensive start to the game.

The Barons, on the other hand, open with a solid single off Allan. I hope Mack's not about to pass out from an anxiety attack behind home plate in his lawn chair. The number-two hitter grounds to Pat at short, and he flips the ball to Bobby at second for the force-out. Bates decides to test Major's arm early—bad choice. Major uncorks a bullet to Bobby, who makes the catch and tag in one motion to complete the caught-stealing work of art for out number two. The third batter grounds out to short to end a very busy first for our middle infielders.

The Panthers manage a single in inning two but no score.

Allan faces the minimum in the bottom of the second on two fly outs to the outfield and another groundout to Pat. That's three chances he's handled perfectly in the first two innings.

Hunter is up again to lead off the third, and I'm hoping the guys will be better hitters the second time around. But nothing doing this inning. Hunter grounds out to short, Danny to first, and Major to third, *ugh*.

After one out in the Barons' half of the third, they load the bases on a single followed by two walks. *Yikes, scary time; hang in there, Mack.* But Big Al knuckles down and gets a high pop-up to Bobby at second for out number two and then Ks the next man to leave the bases loaded. *Whew. That's huge.*

Woody leads off the fourth with an infield hit when he beats out a slow roller to third. Coach Pat calls for another sac bunt from Terry; he's had a knack for getting that job done all season. This effort is a short pop-up toward the first base line. The pitcher and the catcher both dive to make the catch, but the ball bounces off the pitcher's outstretched glove and into the Bates' dugout. So now we've got Woody at third and Terry at second with no outs. Not what Coach Pat expected, but we'll take the good fortune, and I'm thinking, *Let's make some hay, boys.*

Luke produces the first run of the game with a sacrifice fly to center field that scores Woody from third. After a sacrifice bunt moves Terry to third, Bobby singles him home and reaches second when the right fielder bobbles the ball. All right, two runs in and a man on second. A couple of pitches into Pat's at bat, Bobby takes off for third. Pat rips a liner that's past the third baseman on the shortstop side, but it slams into Bobby like a laser-guided missile. Bobby goes down in pain, and the inning's over, since it's an out when a batted ball hits the runner. I'm thinking the ball hit Bobby high on the outside of his thigh but find out after the game that the rocket hit him in the cup. *Ouch!* Thank goodness he wasn't seriously injured and he's able to stay in the game.

This inning has been another great example of baseball. A popped-up sacrifice bunt that could have turned into a double play gets runners to third and second with no outs, and then a solid line drive that should have been an RBI single nearly takes our runner out of the game. Go figure. The game is half over, and the Panthers lead two to zero.

Allan gets the Barons one, two, three for the second time, and the Panthers come back to bat looking to build their lead. This is totally acceptable so far.

Hunter leads off the fifth by beating out an infield hit. Danny follows with a line drive smash to left center that the fielder makes a good running catch of for out number one. Major reaches base when the center fielder drops his fly ball, but the threat ends with two runners stranded.

Big Al gets his third one-two-three inning in the bottom of the fifth. That's strong, and things are looking and feeling good so far. The only bad news is my batteries are running out, and I don't think I'll be able to tape any of the second game; maybe they'll last.

Luke leads off the Panther sixth with a strikeout but reaches first when the ball hits the dirt and eludes the catcher. Phil successfully executes another sacrifice bunt to put our runner on second. *Good job, now let's get that run home.* And Bobby does just that, delivering his third hit in a row, a double that scores Luke. Mr. Birdsong is stranded at second when the inning ends, but it's a three-to-zero lead with six more outs to get. Dare I breathe easy?

The Barons respond in the bottom of the sixth. Imagine that, trouble for the Panthers in the sixth. The leadoff hitter singles to open the inning. Then the second man up golfs one over the left field fence, and suddenly the three-run lead the Panthers worked six at bats to build is reduced to one. Al comes back to strike out the next batter and stem the flow of momentum Bates is riding. The next two batters are outs also, so it's three to two at the end of six. No breathing easy now.

The Panthers answer back in the top of the seventh to

ease my jagged nerves. Major doubles after one out, and Woody follows with a sharp single to left that is hit so hard the left fielder is almost able to get our runner coming from second to third. With runners at first and third, Terry smacks a grounder to short that turns into a six-three fielder's choice but most importantly results in an RBI and a four-to-two lead. The Sandy Pines' at bat ends with the Panthers up by two and only three more outs to get to win the first game. *Just three more outs, guys.*

The bottom of the seventh opens forebodingly with a ringing double by the leadoff man. The next batter rips one to center that Danny hauls in for out number one. Thank goodness that one was catchable 'cause that was two hard-hit balls in a row. I sure hope Al's not running out of gas. After two consecutive singles, the lead is down to one. Men are on first and third with one out. The home crowd is roaring, and my guts are in square knots. *Come on, guys, stay strong; don't let this one get away.*

Allan gets a short fly ball to center field for out number two. And with Danny's strong arm out there, the Barons know better than to possibly make the last out of the game at home on a tag-up. They know Danny's signed with a Division I university as a pitcher and don't dare test him at this juncture. One more out to get, and I don't know whether to hyperventilate or hold my breath.

The next batter is the number-two man in the Barons' lineup, the powerful right fielder who homered in his last at bat just last inning. I opt to hold my breath. Al fools him with a slider on the first pitch. But he connects solidly with his next swing. The ball is heading to the gap in left center field, almost the same spot where his homer flew out last inning. I'm gasping for air now as the crowd roars. Phil is racing over and back from his left fielder's position, and Danny is racing over and back from his center field position. *Lord, help*!

As they converge, Phil sticks out his glove hand at the last instant and snags the rocket. Game over! Panthers win four to three on a play that proves again that baseball is a game of inches. If that ball is a few more inches higher, the Panthers lose, and the Barons ride a tidal wave of momentum into the second game. They would not only have the one-game advantage but also a world of confidence and a raucous crowd that would surely have believed they were unbeatable had they gotten their twenty-third win in a row. I'm no expert on baseball or psychology, but I believe this win, coming the way it did, is almost as huge as the Barons' victory in seventeen innings in the first game eight years ago. We shall see. Boy, it's nice to breathe again. And I've got thirty minutes before the next game to enjoy an unrestricted oxygen flow.

Between games, some threatening clouds begin to roll in, and as I'm standing in the bleachers watching their progress, I'm reminded of the movie *The Natural*. I recall the lightning strike and storm before Roy Hobbs's first at bat, when he knocked the cover off the ball. And then there was the lightning in the sky during his final, climactic at bat in the league championship game. Yeah, I'm fantasizing a little about Woody hitting a big homer, but in 2002, if the lightning does come, nobody will have the opportunity to hit.

I check out my scorebook during the break and see that Bobby went three for three in the first game, with a double his last at bat. That's darn good, especially hitting a double after suffering a rocket to the crotch in his previous at bat. Woody collected two hits in four at bats. Major added the crucial double in the seventh inning, and Hunter, Luke, and Terry all added singles in the Panther victory. Terry also had two critical sacrifice bunts in that first game. Nine hits and Allan's complete game make for a great start. But game one's history, and game two is coming up.

State: Quarterfinals, Game Two versus Bates Barons

Bates's ace is pitching the second game. He's the third baseman from the first game, and he looks more like he should be a coach than a player. He's huge, thick, and adult looking. But he doesn't seem to be throwing especially hard during warm-ups. The Panthers are batting as the home team in this game, and Danny is on the mound for Sandy Pines. I know Mack and Becky will be able to relax a little more for this game after Allan's fine performance in game one. It's time for the first pitch, time for the belly to rumba.

Danny has a great first inning, striking out the first two batters. The third man grounds out to short; there's the busiest man on the field today, Pat, making another put-out.

Sandy Pines also goes one, two, three in their first at bat. Hunter and Danny both ground out, and then Major is called out on strikes. Of course, he is sent back to the dugout with the hateful "step, step, step" salute.

Things don't go so well for the Panthers in the top of the second. After the leadoff hitter singles, the next two batters are retired. Then the bad things start, the very bad things. The next batter hits a grounder to Woody's left. He makes a good lunging dive to glove the ball and scrambles to his feet to make the throw. But he has to rush, and the throw is in the dirt. Terry can't dig it out at first, and the runner is safe. There's also a man at third now, having reached second on an earlier wild pitch. *Oh no.* I'm stunned at the bad turn of events, and I'm betting Woody is too. We could possibly have been out of the inning if the throw had been perfect, but nobody's perfect. I'm hoping Danny can get that third out before any damage is done, both for the team and for Woody's confidence for the rest of the series. We can't have him get tentative at the hot corner during the state playoffs. And right now, in the depths of *Oh no*, is the time that I am most grateful that the Panthers won the first game. But in this inning, in this game, the nightmare has just begun.

The next batter doubles, and then three singles in a row later, Danny is pulled; well, that's it. The dam's busted. Mike enters in the midst of the disaster with men on first and second and four unearned runs across for the Barons, *ugh*. But Mike slams the door with a strikeout, what a beautiful thing. Now let's see if the rest of the Panthers can respond and climb out of this four-run hole.

Of course, Woody leads off the bottom of the second. I mean, of course. And he gets things started with a single. *Good job, son. You just loosened that paralyzed knot in my gut.* And just as in the first game, he's the first Panther to cross home plate. After Terry lines out to center field, Luke collects the second single of the inning. Then with two outs, Pat delivers a clutch hit, and Sandy Pines is back in it at two to four when their half of the inning ends.

Mike picks up where he left off, striking out the first Barons batter of the third. The next man reaches base on an infield hit before Mike gets the next two hitters on fly ball outs to the outfield. I check in with Mack during the half inning, and he says the Barons appear to be chasing Mike's curve and slider. Hopefully he'll stick with those pitches and they will continue to be effective. For now, Mike has stemmed the flow and enabled the Panthers to swing a little momentum back their way.

The third starts inauspiciously for the Panther batters on a fly out by Hunter and a groundout by Danny. But Major smacks a double, and Woody comes to bat with a chance to do some damage. And he does indeed do damage. There are no bolts of lightning; in fact, the threatening clouds have blown away, but Woody delivers a blast that clears the left center field fence by twenty or thirty yards, and the game is tied! Now it's good things. I can't hear our crowd near the backstop fence since we're sitting pretty high up behind home plate, but I find out later that they are chanting "step, step, step" on each of Woody's footfalls as he rounds the bases in a fairly quick home-run trot. It's a great moment for me as a dad and a great moment for Woody. I'm sure he feels some redemption, and that makes it even sweeter. It would have been nice to get in on the "step" shouts, but I'm very, very happy to go to the fourth inning all tied up at four. It's pretty weird thinking back eight years to Woody and me watching these same two schools battle. Woody was such a little kid then.

And it stays four to four for a long, long time. Mike faces the minimum in the fourth, fifth, sixth, and eighth innings with one strikeout in each inning. He gives up a one-out double in the seventh but Ks the next man and gets out number three on a groundout to third. *Whew, that's awesome production from Mike.*

The Panthers suffer an almost-identical fate through the eighth inning. They go down one, two, three in the fourth, fifth, sixth, and eighth inning also. In the seventh, Bobby collects a one-out single. Pat follows with another single, but a four-six-three double play ends the threat and strands a runner at third. That was a darned good play to keep Sandy Pines from getting the winning run home when they had two runners on and only one out. I really thought the Panthers might end it there.

Mike gives up an infield hit to open the ninth. The next man moves the runner to second with a sacrifice bunt, and Coach Pat brings Pat from shortstop to pitch in relief of Mike. Six scoreless innings by Mike is awesome. And then Pat strikes out their next two batters to end the Baron ninth. This has got to be the best pitching the Panthers have had in any two-game stretch this year.

Woody is leading off the inning for Sandy Pines, and maybe that's a good omen. My nerves and gut have settled down into a neutral state over the last few innings. I'm hoping maybe Woody can score the last run of this game after having scored the first a long time ago. But he grounds out to the shortstop, so it will have to be someone else scoring the winning run if it comes this inning. Terry singles and moves to second when Luke draws a walk, and my gut stirs to action. Bobby sac-bunts the runners to second and third, and we're close—really close, really, really close. I'm thinking, *Let's get 'em now, guys.* But a groundout to second ends the inning and the threat, *ugh.* Is this game going to be another seventeen-inning marathon? So far it's playing out like a heavyweight title fight.

Pat gets the first two Barons on groundouts to start the tenth. The next batter, who happens to be the first game's pitcher, launches a high fly to center as Danny races back and the Barons' crowd starts to roar. It's a fence scraper that just gets out, but it's out. That's a knockdown in this heavyweight bout, but we'll have to wait for the Panthers' last at bat to see if it's a knockout. Pat Ks the next batter to end the Barons' at bat. My guts are up to about a hundred RPMs as my mind flashes between thoughts of the four unearned runs in the second inning and my firm belief that Phil can take them in game three; they can't possibly have as good a number-three pitcher as Sandy Pines.

Speaking of Phil, he leads off the Panther tenth. Unfortunately, he grounds out for out number one. That's okay. Our leadoff hitter, Hunter, is up next. Hunter looks at a called strike three for out number two, and it begins to look like that home run was indeed a knockout blow. RPMs have now reached two hundred. Danny steps in with no hits in eight at bats today, and when the count goes to no balls and two strikes, it feels like the ref has reached a count of nine on the Panthers and is about to declare a knockout. But no, not today, brother! Today Yogi and his magic are still in the Panther dugout.

Danny launches the zero-and-two pitch into left center, and it takes a huge hop over the fence for a double. Both crowds are roaring now as the Panthers are back on their feet. Major follows, and he wastes no time in smashing the first pitch to left field for an RBI single to tie the game up and rock the Barons and their fans back on their heels with an awesome counterpunch. They're reeling now, and one more big blow could end it. Woody steps in, and I know he's going to try to deliver that big blow. He's a little too eager and tops a breaking ball to third for out number three. I can tell from his body language that he's disgusted. I know how much he wanted to knock in that winning run; it would have been so sweet. The inning is over, but the Panthers have gotten up off the mat. Danny and Major have tied the game again at our last gasp just like they did against Southpark, and this time it's in extra innings! It's another unreal comeback from the brink, but only time will tell if it was just a temporary reprieve.

Bates comes out swinging again in the eleventh round; make that inning. After a sky-high pop-up that Bobby grabs at second, the second batter doubles over Phil's head. The

The Final Season

next man grounds slowly to third, and Woody charges, comes up with the slow hopper, and fires to first. But Terry sees the runner break from second for third, steps toward Woody's throw, grabs it, and immediately guns the ball to third base. Sophomore Andrew Smith came on to play shortstop when Pat moved to the pitcher's mound. And he has played his position perfectly, coming over to cover third when Woody charged the slow grounder. Terry's throw is on the money, and Andrew reaches up to tag the leg of the surprised runner who's trying to jump over the tag as it's too late to slide. Great play, huge out, and it's a shuttering counter-punch to the Barons' midsection! They are further staggered when Pat Ks the next batter for out number three. Holy mackerel, this game is getting more fantastic with each successive play as we build to what could be some kind of gigantic finish.

Bates finally brings in a new pitcher for the bottom of the eleventh. What a masterful performance by the man wearing number one. The reliever is a junk baller, and he Ks Terry to open the Panther at bat. When Luke grounds out to second, it looks and feels like the marathon is going to continue. Bobby reaches first on a walk, but a second strikeout ends the eleventh.

Round/Inning twelve, here we go again. Pat's in his fourth inning now, but I'm thinking he's gonna have to go seven or eight maybe. He's still strong, though, striking out the Barons' first batter. The next man singles—*uh-oh*—a solid shot by the Barons. Bates is known as a running team, and they try to swipe second. Major comes up throwing and uncorks another BB that Bobby grabs and sweep-tags in one motion again. And again it's an out; caught stealing. Another roundhouse blow rocks the Barons back on their heels when Pat Ks the batter for out number three. Sandy Pines wins the first half of round twelve and carries the momentum into their at bat.

Phil works a walk out of the pitcher to open the Panther twelfth; great start. Hunter puts down a sacrifice bunt and moves Phil to second. That's a right cross to the Barons' chin, and they're staggering again. With the potential winning run now at second, the Panther crowd is screaming encouragement, and the Baron crowd is exalting their team to hold on. My gut is now spinning like a twirling dervish. A wild pitch moves Phil to third; a sharp jab to the Barons' forehead, and they drop to one knee in the center of the ring as the Panther faithful now roar in anticipation of the knockout.

The Barons bring in the outfield and the infield to try and save themselves as Danny, who saved us with the two-out double his last time up, works the count to two balls and two strikes. And then he rips a line drive shot past first base, and as Phil crosses home plate, the Barons crash to the canvas. Knockout! The Panthers mob Phil behind home plate as they pile into a giant mound and then unpile and head for Danny at first base. It's an incredible scene of joy and celebration for Sandy Pines and just the opposite for Bates. The Panthers will play again in the state semifinals, but the twenty-two-game winning streak and the season are over for the Barons.

After the teams exchange handshakes at home plate, I watch the Panthers happily head into the dugout to collect their gear. And then I notice Coach Pat and Sarah in a long embrace, down the left field line away from the players, and I know what a gigantic good feeling this must be after the huge disappointment they felt on this same field eight years ago. And me, I'm just thinking, *How could it ever get any better than this?*

After we congratulate the players and coaches as they come off the field, we head back to their motel to celebrate a little before we start the drive home. On the way I stop to gas up, and Mack and I decide we need a couple of cold beers to toast the victory. I drive us to the motel, and that's all my driving for the day and night as Jess will be our designated driver for the trip home. It's a great atmosphere around the pool and the players', coaches,' and families' rooms. We spend the next twenty or thirty minutes in good-times banter, during which Sarah's father tells me about how far Woody's homer traveled. He says the Barons' homer in the second game barely got out, but Woody's was way, way outta there. He adds that Woody's shot might even have made the small graveyard on the other side of Evergreen Boulevard from the Sandy Pines field if this had been a home game. Now that really would have been a tape-measure job. Coach Pat once told me that only one of his players ever hit one into the graveyard, and that player went on to hold the college career record for home runs for a few years. That's quite a poke for a high school player, but I'm satisfied that Woody managed one today at any length.

It's really neat seeing Sarah's parents at this victory get-together. They've been following Coach Pat's games for all the years we've known the Welsomes, through all the region and state playoffs, and it's great that they were able to be here in this team's moment of triumph. They miss some of the games because Sarah's dad is still playing competitive softball, but I know they're especially happy to be here today. Sarah's sister and her husband, who bought the Welsomes' house and now live next door to us, have a room here at the motel, so we stop by to say hi and enjoy the victories with them also. Woody and I sat in our lawn chairs with them for the deciding game eight years ago when the Barons beat the Panthers for the state title. That makes it even sweeter, to think back and reminisce with the folks who were there eight years ago. But by now, Jess and Becky are ready to head home, so we take off even though I could stay and enjoy this celebration a good bit longer.

Mack and I have a great time discussing today's games and the season on the ride home, while Becky and Jess have some lively, animated conversation of their own in the front.

A few good-natured barbs fly back and forth between the guys and gals, but Mack continuously praises Jess for what a "great job of driving" she's doing.

Jess gives me the option for a restroom stop when we're about halfway home, but I decline, and that's a mistake. The beer backs up bad on me—just a couple can do it. When we finally stop at a Quik Trip on Evergreen Boulevard, I can't even stand up straight to walk inside to the bathroom. So I'm all bent over like an old man, quickstepping to get inside as soon as possible. Becky gets an especially big laugh out of this scene, and she reminds me about it the next few times we're together. Maybe a couple of diet sodas would have been better.

As we exchange hugs and say our happy goodbyes in the Sandy Pines parking lot, I recall the game-time ritual Becky used today and any time Alan is pitching. She was pacing around and behind the stands, silently praying and working her rosary beads as fast as she could. The first time I saw her rosary at a game I had to ask about it, and we traded parochial-school stories for two or three innings. But she bested me by far in the Catholic education department. I had eight years of elementary school. Becky went from first grade all the way through college in Catholic schools. And I guess all those years rubbed off on her 'cause she kinda reminds me of a nun—a sweet nun, that is. She's no nonsense, no debating right and wrong, just like the Sisters of Mercy at OLA. I learned that as condo mates in Florida. But she also has that twinkle of joy and maybe a little mischief in her eyes that you could see when you could get one of the nuns to smile or laugh in school. It was always a great accomplishment to me to get a nun to smile, kind of like getting God to smile.

I remember when I was in the eighth grade and the whole school was in the church practicing Christmas hymns. I was sitting near the front of the church, at the end of a pew, and my buddy was sitting next to me. Sister Gilbert, who was conducting the practice, was tall and thin, and when she moved rapidly up and down the aisle during the singing, her black clothing would flow back at her sides, and she made quite an intimidating figure. She had just made a point of emphasizing how not to sing the last "Gloria" in a hymn. We were not to finish the word *Gloria* with a hard "ia" sound but just let the "Gloria" fade out. As the music started, she took off toward the back, garments flowing to the side, stepping quickly with that look on her face like she really meant business and we better know it.

You couldn't see too much of a Sister of Mercy's face since the white habit came down on top to almost the eyebrows and also covered their throats up to their chins. So it was like that stern look was magnified tenfold. As the song neared the aforementioned spot, I turned my head a little toward my buddy and nudged him with my elbow and then let out a very emphatic "ia" sound exactly as I had been instructed not to do. My buddy and I giggled as I noticed something beside me in my peripheral vision. I turned, and there was Sister Gilbert, perched over me like a hawk ready to peck my head off. And the stern, hawk-like glare was there too, but suddenly it changed to a huge grin! As my eyes settled back into their sockets, she turned to begin the next instruction. You can't tell me nuns don't have a sense of humor. Now, sometimes I tease Becky by calling her "Sister Becky." I don't think she minds it much at all.

That night in bed, waiting for sleep, I realize this is by far the most satisfying day and night I've experienced in the past thirteen years of Woody's baseball. I hope the players realize how special this is. They've made it to the final four of the state championship tournament. And they evened an old score in getting there.

Chapter Forty

Saturday morning we discover that Sandy Pines's opponent for the semifinal match-up has yet to be decided. Another of our county teams, Mackenzie, is battling last year's champ, Stamps County, for the right to face the Panthers. Even though Sandy Pines and Mackenzie are in the same county, they haven't met this season because they're in different regions. We're hoping for an all-Cobb-County match-up since we'll be traveling again in our semifinal series. A thirty- or forty-minute ride beats a four-hour ride any day of the week. Mackenzie and Stamps County are to play their deciding third game on Monday. The other two quarterfinal series will also resume Monday since rain in the Atlanta area postponed the games on Saturday. Both games are in the same area as my office, and their starting times are separated by an hour. You know I'll be checking those games out.

Saturday morning I also make arrangements to get a tape of the Bates games from Pat's dad, who pretty much tapes every play of every game. And that's lucky for me since my batteries fizzled out on me halfway through game two. Pat's dad has my copy ready in the early afternoon, and I'm totally excited when I get back home with it. I've been watching bits and pieces of *The Natural* for the last week or so, which probably explains why I had the connection with the rain clouds and possible storm at Bates. I have always liked to watch *The Natural* at the beginning of each baseball season, and this year I've continued to watch parts of it all season. But now I'm ready to watch those two Bates games again. And I admit, I fast forward to Woody's home run to start the viewing.

Pat's dad films from ground level, through the backstop on our side of home plate, and his coverage of Woody's big fly is so much better than mine would have been. Heck, his tape looks like the game is played in the day instead of at night. Modern technology is really something, isn't it? From our seats back behind home plate we couldn't hear the Sandy Pines crowd chanting "step, step, step" as Woody trotted home, but now I get to hear it on the tape, and it's most enjoyable. As I rewind the tape, I decide to watch the home-run sequence in slow motion, and as I am watching the slow-mo replay, an idea pops into my head.

We've got an old stereo system whose components include an AM/FM radio in the amp, a turntable for albums, a cassette player/recorder, and an eight-track tape player—that's right, an eight track. Anyway, in the past I discovered I could tape onto a cassette from the radio or turntable. Now, Woody has also hooked the TV/VCR setup to the stereo system, so I decide to see if I can tape the audio of the climactic Roy Hobbs home run from *The Natural* onto a cassette. And it works; hot dog, now I'm cooking. I play the audiocassette sound effects over the stereo as I watch the slow-mo of Woody's home run. And I'm thinking, *This is too cool; I'm a highlight filmmaker.* The slow motion is kinda jumpy, but I can tell it would be great if a professional video place could match up the sound and the video.

Now I fast forward to the end of the game to Danny's game- and series-winning hit in the bottom of the twelfth.

And when I run that sequence and the game-ending celebration in slow motion, I'm thinking, *Holy cow, the home run and this sequence should be just about right for the length of the audio from* The Natural. As I watch the games from the beginning, I take notes of the times certain important highlights occur so I can go back to them later. I've done this already on my tapes to possibly do a highlight of Woody to send to a college or two. I've also priced the making of such a highlight video and realize the expense is too great for the number of clips I want to use. But when I finish with the two Bates games, I also realize I have about an hour's worth of highlights in studio time for them. So I decide, *What the heck, I know I've got to do* The Natural *highlight video of Woody's home run and Danny's game-winning hit, so I might as well see if I can do both games also. Oh, this could be good; this could be really good.*

On Sunday I head for the video joint to make the highlight tape. I'm hoping I can get the whole thing done in an hour of studio time. But I have no idea how long it will take to do my number-one priority: the home run and the game-winning hit in slow motion to *The Natural* audio.

Well, the first part of the studio session goes very smoothly and rather quickly. The young guy doing the tape seems to be a whiz at it, and I'm sort of stunned to see how he gets the sound aligned perfectly between the video of the ball coming off Woody's bat and the audio of the same shot from *The Natural*. And the two film clips fit almost exactly the time frame of the audio, from the pitcher delivering the ball on Woody's home run to the two teams shaking hands after Danny's game-winning hit. I'm thoroughly impressed at the technician's work and way too excited over a video for a man my age.

The two-game highlight video comes out almost perfect also. The studio time is a little more than an hour, but it's worth every penny to me. I can't wait for Woody, Jess, and Kim to see it. And I hope the rest of the parents and players will like it as much as I do, or at least almost as much.

All of my family loves it. Woody doesn't say much, but he has a kind of stunned look on his face while watching his home run, and I know he likes it. Kim and Jess both think it's great, with Jess tearing up during Woody's home run and the game-ending hit sequence.

On Monday afternoon, I leave work early for the four p.m. start of the Berkwood game against Stamps County's rival, Masterson. The other quarterfinal series pits Berkwood's archrival, Pierce, against a team from Savannah. The way the brackets are aligned, rivals could face off in the semifinals or the state championship series. Stamps County could face Masterson in the finals, or Pierce could face Berkwood in the semis. Of course, we're hoping Stamps County won't figure into the equation when it comes time for the finals.

Berkwood jumps on Masterson early and often. They are led by their *can't-miss* prospect, who plays first base and pitches some, mostly as the closer. This kid is listed at six foot three and 220 pounds, but he looks even bigger than that to me. He's a lefty with unequaled power for a high school player. He smashes two tape-measure home runs in the three at bats I see; he was issued an intentional walk in the other one. *Whew, this kid is amazing.* He's got twenty-one homers now, and he didn't hit one until their twelfth game of the season. And to top it all off, he's only a junior.

I leave after four innings with Berkwood up eight to zero and head over to Pierce for that series. Pierce loses the first game one to two and falls behind zero to three in the nightcap before I head home. Well, there's still some game to play, but it looks like it will probably be Berkwood hosting

The Final Season

Riverhill from Savannah in one semifinal. That night on the eleven o'clock news sports segment, I learn that I was right about Berkwood and Riverhill, and I get the really good news that Mackenzie has beaten Stamps County, so we won't even have to travel out of our county for our semifinal match-up. And that also means that this year's 5A state championship will be hosted in our county, either by the Panthers or the Mackenzie Warriors.

We get Mack and Becky to come by and watch the video of the Bates games on Tuesday evening while the team is practicing, and they love it too. I'm really glad my camera couldn't do the job at Bates so I had to get the copy from Pat's dad. Funny how things work out sometimes. I made a few extra copies of the tape, thinking some other parents might want them, so I give the Christophers one. And Mack comes up with an idea to show the tape to the team and parents. The annual Home Run Derby contest is Thursday, so we arrange with Coach Pat to do a showing after the Derby at the field for all who can attend.

The derby is a home-run contest after practice between all the Panthers who have hit home runs during the season. It's a lot of fun for the guys, and we figured we could make it a little more fun with the video. Jason's dad sets up the TV and VCR player that Coach Pat got from the school at the bottom level of the home grandstands so everyone can have a good seat for the showing. About half the parents are able to make it tonight.

The players' attention is naturally focused on the Home Run Derby, so they don't pay much attention to the setting up of the equipment. But I must say that the parents were quite antsy to see the tape, especially those that weren't able to attend the games.

I titled the tape "Eight Years After" to tie this year's games into the previous visit to Bates. And it turned out to be quite a hit. Everyone thought I did a great job, but all I had to do was pick out the highlights from a tape that Pat's dad recorded. And modern technology and an expert technician did the rest. I am glad I had the idea and followed through on it, though. I knew it would probably have the most meaning for Coach Pat and gave him one of my extra copies.

Chapter Forty-One

Well, it's Friday. Time for the team to start on a new highlight tape. Mackenzie is about twenty miles from Sandy Pines, mostly to the west. A couple weeks ago I was there for the third and deciding first-round game between Mackenzie and our nemesis, Hammond. Hammond tailed off some at the end of the season, but they did beat us twice. That third game was primarily a pitcher's duel with Mackenzie coming out on top. The most surprising, even startling, part of the game was Hammond's final at bat. Their three best hitters all struck out, even their power-hitting leadoff man who took a called third strike on a three-and-two count. I hope the Panthers can handle the Mackenzie pitching better than the Lancers did in that third game.

When I was here before, I set my chair up out beyond the fence down the right field line on a plateau that allowed me to see over the fence. But for our games I'll start out jammed into the visitors' stands with most of the other Sandy Pines fans. Besides being pretty far from home plate, the plateau is also down from the home team dugout, behind enemy lines so to speak.

The first game is scheduled for a five o'clock start with game two to follow. Graduation for our boys is tomorrow afternoon, so a third game, if necessary, will be played on Monday. That's another reason to be thankful that we don't have to play four hours away, possibly on a Friday and a Monday.

State: Semifinals, Game One
versus Mackenzie Warriors

The state semifinals. It's hard to believe the next-to-last round of the playoffs is already here. Time really does fly.

The Warriors send their ace to the mound for game one. He's a tall right-hander who looks to bring it up there pretty quick.

Hunter starts it off for the Panthers with a walk. But the good fortune doesn't last long as Hunter is picked off first and Danny grounds out to the first baseman. Major follows with a strikeout so the first at bat is short but not sweet. Our ace, Allan, is also on the mound for game one. The Warriors put their leadoff man on first via a walk. Mack mentioned to me before the game that Allan said his shoulder hurt, but Mack thinks he was just complaining, and we both hope there's no real problem. The number-two hitter launches a high fly ball to right field, and the wind is blowing out. But Hunter settles under it and makes the catch for out number one. The three-hole hitter rips a single to center, and the man on first flies around second and heads for third. Danny charges, grabs up the hot grounder, and makes an excellent throw to Woody at third. Woody takes the throw and blocks the bag, à la a catcher at home, and tags the speedy Warrior out as he slides in. Thank goodness for a strong arm in center field. Their clean-up hitter smacks a grounder to Woody, and he scoops it up and fires to first for out number three. Doesn't appear to be any hesitation in Woody's fielding today; he looks confident.

Woody leads off the Sandy Pines second with a comeback

grounder to the pitcher for an easy out number one. Terry draws a walk but is stranded at second when the third out is made. The Panthers take the field for the bottom of the second, not knowing that it will be more like one of their nightmare sixths.

A Warrior leadoff single is followed by a walk, and the walk is followed by a bunt that turns into an infield hit to load the bases. *Oh good, it's fear time already.* Allan comes back to strike out the next batter and then gets a pop-up to short for out number two. Whew, I'm thinking we might get out of this mess. But the next batter is the speedy leadoff man who also hits for power. Coach Pat says he has the quickest bat he's ever seen—yikes. Allan gets ahead of him one ball and two strikes but leaves one up in the strike zone. And blamo, just like that, it's four to zip as the ball rockets over the right field fence. That happened so fast my gut didn't even have time to flip. But unfortunately, the bad things have just begun.

Unbelievably, the next five batters pound out singles. On the third one, Danny, in his haste to come up with the grounder in center and throw out one of the runners, over-runs the ball, which rolls to the fence. Before the ball can be retrieved, all three runners score, and its seven to zero! I think I'm already going into shock. Allan gives up two more singles in a row before Coach Pat replaces him with Mike Drew. That's obviously the most any team has gotten to Allan this season. Maybe his shoulder really is a problem. Mike gets the next batter on a grounder too short to end the disaster.

The Panthers are down by seven early. Let's hope they can get back into this game soon. It doesn't take a genius to realize it's extra tough when your ace is knocked out in the second inning and you're down so many runs so early. But be that as it may, it is still early, and this is a baseball game, which "ain't over 'til it's over."

Phil singles with one out in the top of the third. Two more singles by Hunter and Danny together with an error on the Warrior center fielder plate one for the Panthers. That puts runners at first and third for Major. *Keep it up, guys. That's a start.* But Major grounds out to third, and Woody goes down swinging for out number three, *ugh*. At least Sandy Pines got one run back.

Things go from bad to worse in the bottom of the third when the Warriors score three more runs on four singles and an outfield error. It's ten to one after three innings, and it looks like the game is turning into a huge test for Yogi's philosophy. And now I know I'm in shock. I'm just one big ball of stunned. We're so far down even the adrenaline-pumping station has shut off.

Terry leads off the Panther fourth with a single to left field and is thrown out at second trying to stretch it into a double. Luke draws a walk, but then the inning ends on a groundout followed by a strikeout. The game's half over, and we're down by nine. What a revolting development this is.

The Warriors add two more in the bottom of the fourth on a walk, an infield error, and a double. It's twelve to one. Sandy Pines is now down by eleven with just nine more outs left. It doesn't look good. Any chance for a do-over for this game?

The fifth starts well for the Panthers when Phil reaches first after the pitcher makes a bad throw on a grounder that comes right back to him. Hunter, Danny, and Major follow with singles, and Woody comes up with one run in and the bases loaded. The adrenaline pump house has restarted with a vengeance, and now my gut is back in the blender. Woody rips one that looks like it might get by the third sacker—*oh, yeah*—but he reacts quickly to his left, snags the hot potato, and fires home to force the lead runner for out number one—*dad freaking gum it!* Terry pops out to the first baseman, but then Luke delivers a two-RBI double, *that's better*. They're still hanging in there.

Unfortunately, the inning ends when the next man grounds out to second. Sandy Pines picks up three, so the margin has been cut to eight—twelve to four—thanks in large part to Luke's clutch double. All we need now is a touchdown and a two-point conversion!

Mike faces the minimum in the bottom of the fifth. This is very good, not to mention very necessary, since two runs now for the Warriors would have ended the game via the ten-run mercy rule.

Phil collects a one-out single to get the Panthers going in the top of the sixth. The Warriors help out with two consecutive infield errors that score two runs and put a man on third with Major coming to bat. The Panthers are back in business. *Come on, Major, how 'bout a long ball?* But that's all she wrote for this at bat as Major takes a called third strike, and then Woody goes down swinging for out number three. I'm back in shock now; it obviously ain't Woody's night tonight, and the Panthers are down by six with just three outs left, twelve to six. Good grief, it's excruciating watching your son strike out in consecutive at bats in the final four. I know he's trying as hard as he can, but sometimes it's just not your night.

To make matters just a tad worse, Mackenzie adds another run on a one-out single and a two-out double in the bottom of the sixth—the always wonderful *sixth*. It's now thirteen to six; *what the heck, lets just go out and get that touchdown and two-point conversion, guys.*

Terry starts the Sandy Pines last-chance seventh with a checked-swing pop out to first base, and my guts, which began churning again with the start of the last inning, have ceased to churn; they've turned to cold lead. Luke bats next and doubles for the second time in the game; youth is leading the way. And then Bobby singles, and Pat doubles. Two more runs are in, and it's thirteen to eight—*five more to get guys; a touchdown here, and we're ahead.*

Phil's up now, and he's got two singles already tonight. But I guess he's trying too hard to make something happen, and he goes down swinging for out number two. The cold lead has dropped all the way to my knees now with one out left. Hunter collects his third single of the game, and it's thirteen to nine with a runner on first, four to go. Danny draws a walk, and Major is hit by a pitch, bases loaded. The Warrior coach calls for a new pitcher. Now the tension can really build for the Pelhams as the relief pitcher takes his warm-up tosses and Woody waits in the on-deck circle, no doubt pondering his last two strikeouts.

As Woody steps into the batter's box, the cold lead spreads north, up toward my lungs. I don't know if I can watch. He's obviously struggling tonight, and I'm expecting he'll be swinging for the fences, trying to get all four runs at once. He does take a mighty cut at the first pitch and fouls it straight back. Dear God, just once I wish he'd get all of one on that first swing, just once. He takes the next pitch for ball one and then fouls another one off for strike two. I think even my fingers are lead now. Woody's in the two-strike defensive mode now; no more big swings this trip to the plate. I'm thinking, *Just make contact, kid; anything can happen if you put it in play.*

He holds back on the next pitch, a curve that's called ball two. You know the pitcher wants it to happen on this next pitch; he doesn't want a full count with bases loaded, even if he does have a four-run lead. I'm holding my breath and squeezing Jess's hand when the pitcher delivers the next pitch.

Woody seems to swing late, but he makes solid contact. The line drive rockets over the right side of the infield and slices toward the right field foul line. I grit my teeth so hard I'm afraid I'll crack all my molars at once—*stay fair, you bugger*! It does; the ball hits a foot inside the line and then spins across the line and into the corner. Coach Pat's arm is wind-milling like crazy at third as the three runners pass by him ahead of Woody, who slides into third ahead of the right fielder's throw with his first triple of the year, and we're within one run! *Thank you, Lord, and thank you, Coach Pat, for the two-strike mode.* Tonight it was just the ticket for Woody.

As the excitement mounts, the Mackenzie coach meets with his pitcher, catcher, and infielders at the mound. Terry steps in to try and bring that tying run in from third. The Warrior meeting gave Coach Pat and Terry a chance to meet also. I'm thinking back on all those good sac bunts Terry has put down this year and wondering if Coach Pat would try a squeeze. Then I realize the lead must have gotten all the way to my brain 'cause a coach wouldn't have his first baseman try to bunt for a hit, would he? As Terry waits for the first pitch, the lead in my gut tries to do a flip-flop. He's not bunting on the first pitch; he takes a curve that finds the outside corner for strike one. *Are my ears actually sweating?* Terry jumps on the next delivery and launches it toward the scoreboard beyond the left field fence, and I'm thinking, *It's outta here*! The Sandy Pines crowd jumps to its feet as one, trying to scream the ball out of the park. But it hits the top of the fence, and Terry has an RBI double to tie the game—unreal. I mean completely and totally unreal. A home run would have been ridiculously unbelievable, but the double and tie score are absolutely incredible in their own right. *Are my feet still on the stands, or am I levitating?* The Panthers have come all the way back to tie this thing up. Did somebody say, "It ain't over 'til it's over"?

Before the shock can even wear off and before I'm back down to earth and in my seat good, Luke strokes one into the gap in right center field, and the Panthers lead; the super soph does it again! The Panthers lead fourteen to thirteen. *No way, man.* No way can I believe this. But it's true; I see it on the scoreboard, fourteen to thirteen, visitors. As I'm sitting back down again, I think I remember possibly screaming an expletive when Luke's shot took off, but I hope I'm imagining it. After Bobby's groundout ends the inning, the Panthers take the field with the lead for the first time in the game and three outs to get. *Holy mackerel.*

The Warriors have their number three, four, and five hitters in their batting order coming up in the bottom of the seventh. That's a tough row to hoe for Mike; he's already pitched four hard innings. And maybe even a tougher row for my nerves. But the tide has turned now. The magic and Yogi are back in the Sandy Pines dugout. Mike takes care of the Warriors one, two, three on two groundouts and a fly out to center for the final out of the game. Unbelievable. The Panthers have come back from so far down it's like they were in China. And I'm sure my blood pressure was as high as the Panthers were down. *You're the man, Yogi!*

The stands are humming and buzzing between games. The Warrior fans are understandably stunned and dealing with disbelief. The Panther fans are also dealing with disbelief, but of the opposite and sweetest kind. I have no idea what to expect in the next game. I might expect the Panthers to maintain the momentum created by an unbelievable comeback in game one. Or I might expect the Warriors to be fighting mad and just rip the momentum out of our hands and score seven or eight runs in the first inning. But since this is baseball, I'm sure I don't know what to expect.

What I do know is that Sandy Pines is playing game two looking for a sweep instead of playing game two hoping to stave off elimination. It's great to know that the next game won't be our last. That would be the hardest part for me, knowing the next game might be your last.

State: Semifinals, Game Two versus Mackenzie Warriors

The Panthers are home team for this game, and Phil Allen is our starter. I'm guessing Coach Pat wants to get Phil back on the mound since he saw no action in the Bates series. Gotta keep all your arrows sharp. The crowd is still buzzing when the first Mackenzie batter steps to the plate. The Warriors are eager, and this leadoff hitter slaps the first pitch toward Woody at third. That gets a surge of adrenaline rolling through the old body and snaps me back to reality from my game-one euphoria. Woody gloves the ball but has to fire hard to first after double clutching on getting the horsehide out of his glove. His bullet throw gets the leadoff man for out number one. The next batter is hit by a pitch, and then a walk puts men at first and second with only one out, *uh-oh*. Phil gets the clean-up hitter to ground one to Pat near second base. Pat scoops up the ball, steps on second, and fires to first to complete the inning-ending double play. That's the way we like it.

In the Panther half of the first, Danny singles after Hunter's groundout. But a good pickoff move by the Warrior hurler makes Danny out number two before Major grounds out to third to end the inning.

The Warrior second starts with another grounder to Woody for out number one. Then three walks precede a single that scores two runs. There's nothing like a good slap in the face to obliterate the final traces of euphoria. The good news is that Jason's throw to Woody at third cuts down the runner coming around from first for out number two. Happily, the third out comes on a pop-up before any more runs score.

Woody leads off the Sandy Pines second with a strike-out—*have mercy*—before the Panthers score two of their own on a walk, two hits, and an infield error. *Good job, guys; way to work.* We head to the third all tied up at two to two.

The third opens with a walk to the first Mackenzie batter, and that leads to a run for the Warriors. Seems like a leadoff base on balls almost always comes around to score, and it seems like I've said that before. The worst thing about the run scoring is that a wild pitch and a passed ball get the runner to third before he scores on a groundout to short. Yuck, we're down by a run without even giving up a hit in the inning when the Warrior half of the third ends.

Hunter opens the Sandy Pines third with a pop out to center field. Then the Panthers get rolling. Danny's single is followed by Major's long home run over the center field fence, and the good guys lead by one. Next, Woody reaches first via the hit-by-a-pitch route. That'll work. If you can't hit it with your bat, hit it with your body. After Terry goes down swinging, Luke draws a walk. Bobby singles ahead of another walk to Pat. Jason reaches base on a shortstop error that scores two more runs, and the Panthers lead eight to three after three. *Dare I relax?* The game's not half over, and anything is possible, but I'm getting the good-nerve surges right now.

The Warriors answer back in the top of the fourth after another leadoff walk bodes ill. And it's not a good defensive inning for the Panthers as two infield errors lead to two runs scored, and it's eight to five when the Panthers come to bat in the bottom of the fourth. The game is half over now, and we lead by three. It's not a five-run lead, but it's a lead. I need to keep myself in the present and not get ahead of things. But that ain't an easy thing to do.

I'm hoping I haven't infected our players with my thoughts when they go down one, two, three in the bottom of the fourth. But still, it's only nine more outs to the state championship series, only nine more outs 'til the finals. Like I just said, it isn't easy to stay in the present. I'm glad no one can read my thoughts. I'm sure I'd be chastised severely.

Phil gives up a one-out single in the top of the fifth but gets the next two. *Oh yeah, baby, just six more to go.*

Luke reaches first on a shortstop error to open the Panther fifth. But a groundout to second is followed by back-to-back strikeouts to end the inning; no insurance for Sandy Pines in the fifth. And now it's time for the sixth inning—the *sixth*.

Phil gets the first Warrior batter on a fly ball out to Jason in left. Maybe this sixth inning won't be so bad. The next batter draws a walk, and then the following Warrior hitter, who's a lefty, rips a line-drive homer over the right field fence, and just like that the lead is down to one, and my guts are turning and burning. A double off the bat of the next batter chases Phil. Coach Pat brings Pat to the mound from shortstop and sends Phil to left field. Pat seems ready to go but gives up an infield single to the first man he faces, and now my spinning innards shift into overdrive.

The Warriors have men on first and third with only one out. All it takes now is a fly ball to the outfield, and this thing's tied up. Pat gets the next batter to ground one back to him, and after checking the runner at third, he throws to first for out number two. That's huge. The runner at first advances to second on the play, so a two-out hit will now give the Warriors the lead. The next batter works the count to three balls and one strike, which puts the entire Panther crowd in near-meltdown mode. *Are my ears sweating again?* The batter then takes a mighty cut at a curve ball but tops it and sends a slow, hopping, chipmunk grounder toward third. *Oh no, this can't be happening; it just can't be.* My heart's in my throat, and visions of past chipmunks are racing through my mind as the scene seems to unfold in surreal slow motion before me. My head bobs with each hop of the ball. Woody charges the bounding hopper as the runner at third heads for home. As Woody reaches down with his glove, an instant vision of the between-the-legs opening-game error flashes across my mind. I grind my teeth and hold my breath for the twentieth time tonight.

Now the scene jumps back to real time as Woody calmly scoops the horsehide and delivers a bullet to Terry at first for out number three. *Great freaking balls of fire, Woody did it.* He corralled the chipmunk ball from hades! I think that last play will be the one I remember most vividly from this whole season. As that slow skipper was headed for Woody, I agonized that fate would be so cruel as to put him through this test again. But this time he came through. He really came through and conquered the chipmunk demon.

I'm hoping for a little insurance this inning, but it's almost as if the Panthers seem eager to get this game over with as they go down one, two, three again in the bottom of the sixth. I wonder what sort of gut-twisting scenario awaits us in the top of the seventh and possibly final inning.

As it turns out, the guts are spared. The game and series end without further drama as the Warriors bow out on two infield pop-ups and a final strikeout. As the players celebrate wildly on the field, I realize the Sandy Pines Panthers are going to host the state championship series. The hope that was born back in the gloomy cold of February has become a reality; we're playing for state. Actually, they're playing for state. What the heck, they climbed the mountain, but I feel like I climbed it with them.

Saturday is graduation day for Sandy Pines, and knowing they're in the state finals makes it an even happier occasion for the eleven Panther seniors. We meet Becky, Mack, and David at the huge Baptist church where the ceremony's being held and sit with them in the large balcony section. The graduating class is on two sides of the stage, and the Pelhams get the luck of the draw. After the seniors parade in, Woody ends up on our side and just about as high up as we are.

Again I'm struck by how fast time flies. As the graduates' names are called, I recognize some that I coached when they were ten or eleven but haven't seen in five or six years. And here they are graduating from high school in what seems like the blink of an eye. It's amazing to me how fast the last four years have passed. Both my children are out of high school now; it doesn't seem possible.

After the ceremony, the Pelhams and Christophers have dinner together at the local O'Charlie's. Of course, Mack and I are in deep discussion of the upcoming state championship series over a couple of Diet Cokes as we wait for our table. I figure it's time to needle Mack with a little superstitious humor, like the Who Wants to be a Millionaire game on the trip to Bates.

"I tell you what, Mack; I feel a premonition coming on. If you can chug that Diet Coke before I chug mine, Allan will pitch a shutout in the first game."

"Get outta here, Steve! You're talking like you've got a screw loose again!"

I laugh and say, "Well okay, if that's the way you want it. I'm just trying to help. A little insurance never hurts. So you better hope we hear 'Maggie Mae' on game day."

"You're un-freaking-believable!" Mack says, shaking his head with a gnarly grin on his face.

Mack's main concern about facing Berkwood is, of course, their power-hitting, man-child first baseman. If my son was going to take the mound against this guy, he'd be my main worry also. Berkwood pretty much steamrolled their semifinal opponents with their slugger hitting at least one home run in each of the two victories—two in one of them. I think he's got twenty-three or twenty-four so far this season. At least Allan has a week to rest that shoulder ailment, and hopefully he'll be at his best for the finals.

Dinner was great fun with the Christophers, even though I couldn't bait Mack with any superstitious nonsense. Watching our two graduated sons just drove home again to me how fast kids grow up. Now it's just six days 'til game one of the state championship series. I wonder how fast those days will pass. After three months, it's now down to less than a week.

Fast or slow, it doesn't matter because it's really gonna happen. It's what we've been hoping for for a long, long time—a whole lotta years. They've been great years, and it's so cool that the guys get to finish their high school careers, and for most of them, their baseball careers, in the state finals. I'm gonna try not to be too nervous and just enjoy watching these kids play a championship series. I wish it were starting tomorrow.

Chapter Forty-Two

The funeral was devastating. So much sorrow and grief at a time that was supposed to be filled with excitement and joy.

I am Kimberly.

It is Thursday, the day before the state championship series begins, and the fourth day since my dad died. He died in his sleep Sunday night without any warning or sign of a problem. The doctor says it was a massive coronary, nothing to do with his past cancer. Our family is in shock. I'm sure any family that loses its father is devastated, but this feeling of loss is almost unbearable. My mother has tried so hard to ease my and Woody's overwhelming sadness and grief, but she suffers the same constantly.

Woody seems to be consumed by anger. He has yet to shed any tears. After the funeral on Wednesday, he refused to leave the gravesite. He said Major Thomas and Mike Drew would pick him up at sundown, when the cemetery locks its gates, but he wouldn't leave when they came for him. A cemetery official told them he would call the police if he wouldn't leave, so Woody had Major and Mike drive out of the gates and to a street on the backside of the cemetery near the surrounding fence. They talked him out of climbing the fence to get back in.

Woody won't speak about Dad's death or who or what

he's so angry at, but he seems ready to explode. I have told him how horrible and empty I feel, and he has acknowledged that emptiness. The emptiness is the only thing I've heard him say about how he feels. He talked about something we saw in the last movie we rented: *Behind Enemy Lines*. He told us his chest feels the way the giant angel statue looks at the end, after the tank has blasted a hole through it. Practically the entire chest area is a smooth, round hole—empty, nothing there. Woody said that's how he feels—empty—until the anger that boils up inside of him consumes the emptiness.

I am so thankful that Mom's identical twin sister, Monica, was able to get here so quickly. She and her daughter, Jennifer, had planned a short visit to be here for the state finals. Of course, we didn't know for sure that Sandy Pines would actually be in the series, but they wanted to be here just in case. Thank God they are here, but how I wish their trip had gone as originally planned.

We are a family of faith. We attend Mass every Sunday. We offer thanks before every meal. But this is the kind of tragic catastrophe that tests any and every level of faith. My dad was a spiritual person, although not overly religious. I believe I inherited some of his spirituality, and I am grateful now that I did. I remember asking him a question on September 11 last year, after the attacks and the massive loss of life. I asked him, "How could a loving God allow this horror to happen? Where is our loving God today?"

He told me, as he had before, that God doesn't necessarily prevent tragedy or terror on any scale, even the massive. He reminded me that man's ability to commit evil against his fellow man has been evident through the ages. He pointed out World War II as a huge example from only fifty years ago. He reminded me that God doesn't interfere in man's free will even when the result is horror. But I can't apply these facts to the pain I feel now, and I still ask, *Why my dad? Why now? Why does there have to be so much sadness that we can't understand?*

He also answered the second part of my September 11 question: "Where is our loving God today?"

He told me that our loving God was in the love of the victims' families for the departed and for each other. God was in their grief-stricken embraces and in the tears they wept. God was in the compassion and empathy expressed by the victims' friends and neighbors and coworkers who survived. He was in their tears and embraces as well. Our loving God was in the actions of the heroes who saved so many on that day—the policemen, the firemen, all those who rescued and attempted to rescue their fellow men. And he was in the loving actions of our country that wept along with the families of the victims, a nation that shared their grief.

And then Dad showed me a quote he had found in a copy of *Bits and Pieces*, a monthly booklet he receives that contains quotes and other inspirational thoughts. The quote comes from *An Almost Holy Picture*, by Heather McDonald: "It is said that grace enters the soul through a wound." I think I remembered that quote today because the wound we feel now is so real, so deep.

At another time, my dad taught me that God is wherever two or more are gathered in his name. There were more than two gathered for my dad's funeral mass. And in that setting, though the pain of my loss and grief was overwhelming, I did feel the presence of a loving God of comfort. And I understood why there were many friends of my father from different times and aspects of his life who came to share and lessen our grief. My dad was a wonderful father to Woody and me, and I think, a great husband to our mother. But now I understood what a good friend he had been to so many. Not a doer of great deeds, but simply someone who loved to see others, especially his friends, smile. He was a true believer in the power and the gift of a smile and the goodness of laughter.

Once when I quizzed him on his goals in life, he gave me the usual *dad* answer of wanting to be the best father and husband he could be. But I pressed him, and he said he guessed his goal was to make at least one person smile every day. I know he made me smile every day, whether I wanted to or not.

And those times I especially didn't want to smile, he would pull his *open-hand* trick on me. He would tell me, "I bet I can make you smile just by opening my hand." Then he would open his hand, which he had balled into a fist, and on the palm of his hand would be drawn a smiley face. It got so that I would begin to grin whenever he started his routine and I saw his fist. And even those times when I would be so mad that I could suppress the smile until he opened his hand, I always busted into a grin when I saw that smiley face in the palm of his hand, even though I might still be angry.

He told me once that even though he'd never make millions of dollars, maybe he could make a million smiles. I think he must have believed that a smile is more than just physical or mental but somehow a real communication between spirits.

When he was in the hospital for his lung surgery, he wrote Woody and I the same note. He said he'd meant to write us each a letter in case things didn't go well. But with all the pre-surgery goings-on and the cancer fear, he forgot and had to jot something down at the hospital. He wrote simply, *"Remember, your smile is the light in the window of your soul that lets me know your heart is at home."* And then, *"I will love you always."* He said the words were from an anonymous quote, but I like to think of them as his. I believe those words are true. It's hard to explain, but it's like a smile brings a glow along with it, a glow that seems to come from somewhere deep inside, from your soul. When I can feel my heart now, when the emptiness isn't overwhelming, I feel a broken heart. But still, when I think of his smile words and smiley-face palm, I do smile. And my heart, though broken, is warmed.

I will finish his journal because I know that that is what he would want and because it is another way that I can stay connected to him. I've learned to do the scorebook, but I'll leave the videotaping to Mr. Messina. Mr. Christopher has agreed to help me with the baseball jargon.

I hope the team can play well. Maybe Woody will feel better with something else to focus on. That is, if he can manage to focus on something else. Coach Pat tried to get the games postponed a week or even a few days but couldn't since school is already out for the summer.

Woody said he wouldn't stay late at the cemetery tonight. He knows Dad would want him to be at his best for the games that start tomorrow. I think he'll be home soon. It's almost dark now.

Chapter Forty-Three

It's a spectacularly beautiful day for a baseball game. I'm sure Dad would have loved it; heck, he probably has something to do with it. That thought brings a smile to my face and makes me feel better. It's so very sunny, and there's a nice swirling breeze, making the leaves dance like Dad liked. The grill is fired up with burgers and dogs, and the smell-good smoke drifts over the grandstands and up toward the sky. As I watch the smoke waft upward, I'm reminded of the incense representing our prayers drifting up to the ceiling of the church at Dad's funeral mass.

The crowd is buzzing some, not as much as normal or as much as you would expect for the championship series. But it's to be expected after the tragedy our family and team experienced this week. Over the loudspeakers they're playing some of the old standards, not Dad's warm-up songs. I'm sure they don't want to make things any harder than they already are for all of us.

There is a huge crowd; it *is* the state championships, after all. The regular high school games don't draw really big crowds, mostly just families and friends of the players. But that makes for a very close group of fans, the heart and soul of each side's supporters. And our heart and soul are aching right now. The media has spread the news of our tragedy, and even the Berkwood crowd is pretty subdued, at least now, before the game has begun. I'm sure the families on their side of the stands know how much our side is hurting right now.

The team looks pretty good warming up, not real peppy, but not bad considering. Woody did come home last night about an hour after dark, but he still seems angry and touchy and alone. We talked today. I don't know how to make him feel better, but I wanted to remind him how Dad would want him to conduct himself in these games. Of course it made him mad, me telling him what Dad would want. I'm just afraid he'll blow up and get himself thrown out of the game. And if he does, he'll miss the next game also.

I watch Woody walking to the dugout after warm-ups, spitting on his hands, trying to get the dry, dusty dirt off. He hates the way it feels to have the dirt-and-brick-dust mixture stuck to his dry hands.

State: Finals, Game One versus Berkwood Pirates

Allan takes the mound for the Panthers and begins game one of the state championship with a called strike. The crowd seems tense as the count reaches three balls and two strikes. The next pitch is smacked to right center field for a leadoff double. There's a perceptible groan from the home stands as a loud cheer goes up on the visitors' side.

I'm sitting with Mom and Monica, and Jennifer and Becky Christopher in our home grandstands where I always sit. I thought about going down to the left field bleachers like Dad used to, but that seemed too weird. Anyway, Mack Christopher is not down there either today, so I wouldn't have been too comfortable there. He's in the score box above the concession stand running the scoreboard. That's weird too, 'cause Big Mack likes to be down there where he can see over the fence and maybe sneak a smoke.

The next batter hits a ground ball to Bobby at second, and the runner at second breaks for third. Bobby chooses to go for the lead runner and fires the ball to Woody at third. Woody takes the throw and blocks the bag just in time to tag the runner out. Now our side cheers, and Mom and I are especially glad Woody has made a play without any problems. It's good for him to get that first one under his belt considering his state of mind.

But now there's a runner at first, and the Pirates' junior slugger, the one everybody says will be a major leaguer someday, comes to bat. He's huge; he looks more like a pro football player than a high school baseball player to me. And he rips the first pitch from Allan over Hunter's head and off the fence in right field for an RBI double. The visitors' side roars now as they take the lead in their first at bat. Hunter never had a chance to catch the ball; it was a line drive rocket that hit the fence like a bullet. I guess we should be happy it wasn't a home run. But now there's a runner on second with only one out and one run in. A pitch in the dirt sends the runner to third, and then a fly ball out to Danny in center field scores the run. It's two runs in and two outs, and the visitor crowd is cheering confidently like this is how things are supposed to happen.

I'm worried and a little ticked off, and I can see that Woody is letting some anger out, kicking at the dirt and turning his head down toward the outfield so no one will hear him verbalize his anger. Luckily the next batter grounds one back to Allan, and he throws to first for out number three. The Panthers are down by two early. But it is early, and they have their first at bat to see if they can answer back.

Hunter leads off our half of the first inning with a fly ball out to center field. Then the Panther excitement begins. Danny takes a one-ball, one-strike pitch over the right field fence for our first run, and it's our turn to cheer. And before the cheers for Danny's home run die down, Major launches one high and deep that lands on Evergreen Boulevard, and we're tied two to two! The home crowd is roaring now as sound and excitement encircle the field.

It's estimated that there are fifteen hundred to two thousand fans in attendance. They've spilled out of the stands and to the bank beyond the right field fence and all along the Evergreen Boulevard sidewalk, peering through or over the windscreen. A local cable TV station is broadcasting the games live and will show them again on Sunday so the guys will get to see them.

Woody comes to bat for the second time this season following back-to-back homers by Danny and Major. I'm sure he'll be swinging for the fences too. As much anger as he's displaying, I'm certain he'll be swinging as hard as he can anyway, even if Danny and Major hadn't just hit home runs. And he does take a mighty cut at the first pitch, which curves into the dirt—strike one. I know how hard the Sandy Pines parents are pulling and praying for Woody. I'm praying as fast as I can. He takes the next pitch, which looks like it's outside to me, but it's called strike two. Woody jerks his head in disgust, whether at himself or the call, I don't know. He takes the next pitch, which is another curve in the dirt—ball one. But the Pirate pitcher tries yet another curve, and Woody goes fishing again for strike three.

I hold my breath as he stomps angrily out of the batter's box, and I hear Mack Christopher leaning out of the window of the press box hollering, "That's okay, Woody, no sweat! You'll get him next time, buddy!"

I hear some other shouts of encouragement as Woody enters the dugout, but I'm still holding my breath, waiting for the loud bang of his helmet slamming off the concrete floor or cinderblock wall. But I hear no sounds of destruction or even loud curses, thank goodness.

The Panther excitement isn't over yet, however. Terry succeeds in following Danny and Major's lead, smacking one over the left field fence and off the retaining wall for the third home run of the inning and a three-to-two Panther lead! The crowd is really going wild now; we're all jumping and hollering like we've won the game. I know it's early. I'm well aware of Dad's favorite Yogi quote, "It ain't over 'til it's over," but this is our family and team's first taste of joy after almost a week of grief, even if it is just the first inning of a high school baseball game.

Luke bats next and reaches first on an infield error. But then a fly out ends the inning with the Panthers up three to two.

Allan shuts the Pirates down in the second. The first out comes on a grounder to Bobby at second, and then Big Al finishes 'em off with two strikeouts in a row for a one-two-three inning. And that gets the home crowd cheering almost as loudly as one of our homers.

The Pirate pitcher continues the string of Ks by striking out our first batter in the second. After a groundout to third, Hunter bats for the second time. And he produces the fourth Panther run with the fourth solo home run of the game! Now we're going crazy again in the home stands, and I think I even see a hint of a smile on Woody's face as he and the rest of the team greet Hunter at home plate. That's all the Panthers get in the second, but a four-to-two lead after two innings isn't bad.

Allan Ks the first hitter of the Pirate third to give him

three in a row. That brings the top of their order up for the second time. But no worries for Al. The next two batters go down on a fly out to center field and a slow grounder to Terry at first. That's Al's second one-two-three inning in a row.

Sandy Pines also goes one, two, three in the third. Woody reaches first with one out when he's hit by a pitch. When the ball hits him, I'm afraid he'll go after the pitcher, but he just trots down to first. I'm thinking maybe he's happier about getting to first than mad about getting hit. But Terry grounds one to second, and a double play ends the Panther third.

The Pirate slugger leads off the fourth with a long home run over the right field fence that bounces off the roof of the indoor hitting/pitching building. I've never seen that before. Al comes back with a K for out number one. A single is followed by another strikeout, and then the inning ends on a grounder back to Al. But the lead's been cut by one, four to three.

The Panthers go one, two, three in the bottom of the fourth on three fly outs to the outfield.

The first batter reaches base on a walk to open the Berkwood fifth. Out number one comes when the next hitter fouls off a two-strike bunt attempt for a strikeout. Then a single puts runners on first and second. The following batter grounds one sharply to Terry at first for out number two, but the runners advance to third and second. And up comes the Pirate slugger who homered in his last at bat. Coach Pat is taking no chances this time, though, and puts the slugger on first with an intentional walk. Bases are loaded with two outs. Al is up to the challenge, getting a soft pop-up to Terry in foul territory by first base for the third out. That was too close for comfort.

Sandy Pines doesn't make anything happen in their half

of the fifth, going one, two, three again. This is getting to be a nasty habit.

The Pirates open the sixth with a single. Allan gets the next batter on a strikeout but then puts a second runner on with a walk. The next hitter launches a long fly to right field that Hunter catches just in front of the fence. Both runners tag up and advance, putting runners on second and third with two outs. Things are getting scary now.

When the next batter draws a walk to load the bases, it's definitely nail-biting time. The Panther fans are holding their breath when the next batter smashes a high fly deep to center field. Danny races back to the fence and hauls the long blast in for out number three. *Whew,* Sandy Pines still has a one-run lead after what could have been a disastrous sixth.

Major leads off the Panther sixth with a single. Woody finally gets one he likes and smacks it toward third. But the third baseman makes a stab to his left, shags the grounder, and fires to second to force Major. The second baseman turns and throws to first just in time to beat Woody and complete the double play. Woody shouts something indistinguishable through clenched teeth and shakes both fists in front of him as he heads back to the dugout. But again I don't hear any explosions from the dugout, and that's one thing to be grateful for. Terry bats next and keeps the inning going with a two-out double. Then the Pirates bring the big slugger from first base to the mound to try and shut down the Panthers. And this guy can really bring the heat.

Luke is patient, though, and manages a walk as the big guy is working to find the strike zone. Bobby comes up with two on and two out and gets ahead as the first two pitches to him are balls. But then the pitcher finds his groove and fires two strikes in a row to even the count. Bobby fouls one off and then takes ball three for a full count. The home crowd encourages Bobby with shouts to "hang in there" and then roars with one voice as he bloops one over the second baseman and in front of the hard-charging right fielder. Terry scores, and the Panthers lead five to three. The Pirate hurler strikes out our next batter on three straight pitches to end the sixth. It still "ain't over yet," but a two-run lead with just three more outs to go isn't half bad.

Allan goes to the mound for the seventh, but his mom is wondering how long Coach Pat will leave him in since he seems to be tiring. The first Pirate up smacks one hard between short and second, but Pat scoops it up and makes a good throw to first for out number one. And it's a good thing that man didn't reach base 'cause the slugger is up now. And he wastes little time, blasting the second pitch he sees over the center field fence, the retaining wall, and fence and onto Evergreen Boulevard. Thank goodness for that run last inning. We're still up five to four. The next batter singles, and Coach Pat brings Pat in from shortstop to try and preserve the win for the Panthers and Allan.

I think Allan's mom, Becky, is relieved when the crowd gives him a standing ovation as he comes to the dugout. Pat gets a grounder to Bobby from the next batter. But it is toward first base, and Bobby has to throw there for out number two as the runner advances to second. Now there's one more out to get with the tying run on second. Mercifully, the end comes quickly when the next hitter smashes a line drive at Woody, who gets his glove up in front of his face to snag the bullet and save his teeth. Game over. Panthers win!

Wow, what a great game and what a great win. All the Panthers—players, coaches, and fans—are excited but subdued. Subdued because we all know that's just one game.

We have to win another one, and everyone realizes that this Berkwood team is very capable of winning two in a row from us, especially considering their star first baseman. He batted four times in the game with two homers, a double, and one intentional walk. I'm convinced now that we're watching a future major leaguer.

Of course, with the tension of the game over now, my thoughts go to my dad and how excited he would have been. I turn to Mom next to me as I begin to fight tears, and she looks at me with tears in her eyes also. Monica and Jennifer are also tearing up as we exchange hugs, and then Becky Christopher gives us each a quick hug as she heads out of the stands to congratulate Allan. I'll be glad when the next game starts in thirty minutes.

State: Finals, Game Two versus Berkwood Pirates

The weather's still beautiful although the sun is starting to sink low in the west behind the trees and shadows are beginning to creep onto the field. The grill is still smoking as the Pirates take the field as home team in game two. Danny will pitch for Sandy Pines, so Phil will play center field, and Jason will be in the lineup in left field.

Major gets the first hit for the Panthers, a two-out double. But the inning ends on Woody's fly out to right field. He's muttering to himself on the way to take up his defensive position at third base, but I think his anger burner is on low for now at least.

The Pirates get a two-out double from their slugger; the guy seems unstoppable. But Pat makes an excellent play on a hot grounder, and his throw just beats the runner at first to end the Pirates' first.

Terry starts the Panther second with a long fly to left field that doesn't quite have enough to clear the fence, and the left fielder snags it for out number one. Bobby singles, and then Pat and Jason draw walks to load the bases. Phil delivers a sacrifice fly to right field that scores Terry for the first run of the game. Unfortunately, that's all the Panthers get as the inning ends on Hunter's groundout.

The Pirate second heats up on a one-out double that puts the tying run on second. A groundout then moves the runner to third with two out. A solid double ties the game, and then a home run that just clears the fence in right field puts Berkwood up three to one. And that's the score when the inning ends. The Pirates clearly gained the momentum in the second, and their fans' cheering has increased with the change in the score. We'll see if the Panthers can take the momentum back and get us up on our feet again.

It doesn't happen in the third as Sandy Pines goes down one, two, three. A strikeout and a fly out to center precede Woody's grounder back to the pitcher; nothing doing this inning.

Danny keeps the Pirates right where they are. He gives up a two-out single but gets a grounder to short to end the inning.

Terry draws a base on balls to open the Panther fourth, and the home crowd stirs a little at the good start. Then a groundout is followed by two strikeouts, and the Panthers don't score in the fourth.

The Pirates go one, two, three in their half of the inning, so the Panthers are still down three to one going into the fifth. And they're still down three to one an inning later after they go one, two, three in the top of the sixth. Well, this is getting to be nerve wracking; we've only got three more outs, and I think I've inherited Dad's gut bombers. Let's hope we can keep it at three to one for our last at bat.

No such luck as the Pirate slugger opens their half of the sixth with another home run, and it's quickly four to one. And that's just the beginning. Three hits and three walks later, the score is six to one, and the bases are loaded for the slugger's second trip to the plate this inning. And he cleans them off with a huge blast over the center field fence and onto Evergreen Boulevard again! Their crowd is understandably going wild as I realize how unreal the slugger has been—two home runs in one inning and four today in two games. This guy is unbelievable.

The Panthers come to bat for the last time, down ten to one. And that's how it ends. A huge win for the Pirates definitely swings the momentum their way for the deciding third game tomorrow. And the way their crowd is celebrating, you'd think that they'd already won game three. Our guys look pretty awed by the Pirates' performance in game two, but hopefully they'll be rough and ready tomorrow when it's game time.

Mack, Becky, and David Christopher come by, and we all eat fried chicken and try to cheer each other up for the big game tomorrow. Coach Pat and some of the dads take the team to Arby's for a quick, late supper. I'm guessing he wants to keep them together as long as possible tonight so hopefully they'll go home and get some sleep for tomorrow's game. I'm also guessing he wants as much company as possible for Woody now. Woody didn't seem any more down than the other players after the game, but he's the smoldering volcano again when he gets home. Again I'm so glad Aunt Monica is here to help shoulder the emotional load for Mom and us. I think it is especially helpful for Woody to have her consolation. It's sort of like having a mom-and-a-half.

Everybody is quite exhausted and heads for bed except for Woody and me. He bums a cigarette from me and heads to the back steps that lead down to the ground from the deck to light up. His level of uneasiness seems to have grown a great deal since he first got home, so I follow to see if I can get any idea at all about his state of mind.

As we sit and smoke, I try to assure him that he'll do fine in the game tomorrow because I can't think of any other way to start a conversation. But he gets even more agitated and says I don't understand, that he knows he's screwing up his last chance to do what Dad wanted most: to get a scholarship to play college ball. He says his only chance now was to have a huge state championship series, hit at least a couple of home runs and a bunch of doubles or triples, or get a hit every time up or something like that! But he's screwing it up totally, and there's just too much pressure; it's crushing him. He's letting Dad down; he's failing at his last chance to make Dad proud.

I tell him that's not so, that I've read Dad's journal, that I know that all Dad wanted is for him to do his best, have fun doing it, and not worry about playing college ball.

I tell him, "You know Dad loves us and doesn't require any special success to be proud of us. You don't have to be a baseball winner for him. Two of his favorite movies, *Rudy* and *Braveheart*, weren't about traditional winners. They were about people who were winners because they never gave up. That's what winning is to Dad, never giving up. It's not important to him that you get signed to a scholarship but that you don't give up trying to play in college if that's what you want. Don't give up if it's in your heart to play. That's all you have to do to be a winner in Dad's eyes."

Woody just says, "You don't understand. I've got to get a scholarship. I've got to keep playing. I know that's what he wanted, and that's what I've got to do. I've got to do it! I have got to do it!"

I tell him, "Woody, Dad loved you unconditionally, just like he loved me unconditionally. You saw that he didn't stop loving me when I kept getting into trouble or even when I ran away. You know that, Woody. You know you don't have to do anything for Dad's love."

But he says, "Oh yes, I do. I've got to do it somehow, even though I've blown it so far. I've got to do it!"

We just sit quietly for a while, and then I try to get him to go to bed, but he says he can't; there's no way he can go to sleep now. So I go on back into the house and head for my room. As I pass through the den, I notice a wall hanging Dad brought back from one of his audit trips: a weaving plant in North Carolina. I stop dead in my tracks when my eyes find the words.

The Weaver
My Life is but a weaving between the Lord and me;
I cannot choose the colors; He worketh steadily.
Oft times He weaveth sorrow, and I, in foolish pride,
Forget He sees the upper, and I the underside.
Not til the loom is silent and the shuttles cease to fly,
Shall God unroll the canvas and
explain the reason why.
The dark threads are as needful in
the Weaver's skillful hand
As the threads of gold and silver in
the pattern He has planned.

Dad said he noticed it on the wall of an office where he was doing interviews in the plant. He asked about it and was told that it is an anonymous work attributed to a lady who worked as a weaver in the industry years ago. He bought a version as a wall hanging at a craft store and brought it home because he thought it was a wonderful description of a life of faith.

And he showed me the difference between the upper side and underside of a woven throw. The upper side is the precise design of the weaving, and the underside is different shades and shapes and barely recognizable as the pattern.

As I climb into bed and repeat the words in my head, the tears come, and I pray that Woody can escape the dark threads at least for a little while.

Chapter Forty-Four

Saturday is another absolutely perfect day for a game, maybe a little more windy. And I'm still wondering if Dad isn't somehow pulling some strings somewhere to get this perfect weather. At least Woody was asleep in his bed this morning. I don't know for how long, but he did sleep some. Unfortunately, he's still uptight when he heads for the ballpark. Mom's worried about him, but I try to ease her anxiety by telling her he'll be okay once the game starts, even though I don't really believe it myself.

The ballpark is an exact duplicate of yesterday except that the game is starting an hour earlier today. The smell of grilling burgers is in the air, the tunes are playing, and the crowd is growing. The Berkwood crowd seems confident, and that's easy to understand after game two yesterday. By game time the crowd is even larger than last night, and the atmosphere is charged. This is it—one last chance and one final championship game.

Mom and I are tremendously relieved when Sandy Pines wins the toss of the coin and gets to bat as home team. Mom can't stand it when the other team gets to bat last. We're all in our same places in the stands with Becky sitting with us again, and again Mack Christopher is in the score box above the concession stand instead of down the left field line.

State: Finals, Game Three versus Berkwood Pirates

Phil is on the mound for the Panthers today. Dad figured no other team has as good a third starter as Phil. So that's the mindset I'm taking. We've got the best pitcher today. Woody looks pretty good during infield warm ups, focused but very intense. He bobbles a couple of grounders but fires them so hard to Terry at first that I'm almost surprised to see him catch them.

And then, almost suddenly it seems, it's time for the first pitch. Phil delivers a called strike, and the final game of the final season is underway. The Pirate leadoff man takes ball one before fouling off the next pitch for strike two. Then he hits a sky-high pop-up on the third base side of the infield. Woody circles under it and makes the catch for out number one. He also gets out number two when the next batter pops one up. Two down and nobody on when the Pirate slugger steps up for his first at bat of game three. He smacks the first pitch, but it's on the ground to Pat at short, and he scoops it and fires to first for out number three. No problems for the Panthers in the top of the first and thus no worries for their fans yet.

Hunter leads off the Sandy Pines first with a solid single to left field, bringing the home crowd to its feet, cheering mightily. Major also records a single after Danny's strikeout, but Hunter can't advance to third, so there are men on first and second when Woody comes to bat. I watched him in the on-deck circle while Major was batting, and he was so intense, swinging the weighted warm-up bat almost violently. It makes my stomach queasy to see him so worked up, so on edge, and it only gets worse when he swings and misses at strike three and trudges angrily back to the dugout, obviously muttering to himself. Dear God, I wish he could calm down, and I send a quick silent prayer out for that intention. We all cheer loudly for Terry to come through and knock Hunter in. But the inning and the Panther threat end on Terry's groundout to second base. *Darn, that was a good chance to take the lead.*

The Pirate second starts similarly to their first. The first two batters hit fly balls to the same fielder. This inning it's Hunter who catches a foul fly for out number one, and then a long one takes him to the warning track before he gathers it in for out number two. But that's the last of the similarities. Phil hits the next batter after getting ahead in the count two strikes and no balls. The next batter makes him pay dearly, bashing one over the left field fence for a two-run homer. Ugh, it's totally no fun being behind in the championship game. The next hitter grounds one to Woody at third, and he makes a smooth scoop of it and fires to first for out number three. He's gotten three of the first six put-outs for Sandy Pines; he's playing solid defense. Hopefully his offense will follow suit in his next at bat.

The Panthers come to bat down by two in the second and soon return to the field still trailing by two. The Pirate pitcher takes care of all three batters himself by striking out the first two and then fielding a high bouncer and throwing to first for out number three. Our two batters who struck out were called out looking, and the crowd murmurs uneasily at the Pirate pitcher's mastery of our Panthers so far. Of the first six outs, four are strikeouts. Let's hope our hitters are used to him the next time they get up.

The Pirates add another run in the top of the third on two singles and an error on our center fielder. The only good news is that Phil battles hard and gets out number three on a strikeout. I don't like being behind by three runs. I don't like this at all. It's still pretty early, but I really, really don't like being behind.

Things don't start well for the Panthers in their half of the third as the Pirate pitcher returns Phil's favor and Ks him for out number one. But Hunter draws a walk, and Danny is hit by a pitch to give us runners at first and second with only one out. Out number two comes when Major grounds one to the third baseman, who knocks it down, grabs it, and scrambles to his feet to step on third base to force the lead runner for out number two. Still, we have men on first and second when Woody comes to bat.

I see Mom squeezing Monica's hand tightly as she shouts encouragement with the rest of our fans to Woody. He takes the first pitch, which is high, for ball one. The second pitch makes him jump back as it comes inside, close to hitting him. I inch forward in my seat as the pitcher delivers the next throw. Woody smacks it hard, and I think it will get through for a hit, but the second baseman dives to his left, snags the ball, and manages to throw to first for out number three and the end of the inning. Woody scares me to death after the play when he jerks off his helmet and rears back like he's going to smash it to the ground. But he doesn't, and luckily Mom had shut her eyes after the out and didn't see him.

The first Pirate batter in the fourth launches a long, high fly to the center field fence. "Oh no," I mutter as Danny turns and races toward the fence. He turns to look over his left shoulder as he hits the warning track, takes two more strides, and then leaps against the fence, reaching over the fence with his glove as the ball sails out. He crashes to the ground and gets up with the ball in his glove! Out number one is the most thrilling play I've ever seen, and the crowd, which is surrounding the field again today, goes nuts. *Holy cow, that was great!*

The next batter singles, and that brings Coach Pat to the mound to make a switch. He brings Mike Drew in to pitch and sends Phil to left field. That means Jason has to come out of the game. I feel bad for Jason; that's probably the end of his high school career. It did seem to go so fast. I remember when his mom would drop him off to ride to Sandy Pines with Woody and me when they were freshmen.

Mike has a rough start, hitting the first batter he faces. That puts men on first and second with one out. But he comes back to strike out the next hitter for out number two, and then he grabs a grounder from the following batter and throws to first for out number three. That was good damage control by Mike, as Dad used to say. The game's half over, and Sandy Pines is down three to zero. *Come on, guys, we need some runs.*

Terry starts the Panther fourth with a single; *that's better.* Mike bats next and puts down a sacrifice bunt that gets Terry to second with one out. Then Pat doubles to right center field to score Terry, and we've got our first run! The fans are back in it now; the cheering is loud and long. And the cheering gets even louder when Bobby hits a slow roller between first and second. The first baseman fields it and then flips it over the head of the pitcher, who has run over to cover first. Bobby is safe, and Pat has come all the way home to score our second run!

Phil bats next and attempts a bunt but pops it up to the pitcher for out number two, *yuck*. Hunter then draws a walk that puts the potential tying run at second. There are runners at first and second for Danny, but the Pirate hurler wins this duel, striking out Danny for out number three. I really thought we were gonna at least tie it up. But the Panthers did rally to get within one at three to two.

The first Pirate batter of the fifth singles to quiet the home crowd and excite the visitors. He steals second on the first pitch to the following batter and gets to third when the batter grounds to second and Bobby throws him out at first. This isn't good; they've got a runner on third with just one out. Our side is dead silent, and the visitors' side is rocking. And it rocks even louder when a wild pitch scores the runner from third and the Pirates increase their lead to four to two. My stomach cries out for some Pepto when the slugger bats next. This is way scary. He might break our backs with a home run now. But even as the gastric juices swirl, he hits another grounder to short that Pat handles and throws to first for out number two. Whew, at least Slugger hasn't slugged one out. The following batter also grounds out to short to end the Pirate fifth as our crowd roars and my tummy settles down.

Major opens the Sandy Pines half of inning five with a single, and it's our turn to cheer again. Woody steps up to the plate as my nerves jump and jangle. I pray silently as fast as I can but to no avail. After two fouled bunt attempts, Woody goes down swinging, striking out for the second time in the game. He slams the head of the bat down on the ground on his way back to the dugout, and I hear his metal cleats click across the concrete as he kicks at the floor. I also hear his hands slap the batting helmet on his head as I'm sure he struggles to maintain some control. "Sweet Jesus," I pray, "please help him calm down, please."

Terry follows with a single, and our crowd is cheering again. I believe all our fans are suffering with Woody, and it's a great relief to be able to cheer and holler and clap away the stress. We've got runners at first and third now with Mike Drew coming to bat for one of the few times this season. He tries to put down a sacrifice bunt but winds up striking out. Two outs now with men at first and third. Pat comes through with his second double to score Major from third and push Terry over to take his place. Runners are at second and third with a run in and two outs. Bobby draws a walk to load the bases, and our side is going crazy now. Thank goodness no one can focus on Woody's strikeout right now, hopefully not even Woody.

Phil comes up to bat, and we really need him to come through. But the Pirate pitcher comes through first—for us, that is—by balking and sending the tying run home. I don't know what a balk is, but he did it, and we're all tied up. Our crowd gets in a few more moments of cheering before the angry Pirate hurler strikes out Phil to end the inning. But hey, we tied it up! It's a new game with two innings left to play.

The first Pirate batter of the sixth blasts one to right field that Hunter races back for and catches with his back against the fence—*gulp*. Mike gets the next hitter on a grounder to second and the following batter on a grounder to Woody at third. He's playing great defense, anyway. Three up and three down for the Pirates; my nerves needed the rest. And that was the hated and feared sixth inning. Maybe that's a good omen, getting to our turn in the sixth with the score still tied four to four.

Hunter opens the Panther sixth with a double, and we're rolling again. The Pirates bring in a new pitcher; it's not Slugger. We find out after the game that his elbow is hurting, so he's not available to pitch. Danny greets the new hurler with an infield single that moves Hunter to third but not home; we're still tied. Major comes to bat and draws a walk to load the bases for Woody. I so wanted, hoped, and prayed that Major would get the go-ahead run home before Woody came to bat. The pressure of the game and the pressure he is putting on himself must be unbearable now. And I can't bear to watch and squeeze my eyes shut with each pitch.

And the Pelham family trauma continues as Woody swings at strike one, then strike two, and finally strike three. Our crowd falls silent, and my heart sinks as Woody storms out of the batter's box, banging his helmet once with the bat before disappearing into the dugout to sounds of bat bags and equipment being slammed about. I hold my breath as I look from the umpire to Coach Pat, and they both are looking elsewhere, giving Woody the benefit of his grief, a benefit he needs so much right now. I really don't know how he can stand it any longer, the incredible pressure of the game on top of his desperate desire and efforts to do something spectacular to secure a scholarship. We've never been really close, but we've grown much closer, brought together by grief and his panic to succeed. I think the visitor crowd even feels for Woody right now. I'm sure they all know the story of this past week's events.

Terry steps in and works the count to two balls and one strike. And then he saves our side and the Pelham sanity, launching one high and far over the left field fence and off the Evergreen Boulevard windscreen! I'm in the midst of a sea of pandemonium now, cheering, screaming, and crying. I truly believe our fans are as relieved and happy for Woody as they are that the Panthers lead eight to four. I really believe the cheering is as much to say, "It's okay, Woody," as it is to celebrate the lead. Our family group is reduced to happy sobs and hugs and joyful jumping up and down. The next two Panthers make outs to end the inning, but none of our fans care. We're ahead; we lead by four runs with just three more outs to go. And Woody is safe. The team is carrying him through his grief-driven nightmare.

But like Mr. Berra said, "It ain't over 'til it's over." The first batter for the Pirates is hit by Mike's first pitch. The next hitter singles before Mike hits another batter, and the bases are loaded with no outs. This is really getting to be too much. The Pirate crowd is roaring for their team to score, and our crowd is roaring for our guys to get them out. Coach Pat brings Pat in to pitch, and Brian Smith comes in to play short. The next hitter smashes one between Woody and Brian. Woody dives to his left and gets a piece of the ball, knocking it down and keeping it on the infield dirt. The ball rolls toward Brian, but before he can retrieve it, a run has scored, and the other runners are safe. It's eight to five; bases are still loaded and no outs. Woody is livid. He's kicking the dirt and gesturing like he's in the middle of a prizefight. Coach Pat calls time and goes to talk to Woody to try and calm him down.

Woody made a great play. He did all he could do, but I know he's about to explode with frustration. If he had snagged that line drive for the first out, it could have redeemed him. It could have set up a possible inning- and game-ending double play. He listens to Coach Pat, or pretends to, but I can tell he is still at his wit's end when play is resumed. And I realize that we dodged a bullet there. Woody saved at least one run with his defense. But oh no, the slugger is coming to bat now. *Come on, Pat, bear down. Don't give him anything good to hit.*

The place is electric; everyone on each side is standing and yelling and clapping. Pat delivers a curve ball that Slugger takes for strike one. Our side roars. Pat delivers the next pitch, and Slugger deposits it over the center field fence and off the retainer wall for a grand-slam homer. Pirates lead nine to eight. Just like that, like lightning, we're behind again. The air goes out of our side like a punctured balloon.

We get the next three batters out, but the damage is done, and the momentum has shifted. Or has it? The team races off the field and gathers around Coach Pat—except for Woody—the way they always do before they need one last-bat rally. I watch Woody jump down into the dugout and hurl his glove and then his hat as hard as he can at the back of the dugout.

Then goose bumps explode all over me as the speakers blare to life with REO Speed Wagon's "Roll with the Changes," my dad's music. I see Woody's body tense angrily, and then he makes a fist and rears back to throw a mighty punch as he steps forward toward the back of the dugout and out of my sight. This music hasn't been played in the series, but that's what Mack Christopher is really doing in the score box. He's playing Dad's music, urging the team to keep on fighting. The crowd feeds off the team and the music, raising our cheers to a crescendo. I turn to Mom, torn between my fear that Woody has injured himself and the emotion of the moment, and see that, like me, she is about to come apart at the seams. The music together with the contest and all the grief of the week has now created a knot of nausea the size of a grapefruit in my stomach and a searing lump the size of a lemon in my throat.

Bobby leads off the Panther seventh with a hard grounder that the shortstop mishandles, and we've got a runner on first. And the home crowd is crazy. Phil bats next and puts down a sacrifice bunt, but the catcher grabs it up and rifles a throw to second to cut down the lead runner for out number one. Our crowd moans as theirs cheers wildly. There's still a man on first but one out now. Hunter bats next and works the count full. The atmosphere goes electric again as Hunter launches the next pitch deep to center field. But their center fielder runs under it and makes the catch on the warning track for out number two. This is getting really bad and really scary, and my stomach is about to explode. The moms are fighting back tears as Danny draws a walk, and Major comes to bat with two outs and two on.

I look at Woody as he heads into the on-deck circle, happy to see he's able to grip the bat but fearful to see a bloody, swollen right hand. But his hand appears unharmed. And something is different. Something is very different. He's not gritting his teeth and swinging the weighted bat feverishly. He's not kicking at the dirt and muttering to himself. Woody is totally calm. Oddly, I think there might even be a hint of a grin on his face. I turn to tell Mom to look when everyone around me screams, scaring me half to death. Major has just smacked a single to left field, but it was hit so hard that Phil has to stop at third. The bases are now loaded with two outs.

And then the chant starts. Woody's buddies in our stands are starting the "Woody" chant, just like they did in our last at bat of the Sebastian game. As Woody heads for the batter's box, the "Woo-dy, Woo-dy" chants with the staccato clapping increase in volume.

I tell Mom, "Look at Woody. There's something different with him; something's changed."

And she says she knows; she can see it too, and she can feel it. He's not angry anymore. The goose bumps are back in double-decker style as the chants end and Woody steps to the plate. Wouldn't you know it would all come down to this?

My stomach churns harder as I hear Mr. Christopher holler down from the score box, "Your pitch, Woody. Look for a good one!"

The Pirate pitcher checks the runners, and I hold my breath as he begins his delivery, but I don't shut my eyes this time. Here it comes. And then there it goes.

Woody puts the smoothest, sweetest swing I have ever seen him make on that ball, and it takes off like a rocket! It's high and deep and way out there. It's over the center field fence, over the Evergreen Boulevard fence, and out of sight!

And I think I'm dreaming or maybe just losing my mind because now I hear the call from the climatic home run in *The Natural* over the loudspeakers. I see Woody take slow steps out of the batter's box, look skyward, and raise his right thumb in the air. I remember that gesture from years ago in youth ball. It's their signal that everything's okay; it's his thumbs up back to Dad.

And then I see Mack Christopher, wiping at his eyes, hanging out of the score box window, hollering, "You go, Woody Pelham! You go, boy!" And I know he's playing the tape; he's putting Dad's fingerprint on this fantastic moment.

The crowd is now total pandemonium, screaming, hugging, and crying, like an epidemic of weeping has hit the stands, but these are tears of joy and not just for a ball game that's won. It's much more than that.

Then something strange and wonderful happens. As Woody rounds first base and approaches the huge Pirate slugger, the slugger raises his hand and gives Woody a congratulatory fist tap as he passes. And the crowd's roar surges even louder. Then the second baseman follows his team leader's example and fist taps Woody as he passes, and then the shortstop and then the third baseman follow suit. And somehow the sound of the crowd seems to surge louder with each salute. What we're witnessing isn't just sportsmanship; it's more a display of some kind of kinsmanship or humanship. I don't know what to call it or how to explain it. It's players and fans of our opponent recognizing that this moment is much more than a victory in a championship ball game. It's a triumph of spirit over grief, of life over loss, and it's shared by all who are a part of it in any way. It's a baseball game, but today it's a channel for much more than that.

As Woody approaches home plate and before he's swallowed up by his teammates, I see his smile and his tear-streaked cheeks, and I know he's all right for now.

When we see Mack Christopher after the game, he tells us that Woody's home run cleared Evergreen Boulevard, landed in the graveyard, and ricocheted off a headstone and up into the trees. He says no one has been able to find it yet. The team and families go out to dinner together, and I think everyone is still in a daze of extreme happiness when we say our goodnights.

Mom and Aunt Monica and I talk late into the night about the games and how excited Dad would have been. And we all agree that really he was excited and he was there in a way we can't completely understand. We are grateful for the games and the easing of our grief.

I'm so wired to find out what happened to Woody that last inning that I'm still up when Woody gets home around three thirty or four in the morning. We head to the back deck steps and take a seat to talk the remaining darkness away.

"Okay, Woody, I've been dying to know what happened when you stormed into the dugout before the last of the seventh. You threw your glove and your hat, and I saw you rear back to punch the dugout wall. I expected to see your hand all bloodied when you came on deck, but no injury, and you were all calmed down. What was it?"

"I was about to totally crack up. I was so mad and frustrated and messed up over Dad that I felt like my head was gonna just blow up. I couldn't even huddle up with the team. And then the music, his music, starts, and that just pushed me all the way over the edge. I'd already thrown my glove and hat as hard as I could, so I just decided to punch a hole through the wall of the dugout. I really intended to put my fist through the wall. You know I've done stupid things like that before. But when I drew back my arm, it all flew out of me; it was gone in half a second, just gone like somebody flipped a switch. And then a feeling of calm and relief was all over me like I'd stepped into a waterfall of it. And that empty cold hole in my chest filled up with warmth. Then I knew that what you had said was true. Dad was already happy with me. I didn't need to do anything else to make him happy. I didn't need a scholarship. I didn't even need to ever bat again. He was already happy. I don't know how it happened, but something got done to me. I've never felt anything like it, and I don't think I ever will again. As I walked to the on-deck circle, I thought of a cartoon of a crane trying to swallow a frog. And when I remembered Dad always saying, 'Just watch the ball,' I knew I was going to hit it; I didn't know how well I would hit it, I just knew I would."

I think, *Grace found the wound*, and then I ask, "Do you think Dad helped you hit that home run?"

"No, somehow he just let me know it was all right if I didn't."

"Well, you know they can never make a movie about this game, don't you?" I ask.

Woody replies, "Why not?"

"Because that homer was just way too cliché," I kid and poke him in the ribs.

Woody says, "Well, they say that fact is stranger than fiction, so I guess sometimes fact can be stranger than cliché too!" And he gives me a little shoulder shove.

Then, as our talk naturally turns to Dad times in our lives, we begin to recall his love of Yogi's sayings, especially, of course, "It ain't over 'til it's over." And we recall his story of buying *The Yogi Book: I Really Didn't Say Everything I Said* as a Christmas present to himself one year. How he was reading it in the aisle of the bookstore and laughed so hard that he had tears in his eyes and was afraid the other customers would think he was crying over something sad he was reading.

The first light of dawn begins to sneak into the dark as we continue to talk and laugh so hard that we cry and then cry until we can remember another story that makes us laugh again. We realize how lucky we are that baseball has given us Dad's journal of his final season and that we can relive the fun he had these past few months. And we also realize how amazingly fortunate we are that Woody received what we call the Divine Dugout Intervention. Without that, who knows what our last memories of the final season would be.

The horizon is beginning to turn bright pink when Mom finds us and squeezes in between us on the steps. After we relate our Yogi discussions to her, we all fall silent and watch more and more of the sky glow from pink to crimson with the coming of the new day.

As a slight breeze begins to ruffle the leaves of our cherry tree, Woody says, "You know, I think Dad out-Yogied Yogi yesterday."

Mom asks him how, and he says, "We all know how Yogi said 'It ain't over 'til it's over.' Well, yesterday, I think somehow God and Dad proved that sometimes it ain't over even when it *is* over."

Mom says, "I believe you're right, Woody. I believe you're right." Then she puts her arms around us and gives us a good, big hug and each a kiss on the cheek. After a little while, she gives us another longer, harder squeeze.

I ask her if that last hug is for Dad, and when she answers, "And from him," a warm smile that starts out somewhere deep inside me spreads across my face, and I realize that Woody is so right. It really isn't over.